Wolfhammer

Legends of the Starborn

STEPHEN PHILLIPS

This story is a work of fiction. Any similarities to
names, people,places are purely coincidental.

DEDICATION

To my family and friends and all those helped me put this story together.

ACKNOWLEDGEMENT

A resounding thank you to Matt Petersen for the cover art.

Table of Contents

Chapter 1

Bad Day

The light breeze still hung heavy with smoke; the sound of weapons no longer lingered in the warm air. Jace's chest heaved as he ran from the alien patrol, still in pursuit. He struggled with his pack, now heavy with fresh supplies. He and the others were lucky to find an unsecured truck making deliveries just outside the city. He, like many thrown aside, now clung to hope of release from the aliens who attacked almost a year ago.

Life wasn't anywhere near being normal for those like Jace. They had to fight to survive every minute. If you were lucky and had a chance to reenter the cities, it still wasn't easy. The new leaders examined everyone and had to be deemed worthy of staying. Anyone labeled as a burden was cast out. If you were healthy, beautiful, faithful, and of course, wealthy, you might have a chance. The rest weren't so lucky.

Needing to rest, Jace ducked into some nearby rubble, his lungs burning for relief. After finding a spot, he pushed debris against the opening. Jace remained tucked silently into the hole to avoid detection. Out of habit, Jace found himself staring up into the sky, his mind wishing it was dark so he could see the stars. He looked around as the world quieted, the Daak patrol passing him. Jace knew what to do; he had done this so many times before, and as per the plan, would double back to the meeting point when things cooled down.

Jace fought back a cough, his body reminding him of why the others had thrown him aside. Quietly, he reached into the canvas bag and pulled out some water and food. Without hesitation, he gulped down some of the clean water that burdened his pack. Jace had learned how to scavenge like this for almost a year now. Every day, he became better at it. He had survived by stealing or working with others as best he could. Things had been this way since the attack on Earth started over seven months ago. Although things were returning to something like normal, it was rough for those thrown aside like him. It didn't change the fact that many still saw the Daak as an enemy for attacking Earth.

Jace had also survived being tossed aside by the aliens, having been deemed too ill. Instead of putting him out of his misery, to his surprise, Jace survived and found himself with this band currently scavenging from wealthy, coddled individuals hoarding government supplies marked for smaller areas. He felt it a privilege to help retrieve the needed items from those few who thought themselves worthy, his mind again rationalizing the same conclusion. *This isn't fair.*

Those in power had taken advantage, some even adopting a faith-based approach to survival as a way to live. If you didn't believe, you didn't survive. It was just a new way to control. Even the Daak found the situation an abomination and tried to diminish it. They sent ground forces to dissuade the small feudal communities that began to appear. In the end, there were a chosen few who carved power out of it all, persuading the frail agreement of Earth's leaders to submit. Those few had finally figured out how to do the very same they had achieved before but on a planetary scale. And they used the aliens to enforce it. Today, however, Jace felt freedom again as he ran from the patrol. Along with the others, he was feeling … human.

* * *

The sun was low in the sky when Jace arrived at the agreed-upon coordinates. The canvas pack Jace carried hung low with its treasure. He presented the haul to Silverton and watched her almost crack a smile as one of the others took the spoils. Jace felt some pride for his efforts. Allison Silverman was the current leader of the Southern New York Resistance. She asked him to come along, even though Jace had made his way to the coast. His only option was staying in one of the shelter cities until the Daak came to "help."

"You're good at breaking into things, Tucker. You did a good job of getting that truck open, according to Cy. What did you do before this again?" Silverman asked.

Jace only replied, "Contractor," making the woman scoff at his response before returning to cataloging his recent acquisitions, which were quickly counted before being put on the truck. Most of the supplies were destined for the shelter city, but some were theirs to keep. As Jace waited to receive his cut, they heard weapons fire off in the distance.

"Tell Terrance to get the others going and move; get those supplies to the shelter. Everyone, let's get out of here!" Silverman yelled as they closed up the truck.

Jace looked toward Terrance Keller. He was the only other person he knew who was in charge. There were even times Jace wondered if Silverman knew of the unofficial raids Keller had others go out on. When Jace arrived, there was something about the man that didn't sit well with him. It wasn't his lack of hair, but the coldness behind his gray eyes. Something inside Jace knew he should watch his back around this man.

There was screaming and the sound of one of the aliens' vehicles off in the distance, but it was becoming louder. Jace turned to see how close and was focusing his eyes out into the forest. As he concentrated, his vision was suddenly filled with stars, and a dull thud rang through his skull. Moments later, he felt the ground come up to meet him.

Jace struggled to roll over. As his eyes were again able to focus, he could see others on the ground. Keller and one of Silverman's guards were kicking them to stay down. As Jace struggled to push himself from the dirt, his vision blurred again, and he heard the gravelly sound of Keller's voice saying, "Leave them. The Daak will be busy picking them up, and we can get the hell out of here."

Bastards! Jace growled in his mind as he fought to stand. He willed his body to move. Jace could only see the shadows of the convoy as they vanished from the crest of the road. Jace cursed, realizing he and the others were left for the Daak.

Jace's senses were still in flux when he turned, his eyes barely making out the alien carrier off in the distance. With his last bit of strength, Jace stood, willing his legs to move, his actions allowing him to hide among the remnants of a nearby building. Jace did his best to stay on his feet and flee, but hearing weapons nearby, he decided to stay where he was. Jace reeled at the distinct echo of the assault all around, his mind suddenly wondering, *When did we get weapons like theirs?*

Jace became curious and moved to investigate. When he was close enough to see what was happening, he found something unexpected. Above the ground floated another vehicle, not the Daak carrier. It looked like an elongated van, mostly silver in color, with small windows and markings Jace couldn't make out. Taking cover behind it were people who looked human but wearing similar, silver-colored uniforms. To Jace, it looked as if they were trying to escape.

From his recent encounters, Jace knew to stay motionless; the alien trackers worked on movement. However, he could hear the others yelling but couldn't understand their language.

"Wad ogge sa? Wi hawe in akkoart um de artefakten fin dize planeet te rieden. Wirom fallke de Daak ús oan?" (What are they doing? We have an accord to save this planet's artifacts. Why are the Daak attacking us?) one of those in silver yelled. *"Witte se net hoe't se it ferskol tuskon us en de firdomden Terran lifenstekens moatte ferteall?"* (Don't they know how to tell the difference between us and the damn Terran life signs?)

"Terranen binne net sa fer fan us, daink? Ik daink da se gewoan warzen onfallen. De Daak slan viersknlik op alles dat liket op Terran, Inuskef us," (Terrans are not that far from us, remember? I think they were just attacked. The Daak are probably hitting everything that looks like it's Terran, including us,) another replied.

Jace winced as the Daak fired, hitting the people in silver as they turned to run. Instinct taking over, Jace turned his eyes, spying a clear path to escape. Jace had a chance but hesitated, his mind processing that he had nowhere to go. He'd just been left for dead. "So much for watching my back, guys," Jace whispered with a grumble.

Jace watched as these new silver-suited combatants tried to escape. He could hear them yelling to alert each other. As they ran, they were picked off by the Daak. Jace focused, then shook his head, giving a subtle laugh. His mind was finally realizing he didn't understand a word of what they were saying. All Jace knew was that they were in trouble.

They're unarmed. Why the hell are the Daak attacking them? But as he finished his thought, Jace felt his gut turn. *Shit, the Daak think they're us!*

Jace placed his hand against the crumbling wall as he shifted forward, his mind racing. He felt a sense of responsibility, but he didn't know why. *Was it because we've fought for almost a year, and now my recent actions were causing harm to innocents?* Jace twitched each time the Daak weapons hit their mark. Every time one of these people fell, they braced before hitting the ground. *They're only stunning them.*

Jace remembered the Daak had promised to teach the people of Earth to be less hostile. But from the number of bodies he had come across, Jace was unsure of their true intentions.

A whispered "Dammit," escaped his clenched teeth as he found himself moving closer.

Jace saw one of the women stand, her arms up. She was yelling something, her words not having any meaning to him.

"Ophald, wi binn net Terran. Dih is in sojav misya fan Anuai. Ophald mei ampuminen. Wi hawe tastimn om hjir te wizen!" (Stop, we're not Terran. This is an Anuai protective mission. Stop firing. We have permission to be here!)

Jace watched as the Daak fired on her and she fell. The carrier's robotic arm then dragged the unconscious to the back of the collection pod. Jace could see the trailer's arm placing each carefully into the rear of the hauler. Jace turned away, his back now against a tree, heart racing. His eyes were staring down the alley before him; he still had a chance to flee. His mind played a thousand iterations on how to lose the aliens in the buildings' sewers and basements, but he

5

again turned to look back toward the transport, his gut telling him he had to save those others.

No! Not the time to grow a conscience, Jace.

Jace waited till the Daak warriors moved further away, leaving only the robot to pick up the remaining incapacitated. With what steadiness he had left, Jace found himself jumping onto the back of the pod and climbing up to look inside. Jace could recognize some, and the woman with others in silver lying on the floor. He watched as a few tried to climb out, only to be sent back down by the electrified rim of the container. Jace looked over the edge, careful not to touch the inside. He could see the long, metallic arms placing people in the bin gently.

"At least they're not just dumping them in." Jace found humor in the actions of those attacking.

He paused, and one of those in silver sat up. He quietly tried to get her attention. She remained unaware of him over the noise of the carrier. Jace tried several times, even pulling himself further over the rim. But by doing so, who- or whatever was running the arms noticed. Jace was able to duck as a metallic arm grasped at him. He avoided its grip, only to be knocked down to the ground as it struck the side of the container. The only thing silencing the thud as Jace hit was the sound of the arm straining to be brought back under control. Jace recovered quickly, scanning the area. *There are too many.* He decided to run.

Inside the bin, the woman in silver struggled to her feet and watched as others tried to escape. She shook one of her fellow crew awake, knowing they had to escape.

"Heralyn, wh … what's our status?" the man asked as he steadied himself to stand.

"Well, Captain, uh, Kralin, we're stuck in a collection pod. Baklet looks injured," Heralyn replied, urgency in her voice.

Hearing that, the other woman raised her arm, yelling in a sarcastic tone, "No. I am good to go."

Heralyn laughed, "Oh, so the blood on your uniform is you attempting to get out of work again?"

The woman shook her head, telling them she was sure she had broken a few ribs and that it was becoming hard to breathe.

"This thing doesn't have a med bay, you know," Heralyn said, trying to make a joke, considering the circumstances. "You okay to move?"

The woman tried standing but immediately fell to the ground. "That's a negative." Heralyn watched as Baklet coughed up blood.

Heralyn turned. "Captain, Baklet needs medical attention. We have to get out of this thing."

"Agreed. I wonder if this has a holding field over the top to keep the Terrans inside." He then tapped the glowing pad on his wrist. "Olivand, this is Kralin. We're trapped in a Daak collection pod. Lock onto my signal. We could use some help getting out of here."

Kralin and Heralyn looked at each other, hearing no response.

"Olivand, do you read?" the captain tried again.

After several attempts, with Heralyn trying as well, they realized they were on their own.

"Do you think they found the ship?" Heralyn asked, concerned.

"I don't know, but even if they had to leave, someone should have responded," Kralin said before a grim look appeared on his face. "Let's see if we can get out of here."

The captain tapped the pad on his arm, making the display glow. With little effort, he then jumped several feet, grasping onto the edge of the bin, only to feel the shock of the electrified rim, making him fall to the floor of the pod.

"Captain!" Heralyn rushed over to see if he was injured.

When she asked if he was all right, the man only replied before going unconscious, "Well, enhancement suits don't seem to help."

Heralyn could see the lacework of burned circuits along his suit as she tried to wake him, but he was out cold. She used her pad to check on Baklet, her display showing internal injuries. And with their severity, her crewmate's suit dispensed a painkiller. Heralyn could see Baklet's pupils were dilated, and she was now entranced as her body tried to repair itself.

"Wonderful, down two, and I'm stuck in a collection pod. How the slac are we going to get back to the ship?" Heralyn said as she sat hard on the container's floor.

Chapter 2

Helping Strangers

Jace ran through the forest, with the city and buildings left behind for the moment. He could feel his heart pounding heavily in his chest, his mind never taking a moment to look back. Only two things concerned him: escape, and he was alone again.

When the Daak initially struck, he was working the overnight shift at the factory. He remembered the anger he felt over how the cleaning crew had left early, leaving him the only one to take care of the building. Jace's memory replayed how he was thankful for the job after the financial collapse hit the economy.

Jace's body was numb from what he was asking of it when his haze was broken by the sudden bright flash to his right. Startled, Jace hesitated, making him trip. He found himself weightless as he fell to the ground going full speed. The world spun as he rolled several times until his shoulder stopped hard against a tree.

Jace fought against the disorientation and sat up, his eyes focusing on the large, shiny metal object he had just found. The words, "It's a fuckin' ship!" escaped him.

Curiosity and excitement got the better of him, and he ran toward the object, muttering, "Please don't be Daak."

Jace was hopeful, seeing what looked like humans around the ship. But his excitement was short-lived and his heart filled with a grim realization. Jace slowed, remaining hidden in the brush. His eyes filled with the sight of what looked like bodies on the ground around the entrance. He counted four near the edge and one on the ramp leading into the ship itself.

Cautiously, he waited a few seconds before moving toward the closest being. Jace touched the person's wrist, gently checking for a pulse, words escaping as he thought out loud, "Jace, what are you doing? You don't know if they're like humans, you idiot."

Jace chuckled, taking a moment to mock himself, feeling a pulse, and sighed with relief. He moved to another and could see the scorch from an energy weapon on her chest. Jace wasn't hopeful, but was surprised to find the woman still alive.

"Guess these people are pretty tough," Jace remarked before hearing a moan from the ramp.

Jace immediately headed up, helping the man off of the strut he was leaning on for support.

"You all right?" Jace asked, then gave a sideways glance, looking into the ship.

Jace's mind reeled, and he was surprised to hear his own words. "Hey, um, can you fly this thing?"

The alien shook his head, and when the man responded, Jace couldn't understand a word.

The man tapped the pad on his wrist and then pointed to his mouth and then to Jace. Jace figured out quickly that he wanted him to say something. "Um, can you fly this thing?"

Within moments the man spoke, and Jace heard an electronic voice version of the man say in English, "The Daak attacked us."

Jace was stunned and again asked if the man could fly and was disappointed to see the alien shake his head. Jace heard the man's next words. "We have a crew out there; they need help."

Jace thought back to the others he had encountered and knew where the rest of the crew were. His dilemma was whether he was going to help them. The Daak were still in the area, and Jace desperately wanted to be somewhere else. He straightened the man up, his action making the alien exhale a grunt of pain.

"I think I know where they're at, but can you fly the ship? We could use it to get them," Jace told the man.

The man shook his head as he grasped his side in pain. Jace hadn't noticed the blood that had pooled on the ramp where the man was, but when he looked at his injury, he knew it was from the blade of a Daak weapon.

"Shit, these aliens are worse than us," Jace mumbled, remarking on how humans attacked each other.

Jace looked around at the others on the ground. None of them had weapons. The Daak didn't take weapons after they attacked. They were always left them where they fell.

Then the man he was holding twitched and said something garbled. All Jace could make out was, "med bay," before the man pointed into the ship. Jace looked, then shook his head as he pulled the man to his feet, making him again cry out in pain. "C'mon, I'll give you a hand. Maybe you can help the others."

Jace paused for a second as he helped the man inside, his mind thinking, *This guy's heavier than he looks.* Jace struggled but was able to carry the stranger into the ship. The man pointed, and Jace took him in that direction; within moments, they came upon a small room with what looked like medical equipment. The man motioned to one of the beds, and Jace hoisted him onto it, his sudden effort making the man again cry out loudly.

"Sorry, you're not that light, you know?" Jace complained.

The man pointed to the console as he lay down. Jace stared at the display, oblivious to what it read, but was startled as an image showing the man's outline appeared on the screen; but nothing else was happening. The stranger rolled his head toward Jace, saying, "Press emergency medical."

Jace moved his hand toward the screen. "What does that look like? I can't read any of this."

His words were met with silence as the man fell unconscious. Jace tried to wake him but was unable. Returning to the display, Jace stared at it; he could see several buttons with symbols. Each was a different color, red, green, yellow, purple. Jace looked around the room, and it seemed similar to an emergency room on Earth. As he noticed another similar screen, Jace muttered, "Green usually means go."

Jace held his breath. He was deathly afraid he'd kill the man on the table. As he pressed the green button, some kind of energy field enveloped the stranger. Jace could see a glittering light where the man's wounds were and what looked like several streams of the same energy lighting other parts of his body. He could see the man still breathing shallowly, but an indicator on the screen was blinking.

"I guess he's still alive," Jace said as he looked at the screen to see symbols next to the button. It was a row of five characters, and the last one was changing. When the second-to-last changed, Jace realized what it was.

"This thing's got a countdown, holy shit!" Jace then thought, *If this is a countdown, then?*

Jace looked at his watch, realizing that they were probably seconds. They were close enough to the changing of the number on his watch. "Shit, if this is right, then it's going to take a few hours for this guy. What if the Daak come back?"

Jace looked around, realizing that even if the stranger could fly the ship, it'd be hours until they could leave. And Jace remembered the others still out there. Jace stepped back and turned to look where he had come in. "I wonder if any of the others would heal faster?" With a semblance of hope, Jace headed back outside to retrieve the other injured.

It took several trips, and Jace filled all the beds. He was disappointed seeing the time for all of them too long to be helpful. Jace knew that the Daak would return sooner than they would heal. Then Jace's mind returned to the three trapped in that machine. He knew at least one of them was still walking.

"Dammit, I gotta go back." Jace shook his head.

Jace had been looking for an escape, but these others needed help. He sighed and moved away from the medical beds. His steps quickened as his decision to head back cemented in his mind.

Jace searched for some kind of weapon, only finding a sharpened metal bar that looked like something you could use to pry open a door. Jace grabbed it and headed down the ramp. At the bottom, he paused, looking at the simple metal bar.

"It'll have to do," he said as he moved quickly to where he had seen the carrier heading.

* * *

It was only a few minutes before Jace could see the carrier. There were no Daak in sight. Jace figured the scouts had already moved on, leaving the automated system to collect those they left behind. He climbed on the back of the vehicle and peered over the edge. He could see the woman speaking into her wrist and yelled with reserve to get her attention, "Hey! You need help?" Jace was hoping she could hear him; even with his muted attempt at a yell, he hoped to get her attention. He ducked down, seeing the observation beam swing around, but as he did, the carrier hit uneven ground, making Jace have to readjust his grip as the vehicle moved forward.

"Olivand, kinne jo my hearre? Grach antwurdja." (Olivand, can you hear me? Please respond.) Heralyn tried over and over to reach their ship. Like the commander, she concluded that the Daak might have

13

attacked them. She was now worried about herself and the rest of the crew.

Jace could see the woman from before standing, speaking into her wrist. He yelled to get her attention.

Hearing a voice, the woman looked back and watched as a man ducked down beneath the edge of the carrier. Heralyn remained focused on the spot where she saw him, and when he appeared, she yelled to him. She was frustrated seeing his confused response.

"Wachtsje, mizae ova de Terran -wurdja?" (Wait, what are the Terran words?) she muttered before yelling, "Can you help us?"

Jace perked up in surprise. "You speak our language?"

Heralyn nodded and then took a moment before responding. "There's a release latch on the back; you need to short the locking servo."

Jace looked at her, bewildered. "How? With what?"

Heralyn shook her head. She didn't know, but as the man showed her the small metal rod he held, she nodded with excitement.

Jace smiled as he climbed down the back of the door. *What the hell does a locking servo look like?* Following the center line down the door, he came to a small, circular recess that held what looked like a latch. *That's probably it.*

As he inspected the latch, Jace found two small holes above it. "I guess that could be a keyhole," he muttered before shoving the rod into one of them, only to be thrown off by what felt like current surging through his arm. He quickly stood, watching as the latch spewed sparks, and as the vehicle hit a dip, the door popped open.

"Well, that worked," he said, climbing onto the vehicle again, pulling open the door.

The woman spoke in her language as she approached Jace, making him tap his wrist to tell her to turn on her translator. He was surprised when the woman shook her head. "It doesn't always work correctly. I'm just happy you were able to open the hatch." Jace looked stunned at her excitement. Seeing his response, she gave a sigh of relief, "Sorry, I'm just, I can speak your language, but we need your help."

Jace followed her as the door swung open and closed over the rough terrain. Jace asked, "How do we get everyone out?"

The woman paused for a moment before telling him that her crew were injured and needed medical attention. She pleaded for him to help get them back to their ship. Seeing him looking at the people in the carrier, she calmly said, "We can't help you. I'm sorry."

Jace stared into the air with anger, his heart screaming, *Why not?* But seeing his fellow Earth people unconscious and how many there were made him realize that if he wanted to survive, he'd have to let them go. His heart now weighed heavy when he told her he'd help get her people back to her ship, mentioning that the beds were all full.

"Wait, you were in our ship?" Heralyn asked, looking at him with a joy he didn't understand. "How did you get the systems to work?" The woman watched his shrug. "I wonder if you're a … never mind, we need to get out of here."

"I'll help you get them back. It's just—I need a favor," Jace said to her.

The woman could feel the torment behind his words before tapping the small screen on her wrist a few times. "All right, I'll grab him, you grab her, and we'll sort this out when we get to the ship."

Jace watched as she picked up the man with little effort as Jace struggled to carry the woman.

"Please be careful with her; I think she has a punctured lung."

Jace nodded and did his best to carry her across his arms as they made their way back to her ship. He watched as the alien moved quickly across the terrain carrying her friend. He struggled, having to stop several times to rest. She stayed close, looking toward the direction of the Daak as she waited.

"You know, your people must live in heavy gravity or something. I'm struggling here." Jace tried not to laugh in frustration as he rested.

Heralyn shook her head. "My suit has a nano-skeleton support system. This world has heavier gravity than ours."

"Wait, you mean like an exo-suit?" Jace asked.

Heralyn nodded, seeing Jace's eyes open in amazement. "Yes, it's about 1.6 times our gravity here. Please, we have to hurry."

Jace didn't disagree. He lifted the woman in his arms, and they were on their way.

After several minutes, they arrived at the ship. Heralyn looked around and saw no sign of the Daak. They both brought their respective loads up the ramp and headed to the med bay.

Heralyn looked at the screens before hitting a panel on the wall and placing the man she carried against it. Jace stood amazed as the man stuck to the small platform, and she tapped a screen next to it.

"How did you activate these?" she asked Jace, who told her he just did the same thing as she. This made her look suspiciously toward him before she tapped another panel on the wall, causing another vertical bed to appear. "Here, put her on this."

Jace did as she said but stumbled and had to steady himself. When his hand touched the panel on the wall, another bed appeared.

The woman in silver smiled. "Oh, you have to be."

Heralyn's moment of discovery was interrupted by an alarm.

"What's that?" Jace asked, nearly panicked.

The woman's face showed fear as she said, "Proximity alert. We have to get out of here. I need to close the hatch."

The woman rushed by Jace, but as her hand was about to touch the door control, she was struck by weapons fire from below. Jace could see the shadow of a Daak warrior coming up the ramp. Instinct took over, and Jace lunged toward him. With his momentum, Jace knocked the alien back several feet into the others who followed. They all landed in a pile. Jace reached around, grabbing onto the Daak weapon pointing toward one of his fellow warriors. As Jace pounded on the alien's arm, the weapon fired. Jace was touching the same warrior and felt a jolt of electricity surge through him, throwing him off. His senses knocked back alive as he hit the dirt hard. With his adrenaline going, Jace ran up the ramp into the ship. As he reached the top, Jace turned and yelled. The Daak recorded him saying, "There's no way in hell you're stopping me from taking this ship!"

Heralyn had been staring across at a display as Jace closed the door. Her hope that they would leave quickly diminished. The screen was showing a warning that the drive reactor was offline. Jace helped Heralyn to her feet; she was obviously in pain. He could see the large burn on her arm as it hung limply to her side. "We have to get out of here, but the reactor is offline," she told him.

Jace looked around, and Heralyn pointed where to go. When the two entered the engine room, Heralyn could see the protection field around the spide crystal had been removed and was thankful that the extractor field was still running.

"We have to seat the crystal to get the ship off the ground," she told him before doubling over in pain.

"How do I do that?" Jace asked.

It took a few seconds for Heralyn to reply. "That room. You'll have to suit up and replace the crystal in the chamber." She pointed to a door before she fell to the ground as the ship shook.

"Sounds like they're trying to break in." Jace looked at Heralyn as she stared at the floor in pain. "Great, now you're of no use. Don't any of you know how to take a hit?"

Jace looked toward the small room, muttering, "Okay, suit up and reseat the crystal. Hope I don't kill myself doing this."

He tried for about a minute before the ship again shook violently—the increased urgency making him decide just to use the gloves. Within seconds of looking at the reactor, he was able to seat the crystal, even with the alarms sounding. Jace shook off the gloves, seeing the palms burned away. He thought whatever the crystal's composition is must have dissolved them. But seeing no injury to his hands, he rushed out to see if Heralyn was functioning.

"I got the crystal in the reactor. Can you fly the ship?" Jace asked, making her shake her head.

"No, I need two arms. But I think you might be able to," she told him.

"Lady, I don't know how to fly this ship," Jace responded.

She pulled on him as he picked her up. "You activated the med bay and ramp. I think you might be able to get us out of here. Get me to the control room; I'll walk you through it."

She groaned as he pulled her forward. She paused, joking, "That suit's a bear to get on, isn't it?"

Jace looked at her. "Yeah, I wound up using only the gloves. Hope that thing's not too dangerous."

"You weren't suited?" she yelled.

Jace shook his head. "I mean, if it's radiation, you can fix it, right?"

She looked at him. "You felt nothing? No burning, no flesh turning to ash?"

Jace looked at his arms. "Don't know what you're talking about, lady. Can you get us out of here or not?"

She nodded and pointed toward the control bridge, seeming oddly inspired.

Heralyn told him to sit in the chair on the right as she sat in the other. She instructed him to place his hand on the display and the other on the stick when the controls became active.

Heralyn started to laugh. "Do you know how long I've wanted to meet someone like you?"

Jace became defensive. "What do you mean someone like me?"

The woman was interrupted as the ship shuddered. "They're trying to break in. We have to launch now."

Heralyn tapped the panel between them, and the screen lit, showing the Daak firing at the ramp door. He looked to her for instructions on how to fly the ship.

"Lift your hand. You fly by moving your hand up or down, turning or dipping up or down to adjust the angle. With your other hand, it's forward or backward and side to side. The farther forward, the faster we go. It's that simple," she instructed.

Within moments, the ship rose from the ground. Jace was unsteady at first, but it took only seconds for him to get the hang of the ship. "You just made my day, lady. We escaped the Daak, and I'm flying a spaceship!"

"My name's Heralyn, please, not lady," she told him, struggling to breathe as if trying to stay awake.

Jace knew the signs of shock from his recent life, and from what he could tell, it seemed these people weren't much different than humans. Jace flew as fast as his courage would let him. He was about to breathe a sigh of relief when they felt the ship lurch again.

"What the hell was that?" Jace asked.

Heralyn struggled to sit up. "Energy weapons. You have to lose them."

Jace did his best, but he was thinking linearly. That allowed the Daak to block their path. "Please tell me this ship has weapons."

Heralyn nodded, telling Jace to press the row of buttons on the display. As he did, he watched the arm with the stick appear, a very familiar-looking item rising from it. "This looks like a fighter grip from one of our planes."

Heralyn nodded. "It's amazing how some things are very similar in the universe, isn't it?"

Jace was about to fire when Heralyn yelled for him to stop. "Don't fire on them. They haven't fired on us from the front yet. The Daak have a very particular way of engaging. If you attack, you'll drag my people into this fight needlessly."

Heralyn tapped the console before her, and an image of the Daak came on the screen. She then sat back, holding her arm.

"Daak commander, your people—"

She was interrupted by the Daak. "Surrender and submit to be taken as prisoners."

"That doesn't sound very nice," Jace said.

Heralyn looked at Jace, and with a hint of disdain, said, "They probably think I'm Terran." She paused. "Daak commander, you have to stop attacking this ship. I am Heralyn Forstrad of the Gilese system Anuai Alliance."

The Daak paused. "You attacked our forces; you are in violation of the agreement."

"No, Commander, you attacked ours; we were on a mission to save artifacts," Heralyn told them.

"Then why is the Terran piloting the ship?" the Daak asked.

"Commander, I am injured."

There were several seconds before the Daak looked concerned and responded, "Are you under duress?"

Heralyn paused for a second and answered yes, but as she was about to speak further, Jace turned to her. "Turn off communications."

"What?"

Jace leaned over, slamming his hand down on the panel, and the screen went blank.

"Why'd you do that?" she asked him.

Jace looked at the blank screen. "They think I'm kidnapping you and stealing the ship. When you bring them on, let them know I haven't hurt you yet."

Heralyn looked at him, confused and concerned.

"You don't want your people in this fight, right?" Jace asked, making her nod. "Good, then bring them on, and I'll do the talking. But let them know I haven't hurt you. Yet."

Heralyn now understood what the man next to her was doing. Jace was helping her save face and her people's involvement on Earth. "You're crazy; you know that? They'll kill you. The Daak punish lesser worlds stealing advanced technology very severely."

"Yeah, well, then it'll just be me. Hopefully, they'll let you go." Jace sighed.

"Why would you do this?" she asked.

"Because I have seen too many people die. Maybe I can at least save someone," Jace replied. He paused before saying, "Turn on the viewer."

The Daak appeared on the screen. "By the actions we have seen, it appears that you are under duress."

"Commander, the Terran has not harmed me yet. But I think we can—"

"Daak commander?" Jace interrupted her. She looked toward him with annoyance.

"I watched your people shoot her and her crew on the ground. What do you have to say about that?" Jace accused the Daak commander, who was now silent.

"I have not fired on your ship, but I will if I need to." Jace tried sounding threatening.

The Daak commander continued to remain silent.

"Commander, your people need to stop attacking us. We did not attack you," Jace told them.

"Incorrect, Terran. Your people attacked a ship bearing a solution to your environmental and energy problem. You declared war on the Daak."

"No, Commander, *you* are incorrect. I learned that it was a few missiles from some of the morons that run our governments. We did not attack you," Jace told them. "I do not want to harm you, but I will if you remain in my way."

"You threaten us, Terran, when it is you who is incorrect. A planet's government speaks for its people."

Jace laughed. "Then you haven't researched us much, have you? If you did, you'd have found out that there are times when only a few people will speak, and it may not be on the people's behalf. It's usually someone trying to be in control or subjugate others. By your actions, you have declared war on many, and on an innocent planet."

"That has not been our findings. Your people continue to fight and attack us."

Jace shook his head. "That is our way when you attack us. Wouldn't you defend yourselves? You need to take a step back and reevaluate this fight."

The Daak remained silent, finally asking, "Then why do you threaten us now?"

Jace sat tall. "I am only warning you, not threatening. I have no wish to kill anyone. But if you remain in my way, I will. I have taken this ship, and I will leave. Maybe it's time you learned something about my people. When you kill us, we kill in return." Jace paused and lightened his tone. "But you're in luck. I am tired of seeing death, and you have a chance to walk away. Know that I attacked your people because they attacked me. And if you attack me again, I will respond in kind."

Several moments passed before the Daak commander spoke. "We must consult." The screen went blank.

Jace sighed with relief. "That bought us some time, I hope. Now we have to find an opening."

Heralyn looked at Jace. It took years for her people to negotiate with the Daak and do what he just did, but it took him only a few minutes.

Jace loosely gripped the weapons controls. "How fast do you think this ship can go?"

Heralyn turned forward. "Tach seven on a good day, but we don't do that in the atmosphere of a planet. Why?"

Jace stared forward, his eyes looking past the enemy as he chuckled. "I want to get past their ships and into open space. You'll have to tell me where to go from there."

She understood and tapped several controls, telling Jace to strap in as she changed the configuration for flight in space. "This is crazy. We still have to get past that ship."

Jace remained facing forward, his teeth gently clenched. "Leave that to me," he said quietly before tilting the ship forward slightly and firing. The shot missed the Daak ship on purpose. His actions made them move quickly out of his way. When that happened, Jace hit the throttle, and within moments, the ship was beyond the Earth's moon. "Wow, this has got some pickup!"

* * *

Back on Earth, the Daak ship was fighting the sudden turbulence created by the Alliance ship.

"Commander, the Terran did not keep his word, but they have left the engagement area," one of the Daak crew reported.

"Damage report to the chase ship?" the commander asked.

"None, Commander. The Terran missed."

The commander looked confused and pulled up the replay of the Terran attack. He noticed the ship tilt as if to avoid hitting the chase ship.

"Centurion?" the commander called over to him, looking for advice.

"Yes, Commander."

"Why would the Terran miss on purpose? The chase ship was well within his sights."

"I do not know the answer, Commander."

"We must consult. Something about this Terran's actions does not agree with what we have encountered on this world."

Chapter 3

DNA Twist

A few days later, Heralyn and Jace made it back to the main ship. After rendezvousing, the Alliance was permitted to stage just outside the moon's orbit, as per their agreement with the Daak. Their accounts about what had happened to the *Olivand* allowed such an agreement to take place. Jace stared out the window, a satisfied smile exhibiting his amazement seeing the Earth and moon together from where the ship orbited. Jace had always dreamed of seeing something like this, and he touched the window. His fingers felt the cold of space as he pressed his hand against the clear glass. It wasn't smooth, like he would have thought; it was different, like ceramic. The wall was similar in texture as he ran his hand across the side of the portal. His imagination didn't do justice to the sight he was viewing. Jace remained mesmerized as Heralyn walked into the room. He barely acknowledged her as she approached.

"The Errtan Council is aware of what you did, Jace. I've made a recommendation that they consider you a refugee."

Jace turned his head slightly, his eyes still focused on the planet in the distance. "And that means what, exactly?"

Heralyn explained that the Daak and Earth representatives wanted to have him extradited. They were requesting to hold a trial to decide his fate. The Daak considered Jace violent, given his attack on several of their warriors. The disruption of supply shipments was added to cement his supposed danger. The Earth's council had provided evidence that he was a known criminal and wanted to punish him for working against the Daak-Earth consortium.

Jace knew his own people better. Whatever they had was made up so they could bring him back to Earth. Normally, they would have just killed him. But when they learned that he was able to fly the ship, they feigned wanting to hand him over to the Daak and then requested leniency so they could punish Jace instead. Heralyn knew what they were doing as well, but that wasn't important. She had other news.

"I'm glad to see we were able to heal you. When the medics evaluated your condition, they were wondering how you were still alive," Heralyn said with a caring tone.

Jace gave a subtle chuckle. "I know, and I had some problems; that's probably why they left me for dead the first time."

"Who? Who left you for dead?" Heralyn asked in disbelief.

Jace turned his eyes, trying to hide his own disbelief. "The Daak, then my people. Guess both figured I'd die, and they'd be rid of me."

Heralyn felt horrified that even the Daak would have left him for dead. Although, she had read through many reports preparing for the mission, and she knew it wasn't unheard of. If they did leave someone unaided, it was done to prevent supplies from being wasted. When she asked him how long he had been fighting, she was again surprised when he told her several months. She was able to view his medical report and knew he was suffering a recurring illness causing scarring on his lungs. But Jace surprised everyone as he continued to survive, even without the help of the Daak or his people.

Heralyn shifted, holding an info pad before her. "I have some interesting news. I asked the medics to run a DNA profile on you while you were being evaluated."

"That's a bit personal, don't you think?" Jace interrupted, startling her.

"It's not what you think! It's standard procedure for our people and the Alliance," she replied.

Keeping with his serious demeanor, Jace told her to go ahead and tell him the bad news.

"I suspected something when you told me you were able to activate the med bay. And when you were able to use the ship's flight controls, I had to be sure."

Jace looked at her. "You mentioned something back when we were trying to escape. What was that about?"

"According to the scan, you're 72 percent Lyri. You would pass as one of us!" Heralyn told him, giving a smile.

"What'ya mean Lyri? I'm not from Earth?" Jace asked.

Heralyn shook her head. "No, you're from Earth, it's just that your heritage is mostly from another planet. Or to be precise, settlers from another world. It happens on planets settled by the Alliance as well."

Jace tilted his head in confusion.

Heralyn explained how the Lyri discovered hyperspace and jump technology over a million Earth years ago. Jace shook his head every time she paused to calculate the differential from her planet's time reference to Earth's to help him understand. Using the info pad, she showed him a descendants' line back to the Lyri home world. She remarked on how his genetics were closer to her people's than those from Earth. She went on to explain that her people, the Errtan, genetically changed when they settled on other worlds.

"So, what's that mean for me?" Jace interrupted.

Heralyn paused before answering in a serious tone. "It means that the council may side with the Daak and hand you over."

Jace started to laugh. "Well, at least thanks for fixing me up to get tortured and executed."

Heralyn could see the frustration hiding behind his humor and was hesitant in telling him the rest. But when he asked, she decided to tell him. "Jace, there are four known races that have or had a natural resistance to spide radiation: the Daak, Duggor, and the Ha'ark all have some resistance, even some from your world, Terra. But there is a group that has extreme resistance to the radiation. The original creators of the spide reactors," she told him.

"Don't tell me—Earth people, right?" Jace joked.

Heralyn shook her head. "No. And we call your people Terrans, by the way. Your people have some resistance, but for the most part, they would burn as fast as anyone without protective gear. The only other race known who could survive the radiation are those from the Lyri system. But it's been mispronounced by your people as Lyra, instead of Lyri."

Jace tilted his head, trying to process the information. "What are you talking about?"

Heralyn glanced over his shoulder out the window into the darkness as she took a slow breath. "I have worked as a researcher for over one hundred of your years. And in all my time, I have never come across anyone quite like you. There are still many of my people who would look down on you for not being of a pure planetary origin. But you, you have just the right combination. A mix of Terran and Lyri to give you an exceptionally high resistance to spide radiation."

"I still have no clue what you're talking about. What the hell is wrong with me?" Jace asked, his frustration growing.

"Absolutely nothing. The only thing wrong with you is you were born on the wrong planet," Heralyn replied as she looked to the floor.

Seeing Jace confused, Heralyn reached out to him. Jace felt her touch; her hand felt warm on his arm. She wasn't grasping or crushing it. She held on as if to validate something was there.

"Your genetics make you closer to my people than your own. Even though you were born on Earth, you have an extensive resistance to spide radiation. It's rare, even among my people."

Jace didn't believe what she was saying. "How do you know that?"

It was now Heralyn's turn to sigh in frustration. "The gloves from the ship."

Jace showed his hands. "Yeah, whatever the crystal was, it dissolved them. Thankfully, I didn't touch the damn thing."

"That's it, you did. You held the crystal with your bare hands. What was left of the gloves would not have protected anyone. The entire suit is designed to be used as a sealed system. You survived direct exposure to the radiation," she told him. "However, if you had used the suit, the gloves may have survived."

Jace looked at her. "What are you talking about?"

Heralyn was having difficulty explaining and could see his confusion. "The shield on the suit was active. You must have turned on the controls when you tried putting it on. However, the controls were all maxed, and gloves and suit not being integrated as a single unit, had started to deteriorate."

Jace stared blankly at her. "If it's so dangerous, then how come I'm not dead, or dust, or whatever?"

In her frustration, Heralyn pulled him toward the screen on the wall and placed her hand on the display. She spoke a few words in her language, and the screen lit.

"This is what happens to people without a protective suit when exposed to spide radiation," she said as she tapped the display.

Jace watched the screen, seeing the person burn to ash as the radiation dissolved them.

"That could have been me?" he said with a sudden horrified fear at the scene he had just witnessed.

"No," was all Heralyn said.

Jace looked at her; he could see the clarity in her eyes as she stared back, saying, "The radiation didn't do anything to you because you have the right combination of DNA. You are closer to being what my people once were; what we used to be."

Jace stood with his mouth open, trying to form words but saying nothing.

Heralyn moved closer. "The Lyri home world was taken by the Duggor over half a million of your years ago. Since then, we have never identified as Lyri. We moved on and became the people of our new worlds. That acceptance has also caused some rifts among us."

"So, what the hell am I? I'm from Earth," Jace told her.

"Yes, you were born on Earth, but genetically, you are Lyri. As I mentioned, it happens among my people as well." Heralyn paused. "My people have a term for someone like you. However, I'm afraid it's not meant to be complimentary."

Heralyn looked ashamed as she spoke. Jace did what he had always done: he faced the news and asked what it was.

Heralyn hesitated. "There are some of my people who would consider you a disgrace. But anyone proven as Lyri is known as a starborn."

Jace gave her a cheerful, sarcastic look. "Starborn. That's kinda silly, isn't it? I mean, who's born on a planet without a star?"

Heralyn smiled but answered, "It's not that you were born without a star nearby. For you and those like you, with a high degree of Lyri descent, you're not considered part of any alliance. The term is used because there is no home planet. You were born among the stars."

Jace turned, walking away as he scoffed, "Wish I was, Heralyn, wish I was. Then at least this would make some sense. So what if I'm part Lyri and Terran? So what if people don't see me as something like them? I don't care what they think."

Heralyn smiled. "You really don't care, do you?" she asked, making Jace shake his head.

"Besides, it doesn't matter anyway. I'm just trying to survive and not get myself tortured or killed. So, how's this going to help me?"

Heralyn didn't know. But as Jace thought, the information gave him an idea.

He leaned in, saying, "If I'm closer to your people than my own, would that put me under the Alliance's laws?"

Heralyn thought for a moment. "Perhaps, but you'd have to convince the Tribunal to take you as one of us. And would have to had committed a crime that would supersede the attack of the Daak and Earth council charges."

Jace thought, giving a subtle smile as he spoke. "Well, Earth did leave me for dead, right? So that's good. As for the Daak, remember, they think I stole your ship; we can play off that."

Heralyn retorted, "But they knew I helped you."

"Yes, but you were injured and were afraid of dying. I wanted to get out of there. If we play it up as though I restrained the crew, then you look like you were helping to save them."

She knew what he was saying would put him in a bad light, but it was something she could tell the arbiter. Jace said he would take it from there. They knew it was a gamble. Too much, and the Tribunal would certainly hand him over to the Daak.

"Okay, I'll contact the arbiter, and we'll get something planned for your defense," Heralyn said as she started to walk away.

Jace could see she had reservations about the strategy. "Hey, I'm not going to make you out to be some weakling, Commander. I'm just going to make it look like I took advantage of the situation."

Heralyn smiled, but it faded as she spoke. "I hope so; otherwise, they'll hand you over to the Daak or your people pretty quickly."

Jace nodded as she walked away, his heart starting to race. He was unsure of anything that was going on. "Yeah, I hope this works too."

Chapter 4

Trial

Jace walked silently along the hallway, flanked by three guards, his mind racing as only the sound of footsteps against the deck filled his ears. He felt his chest tightening as he neared the entrance to the council chamber. Involuntarily, he pulled against his restraints.

The brightly lit hall became a more foreboding, dark chamber as they turned to enter. Within, he could see the Tribunal and representatives illuminated from above. His heart skipped, hearing the door close behind him. He was led to a small, enclosed area where a hesitant arbiter awaited. The few moments that passed seemed like hours to Jace, only broken as the guards turned him to face the Tribunal.

"Remember to face the Tribunal at all times and remain silent. Don't engage the Daak or your people," the arbiter warned.

Jace did as ordered.

The arbiter took a breath. "My name is Dreslin. I have spoken with Heralyn, and your strategy is a bit risky, but it may be our best option."

Jace was just trying to remember to breathe as he replied, "Nice to meet you, Dreslin."

His words brought a loud scolding from one of the Tribunal members. "The accused will remain silent!"

Jace was startled and was about to speak when Dreslin replied, "Members of the Tribunal, the accused is not familiar with our proceedings. And I have not been able to explain how they will commence. I ask for a moment to confer with the accused."

Again, the same Tribunal member broke the silence. "Arbiter, are we to understand that you are not prepared for this Tribunal?"

Jace looked at Dreslin; he could see the man's demeanor change as he replied, "Tribunal and guests, please forgive for what seems like ineptitude. As for this council's assignment, I was just informed two cycles ago by the Terran representatives that the Daak have also submitted a claim against the accused. I have been informed that the accused had been in medical recovery, not allowed any interaction with an arbiter since his arrival. Only that he was held in isolation."

Another of the Tribunal spoke. "Are you saying he was not held with the other Terrans?"

Dreslin confirmed the statement. "That, and he was being housed in a moderately unsupervised location. I have reports from our security staff stating that the Terrans made several attempts to meet with the accused but were turned away since an arbiter was not present. Although, I do not have information on the requested removal of security by the Terrans for that incident either. In fact, I have an internal request for the defendant's transfer, but without proper authorization, it could not be processed."

Jace looked to his side and watched as one of the Daak glared toward one of the Terran representatives, his mind musing, *Oops, someone's in trouble.*

Dreslin continued. "I ask for a few semi-cycles—that's minutes, for the Terrans—to inform the accused of his rights and procedures. Does challenging counsel object?"

Several seconds passed before the Daak representative responded. "We were misinformed about the accused's isolation. Was the isolation requested by the accused?"

Dreslin turned toward Jace. "Do not speak, but nod if you did request it."

Jace shook his head.

Dreslin then announced, "As you can see by the indication of the field, the accused had not requested the isolation, and so far, has not been informed of his rights or procedures. Does the opposing counsel object to my request?"

Jace again faced forward but looked to the side, seeing the Daak quietly scolding the Earth representatives. Jace heard a quietly muttered answer from the Tribunal as the Daak agreed. "You have a quarter-cycle, Arbiter." Dreslin thanked the Tribunal, and moments later, the walls of the box they were in became opaque.

"That is cool," Jace said.

"If you are uncomfortable, we can raise the temperature. I would not mind doing so. Your people live on a much colder world."

Jace laughed at Dreslin's remark.

They went over what Heralyn had informed him about the plan. Jace knew it was risky, but Dreslin also understood that the man before him was not a war criminal. Jace was defending himself and, in some part, his world. In the arbiter's mind, the actions of helping the crew escape were proof of that. And he told Jace that he planned on using that as a defense.

Dreslin looked at the pad on his wrist. "We're almost out of time. Is there anything else you want to add?"

Jace shook his head, and Dreslin started writing his statement. Jace then looked around. "Is the field you talked about what made the walls opaque?"

"Hmm, what?" Dreslin mumbled as he continued to write.

"You know they left me for dead, right?" Jace told him.

The arbiter looked to Jace, a hint of disgust in his gaze. "When you attacked them?"

Jace shook his head. "No, my own people. They brought me to a survival center but then kicked me out." Dreslin asked why, suspecting that Jace was violent, but Jace replied, "No, I didn't have any money or anything of value to them." Jace paused. "But for some reason, since I flew the ship, they want me back."

Dreslin looked toward the opposing counsel, even though he couldn't see them. "That's why they had you in isolation; they were going to spirit you out of there."

Jace nodded.

Dreslin gave an obvious sigh of frustration. "Anything else?"

Jace looked up. "What is that field you mentioned earlier?"

Dreslin smiled. "I almost forgot to inform you. We use what is known as a memoric field. It discerns actual memories from imagined ones. Sort of a …"

Jace looked at him to continue. "What?"

"I don't want to sound insulting, but it lets us know if you are telling the truth."

Jace looked up. "Wow, we could use this back on Earth."

"I'm sure you could. Is there anything else you need to add?"

Jace shook his head. "It works on your people as well?"

"It does. It has to be set for the correct Terran genetic keying, however. Thankfully, Terrans are pretty much all the same," he noted, making Jace laugh.

"What is it?" Dreslin asked.

Jace looked through the pile of paperwork in front of Dreslin. "Heralyn said something about my DNA not being all Terran. Didn't she tell you?"

Dreslin rifled through the papers, pulling out the DNA results of Jace's medical report. "The field is set wrong; it won't react correctly."

Jace said, "Good. The less they know, the better."

Dreslin stood straight. "No, if the field is found to be mis-set, then it is a good chance they will hand you over to them without question. We should inform the Tribunal."

Jace was wary but reluctantly agreed.

When the walls again became clear, Dreslin announced, "Tribunal, something has come to my attention. The memoric field is not set correctly for the accused. May I approach?"

They agreed, and one of the Daak joined them at the Tribunal stand. The Daak looked back at Jace, who remained staring forward. Whatever Dreslin told them, the Daak agreed, and they returned to their original places.

"The Daak were confused that we mentioned the field wasn't set correctly. You could have used it to your advantage," Dreslin told him as they adjusted the field. After it was done, they again asked if he had requested the isolation, with the same result as earlier.

After arguments were presented, Jace answered each question. The Earth representative stated, "He is essential to our people. His skills are something that we have limited expertise in since the attack. We request him returned so we can rebuild our society."

Jace blurted out, "You've got to be joking! You threw me out because of a busted leg and asthma. You left me to die!"

One of the Tribunal reprimanded Jace. But as he did, he noticed that the memoric field didn't react. Seeing this, he turned to the member next to him.

"The accused did not lie with his last statement. Should we note it?"

The council member looked and then consulted with the other; all three agreed. "This Tribunal wishes to inform both the arbiter and the accusing council that the memoric field did not react during the accused's outburst. Please note that the account of the accused is correct to his knowledge. Does counsel wish to withdraw their request?"

Jace smiled as the Terran representative sat down in disgust.

The trial continued.

Dreslin argued that Jace's actions were those of survival and that the Daak were the aggressors in this case. That perhaps the attack was not as warranted as had been maintained by the Earth government. He continued, stating that Jace took the ship to avoid being captured or killed by the Daak out of fear, and that it was a crime of opportunity, since the commander was injured.

The Tribunal asked of the timeline as it occurred. Jace told them how he remembered it, the memoric field confirming his story. When he made it to the part about being on the ship, he mentioned that he just flew the ship.

"But according to the system logs, the engine was offline, having the spide crystal removed to prevent overload," the Tribunal mentioned.

"Yes, I put the crystal back in and took her to the bridge to fly the ship, but she was unable," Jace replied.

"And then you forced her to unlock the genetic locks on the controls, correct?"

Jace shook his head. "Nope, she was a little out of it, and when I asked her how to fly, she told me. I just put my hands on the controls and took off."

The Daak at first objected, but seeing the field not react, they questioned if it was working. When Jace said that the sky was plaid, the field responded. They again asked him to run the timeline from the closing of the main door to flight.

He told them precisely as he had before, hearing one of the Tribunal say, "Those suits are hard to get on. I'm surprised you had any time."

Jace then said, "I didn't put on the suit. I just used the gloves."

Everyone started to laugh, even the Daak, but his reaction to the field not responding made the Daak glare uncomfortably toward Jace. Moments later, the Daak motioned to his counterpart. "Tribunal, we must consult. May we have a semi-cycle?"

The Tribunal agreed but was curious about the delay. Wondering this, one of the Tribunal replayed part of the hearing. His eyes were filled with concern. "I recommend to the rest of Tribunal that we allow the Daak the time. It will give us a moment to contemplate the proceedings so far as well."

Jace watched as the other council members looked at each other, puzzled. But as Jace watched the Tribunal speak, a look of concern came over all of them.

"Is there a way to see what they are looking at?" Jace asked.

Dreslin nodded and tapped the glass before them and enlarged the paperwork they were examining. "It looks like they are looking at your DNA profile. That may be a good thing. Maybe our plan is working."

Jace suddenly felt his stomach tighten. "Yeah, maybe." But something in his gut was telling him that this was not going to turn out as he anticipated.

The Daak returned, only to stand silently. They awaited being addressed before one of them turned, staring at Jace. The alien almost seemed curious about something. When the Tribunal addressed the Daak, all Jace heard was, "We do not wish to continue at this time. The request for extradition is to be withdrawn. We have additional requests but await the ruling of this Tribunal in reference to the accused. There is another matter we wish to offer separately."

This stunned everyone, and the Earth representatives became belligerent, demanding that they continue, or at least allow the Terran case to continue. Jace sat in complete exhaustion before being ordered to stand again by the Tribunal.

The Tribunal agreed, and the Daak withdrew their request as one of the Tribunal spoke. "As for the Terran request, it is denied. You relinquished all claims when you left the accused behind. But that is not why we are rescinding your claim."

The Tribunal continued to issue its statement. "The accused admitted that he did not entice or force the commander to unlock the controls to him; that he flew the ship without her assistance. And that he willingly fired on a Daak ship under treaty with this galactic council. The accused has also admitted that he is aware of his genetics."

Jace suddenly felt his heart start to pound.

"As regards the Terran agreement, the accused had accessed and operated an Alliance ship without aid, effectively stealing the vessel. Due to his lineage, and since this is the case, the accused would fall under Alliance law. This Tribunal recommends that he be charged for the crime of theft."

"I wish to register an objection, Tribunal; this would be a matter of asylum," Dreslin said.

Jace then asked, "What's going on?"

The arbiter just looked at him.

"Arbiter, you are aware of the sentencing for theft of a vessel, are you not?"

Dreslin nodded. "But this would be under asylum, Tribunal."

The council continued. The Tribunal focused, for some strange reason, on Jace's genetic makeup, again recommending he be sentenced under Alliance laws. They also insisted he be held not in local confinement but at the Alliance facility, and that he be remanded over for community service on an outlying colony.

"But, Tribunal, this was not a premeditated crime."

"We are aware; the only other option would be to hand him over to the Terran representatives."

Dreslin looked at Jace. "I need to confer with the accused for a moment."

The Tribunal agreed.

"What the fuck is going on?" Jace asked as Dreslin leaned in to speak.

Dreslin's head lowered. "It looks like our plan worked a little too well. They want to charge you under *our* laws."

"Okay, so what do you get for borrowing a ship to escape being killed?" Jace asked, obviously upset.

Dreslin took a breath. "A quarter planetary cycle, or about four months your time in minimum security. It's still not that easy."

Jace replied, "Okay, and what's the other option?"

"One planetary cycle community service," the Arbiter told him.

"That doesn't sound so bad," Jace replied.

"But they would be shipping you off-world. Probably to keep the Terrans from trying to abduct you. Unfortunately, they've done it before. I'm going to argue that the sentence is too harsh."

Jace took a breath. "No, I'll take what they are offering."

"We can still argue, get less time."

Jace sat down. "I know this is bullshit, but I've always wanted to see another planet. Tell them I'll take the offer."

Dreslin looked puzzled, and when they came back to address the Tribunal, they insisted that Jace say that he understands and accepts the ruling.

When Jace replied, "Yes," the memoric field gave no indication of him lying.

Chapter 5

Heading Unknown

Jace stared out the small window, watching the streaks of energy surrounding the ship flash. He was still in awe of the wonder of traveling like this. He thought it strange that it felt, well, sort of normal. Jace was still trying to wrap his head around hyperspace and how the space surrounding the space they were in could be smaller. The explanations of dimensional compression and density were way over his head, for now—so many things he had to learn.

Jace's mind was overwhelmed by all the new experiences. In the last several weeks, he had flown an alien ship, been taken to a courtroom on a space station, and was found guilty of theft. His mind found the facts funny; after all, he did steal a spaceship. Even though the Alliance takes theft of technology by lesser-advanced planets very seriously, his conviction was noted as per extenuating circumstances. He was only trying to escape the Daak as they occupied his home world.

The outcome was something he hoped would happen, but he hadn't realized that his people were the problem. After the Daak dismissed their claim, Jace avoided being spirited away. The Earth representatives even tried to abduct him with a fake breakout. But right now, his mind was clear. The only worry he had was wondering where they were taking him.

The Tribunal had charged and convicted Jace of theft of a vessel and given him a little over half a planetary cycle of community service. They were sending him to the Brochan star system, as recommended. He was heading to Charon, a small planetary system on the other side of the galaxy. Even with hyperspace tunneling, it took several weeks of travel. The planet was remote, but it did have something necessary.

Charon VII was a small, rocky planet, the atmosphere oxygen-rich thanks to the planetary engineering of the Alliance. And Jace was offered a reduced sentence if he agreed to help mine and process the crystals they used for the jump reactors. Jace's eyes dazed, his mind still reeling from everything that had happened. He had never been off Earth, but in the previous few weeks, he had done things he had only dreamt of as a child. He was filled with a mix of fear and delight as the energy strands flew by. Unfortunately, he wasn't alone.

"Hey, Terran, you still staring out that window? You can't jump out in hyperspace, you know." A man mocked him as he sat across the aisle. Jartal was one of the other inmates sentenced to community service, while awaiting trial on other charges.

"Jartal, you still think you're going to get to me, don't you?" Jace said, still staring out the window.

The man leaned forward. "You know, I think I'll steal your meals from now on, just to mess with you."

Jace laughed as he looked at the man. The alien looked human in every respect. His long hair was wild as he shifted and tilted his head. There was a total of twenty-three prisoners on the ship heading to Charon; most kept to themselves. Jartal was the exception.

The man was belligerent and annoying, even daring the guards to space him if they didn't like his attitude. But Jace knew what was really going on. He had seen it before on Earth. The man was afraid of where they were going and of his sentence. Jace knew Jartal picked a fight with one of the Gel that were now locked in solitary. When Jace asked what race they were, one of the guards warned him not to mention he was Terran. When Jace asked why, he was told, "Gel don't like Terrans at all. They usually kill them on sight."

Jace found out from the guard that the Gel were the original inhabitants of Earth, and when the Lyri arrived, things changed. After integrating the Lyri technology, the Gel left Earth in search of another world to expand. The Gel also lived several thousand Earth years, on average, so they were able to make it to other star systems. The Gel met others and, in turn, updated their technology. But when they finally returned to Earth, they had found that most of their population was gone. The original Lyri had also left, but their offspring remained. They also found that any Gel who stepped foot on Earth aged quickly.

"You know what, Jay-see? I think I'll tell the Gel you're Terran. Don't you think that would be fun?" Jartal taunted, again trying to enrage Jace.

Jace turned to stare back at the man. "It's Jace, you idiot, not Jay-see, and didn't you tell them you were Terran already?"

The man leaned back, disappointed. "Yeah, the guards stopped them. Put them all in solitary."

Jace could see the disappointment and knew for sure what the man was trying to do. Jace had looked forward to leaving Earth. Something inside him wanted to move out into the universe but was afraid of what he'd find. Unlike Jace, the man sitting across from him was scared.

"Jartal, I'm not going to kill you. That's what you want," Jace said, and the man turned his eyes away from Jace's stare. Jace had seen something like this back home; the man wanted to die instead of facing his punishment. But instead of taking his own life, he wanted someone else to do it for him. Jace wouldn't oblige. He knew it would add time to his own sentence if he attacked anyone on the ship. That fact was emphasized in detail before they left. But Jartal wasn't making it easy. Jace watched as the man stared at the guards along the wall.

Jace turned to look out the window when in his peripheral vision he caught a glint of light. Jace's reflexes kicked in, and he pulled his arm up, only to watch a sharpened metal rod pierce through it, stopping near his face.

Jace punched Jartal with his free arm, striking the man dead center on the nose. Jace felt the man's grip loosen on the rod, allowing him to pull away from his attacker. Seconds later, Jace found himself locked tightly in the armored guard's hold. Jace struggled for a moment before realizing who was holding him. As he relaxed, the guard moved him away from Jartal.

"Your actions were defensive; you will not be charged," he heard the guard say. On the other end of the cabin, he heard Jartal screaming as he was held down by the other guards. He could hear them telling him, "Jartal, you have attacked several people on this ship. Your actions will be reported, and additional sentencing will be recommended."

Jace then heard, "No, just kill me. I am not spending the rest of my life on some out-of-the-way planet."

Jace never heard the rest, as the door to the cabin closed.

"Where are you taking me?" Jace tried to free himself from the guard's hold.

"You require medical attention. Do you not feel the injury to your arm?" the guard asked.

Jace peered down, seeing the trail of blood that his arm had left down the entire hallway. He instinctively tried to use his other hand to hold the wound closed but was unable to move due to the guard's grasp. His fight didn't last long. As they entered the medical bay, the doctor quickly grasped Jace's arm to put pressure on the wound. "Put him here," the doctor ordered.

Within seconds, Jace felt some force pull him against the wall, and as he had seen on the ship he had stolen, he was unable to move. He watched the doctor's gray-skinned hands through the clear gloves as he used a device to stop the bleeding.

"All right, anesthetic field is active. Let's remove that thing from you, shall we?" the doctor said as he pulled the sharpened rod from Jace's arm.

Jace felt no pain, but the doctor wasn't finished. Jace watched as the man used several different devices, and the wound on his arm quickly healed.

"Well, that should do it. Unfortunately, the weapon chipped the bone on its way in. It's not a break, so there's no need to knit it. But you may feel a dull ache for the next few days," the doctor said, and Jace fell as he was released from the table.

"Thanks, Doc. Gotta love this hospital tech," Jace said, examining where the hole in his arm used to be.

The doctor chuckled and looked down. "You made a mess all the way here. Don't worry; the cleaning sentinels will have it up in a cycle." The doctor then reached down and wiped some of the blood off the floor with a cloth and was about to throw it away before looking at it closely.

"Hmm, this is pretty dark red for Terran blood. You are Terran, if my memory is correct?" the doctor asked.

Jace nodded. "That's just its normal color. I've seen it too many times to count."

The doctor laughed. "Ah yes, you Terrans and all of your fighting. But let's have a look, just in case."

Jace stood by as the doctor placed the cloth on a device and looked into the lens. "Terran hemoglobin, platelets, plasma … nothing out of the ordinary. But there is a higher concentration of iron in your blood. Usually only see that in low-oxygen environments. Let me run an analysis, and I'll check your file."

Jace watched as the man typed on his screen and looked over the information that appeared. He had been through this before, after the court ruling. He became concerned with the amount of blood they were taking, even after the trial.

The doctor looked over the readings. "No, nothing unusual, just the higher concentration of iron." He then moved to the other screen and read through the results. "Of all the idiots! You can't get good medical help these days, you know that? Even with the Alliance. Why does your sequence show Lyri readings? You're Terran."

He continued to read through. "Oh wait, it does show Terran, but only about 20 percent. That doesn't make any sense. It's like you're not …" The doctor stopped and turned toward Jace.

"I'm not what?" Jace asked.

The doctor leaned back as he sat in his chair and smiled. "On Oppa, my people are asked to perform as medical staff on tens of thousands of ships galaxywide. We learned a long time ago not to judge. And in your case, I am not as well."

Jace shifted his weight as he rubbed his arm. "What is it, Doc?"

The doctor again smiled. "You know, don't you?"

Jace gave a sarcastic response. "I have no idea what you're talking about, Doc."

The doctor stood. "Starborn are not very welcome among Alliance worlds, you know. If you do leave Charon and can't return to your home world, I ask that you consider my home planet as a place to go."

Jace looked suspiciously at the doctor.

"Please, don't get me wrong. My people are empathetic. I am just telling you out of concern."

Jace asked why, and the doctor said, "My world has the highest known concentration of starborn refugees in the galaxy. And to be honest, they are very productive and ingenious beings. They created half of these devices you see. You should take pride in your heritage." The doctor mentioned again that they learned a long time ago not to judge other races and that what Jace was, was nothing to be ashamed of. "They were, after all, some of the first beings to travel the stars."

"I'll take your advice to heart, Doc, but right now, I just want to get to where we're going."

"Don't worry, we'll be planetside shortly." The doctor paused. "And then, you'll be *their* problem."

Jace said, "But, Doc, I thought we were bonding here," before starting to laugh.

The doctor walked forward. "There's been enough violence on this ship. The Gel know there is a Terran on board. Thankfully, they are unloading the lot of you on Charon. There's too much negativity on board this ship. Get back to the holding area. And watch your back. I don't want to see you in here again."

Jace turned and hit the panel on the door and looked at the doctor before leaving. The doctor watched the door close.

"You may have been told what you are, but you don't really know what you are yet. Let's hope you survive long enough to find out."

Chapter 6

Mining Planet

They arrived on Charon only days after Jace was attacked. He was the only one in the holding area for the rest of the flight, since everyone else was held in confinement. Jace spent most of his time staring out the window as they entered the atmosphere. He could see the dark-orange sky as the red hue of the star colored the atmosphere a dull brownish-red. The sight made Jace think, *Looks like Los Angeles on a bad day.*

The surface of the planet had vegetation, water, and what looked like desert. Jace could see animals running in packs as they flew over.

"What are those?" Jace asked.

One of the guards responded, "Raza wolves. You might recognize them a little. They're like the wolves you have from your world. But they've been crossed with raza."

"What's a raza?" Jace asked.

The guard laughed. "They're mean creatures with razorlike claws, and feathers. They exist on several planets I wouldn't want to go to."

"Why the hell would anyone want to do that to a wolf?" Jace asked.

The guard replied, "To make them harder to escape from. And it mellowed out the raza DNA. They were bred to keep people in."

Jace looked at him, then turned toward the window again. "Sounds like a prison planet."

"It was. There's a field and barrier that keeps them from attacking the compounds. I wouldn't want to be out near any of them."

"I'll keep that in mind." Jace realized that he might have just been sentenced to something other than what he was promised. But that would have to be a worry for another time. Right now, his fellow inmates were the problem.

The ship landed, and he grabbed his belongings. Jace was led outside and stood where they told him, watching as the others lined up next to him. Jartal, thankfully, was away from Jace. When he looked over, Jartal seemed very subdued.

There was a pause when the Gel came out, each pausing to look up at the sky and take a deep breath of air. Jace watched as they stood closer to each other and farther from any beings that looked like him. He was wondering if huddling together was something their people did, but when he heard, "This planet reeks of your kind, Terran," to Jartal, Jace figured out what was going on.

Jace looked forward; there were several well-armed guards with substantial exo-suits. He did take a slight look around to get some sort of bearing. He was about to say something to the prisoner standing next to him but noticed him shaking and sweating.

"You all right?" Jace asked.

His question was not answered by the man but by the female guard in front of them.

"It's the radiation. Don't worry, you'll start to feel its effects soon," she said, her voice coming from the speaker in her suit.

Seconds later, Jace watched as three others emerged from the compound door. "Get the others ready to board the transport," Jace heard the one leading them. He had several plates of armor decorated with awards that Jace noticed as he turned to inspect the line. Jace continued to watch as the third officer broke away, walking toward the ship. Jace kept his eyes focused forward but still tried to see what was going on. He could see the ship's doctor handing the one soldier an information pad, and the man returned a very similar-looking one to him.

As the man turned, motioning toward the door, Jace could see the same grayish skin tone on the suited guard's face. The two gray-skinned aliens looked over the pads and when finished, saluted each other. The doctor then turned, moving back inside.

The other guard approached and spoke with the one who had the decorated chest before moving the first prisoner.

"Welcome, everyone. I am Captain Bosh. I run this facility. We will have you inside shortly. However, we have several people who have served their time here, leaving us today. I do hope you will honor them and do your best to surpass their work ethic."

Jace rolled his eyes and thought, *Oh, it's going to be fun here.*

He listened as the captain read off the names of each individual and their planet of origin. When he reached the Gel, he was very good at pronouncing their names, and Jace overheard the captain say, "There are Terrans and non-Terrans here. I do not want any trouble. Your fellow Gel have learned to live with Terrans nearby, and you will as well." One of the Gel didn't like what the captain said and within seconds, Jace felt a sharp pain in his ear. As he recovered, he noticed that everyone had the same reaction.

"You know, I usually have a Terran who sets that off first. They're always troublemakers. But what you experienced was the activation of nerve-induced pain generation built into your aural translators. You would be wise to avoid setting it off too often; it can cause severe nerve damage."

The captain then continued and reached Jartal. "Jartal Ayate, Gilese IV. Crimes, multiple murders. And cannibalism, as well as piracy?" The captain looked at the man who seemed to stare into the abyss. "I see he's been sedated."

The guard next to him held the pad up. "Yes, sir. He attacked several prisoners and guards, severely injuring one of them, who was treated en route."

"What did he do, try to take a bite out of him?" the captain joked.

The man remained serious. "No, but he did impale another prisoner's arm. There was a bio-mat cleanup that had to be performed."

The captain looked at the guard. "If this person's crimes are so severe, why is he here? This is a minimum-security facility."

"Yes, Captain, but we are only holding this prisoner until his Tribunal on Gilese calls for his return," the guard explained.

The captain looked at Jartal. "We have a special place for people like you. Even if you escape, the radiation will get you."

The captain then stepped back and announced, "By now, all of you are starting to feel the effects of spide radiation. Thankfully, we do have extractors running, so for loading and unloading, it is not fatal."

Hearing this, Jace looked to see everyone swaying or sweating as if something was affecting them. He, however, felt fine. Thinking to himself, *Probably a way to soften everyone up before they bring them inside*, Jace remained silent and looked forward, but his attention became focused on the line of inmates surrounded by guards heading into the ship. Just as the captain reached the man next to Jace, the ship's door closed.

"Jace Tucker, Terran." He then watched a few of the Gel trying to get a look before Bosh continued. "Crime, theft of a vessel, and kidnapping," the captain said and looked at Jace, waiting for a response.

Jace was smart; he said nothing and stared forward, but in his mind screamed, *Get the fuck out of my face, asshole!*

The captain leaned toward Jace. "I am surprised that you were not the first to cause trouble. Terrans almost always do."

The captain stood in front of Jace as the ship flew off. Jace felt the air move around him and felt an almost ethereal sense of being. Air blowing through his hair and clothes was something he always enjoyed. But he was brought back to reality as Bosh spoke.

"Are you feeling all right, Terran?"

Jace looked at the captain. "New planet, same shit." He instantly regretted speaking, feeling the burning in his implant.

The captain looked at him with a smile. "You almost had me disappointed." Jace held his head as the captain continued. "Since the Terran has been insubordinate, we will stay out here till the radiation makes him pass out. And, from what I see, several of you may do so before him. Let's prove that there are more resilient races in the galaxy than Terrans."

Several minutes went by, and Jace watched as others sat or fell forward. The captain continued to stand in front of him. "You'll fall, Terran," Bosh whispered, but after that, the gray-skinned guard tapped the captain's shoulder, holding up two fingers before tapping his helmet. He could see them speaking but could only hear the muffled conversation. Whatever it was angered the captain, but the guard handed the pad to the captain as he pointed to something on the pad.

The captain glared toward Jace and tapped his helmet again. "I think you all understand the consequences of being out on the surface without a protective suit. Now follow the guards inside for processing."

They started to lead the others inside, but one guard held Jace for a moment. "When we process you, I have to take some additional readings. You'll have to go last."

Jace turned toward him. "Well, don't I feel special."

Inside the compound, the wait for processing wasn't long, and they seemed very efficient. When it was Jace's turn, the doctor made sure there were as few people present as possible.

"Is it Jay-see or Jace?" the doctor asked. Jace told him what name he preferred. "Well, forgive the theatrics. The captain has to maintain a certain level of control of this facility. I assure you, he has never put anyone on the surface outside the compound to be punished."

Jace sat down. "I'm sure he's a great guy. Seems really concerned."

The doctor looked at Jace, noting his sarcastic response. "Not a fan of this place. Then why did you accept coming here?"

Jace looked down at the floor. "Didn't have many choices. My own people left me to die and then only wanted me back when they found out I could be used. The Daak wanted to take me as well. I'm a man without a world."

The doctor laughed. "That's sort of appropriate, isn't it?" making Jace look toward him, puzzled. "Your being without a world, I mean. Amaian told me what you are—before reporting that you were injured."

Jace looked more puzzled before saying, "You know, I never did ask his name. You're from Oppa, right?"

The doctor nodded.

"Forgive me, are you an Oppaian? Or Oppa? Or I don't know what to call your people," Jace said.

The doctor walked over, carrying a device, and placed it on Jace's forearm. "My people are called Oppan. My name is Tulo. And these—" The doctor hit a button, and Jace felt several sharp pains as needles entered his arm, making him grunt as the doctor held it down tight to the table. "—are the inoculations you'll need to stay here."

"Great bedside manner you got there, Doc," Jace said, rubbing his arm where the device was after it was removed, making Tulo laugh.

"Well, I do the best I can with what's available."

The doctor then pulled out another instrument and took Jace's vitals. "Good to see they fixed you up on the Alliance base. It'll make it easier to keep you healthy out here."

"Thanks a lot, Doc. Any more surprises?"

"Well, we do have a new design for a protective suit. It may get some time off your sentence if you'd be willing to test it."

Jace looked at him with suspicion. "And if it doesn't work?"

The doctor smiled. "You held a crystal in your hands; I don't think it'd matter to you."

Jace couldn't disagree, so he accepted the doctor's offer.

"Good, I'll let Bosh know. He's the only one who can assign the suits. There's only three of them for the moment."

"Now what?"

The doctor walked over. "Tests are done; you're processed in." He then pointed toward a door. "Commissary is down the hall. Get some work clothes and provisions and a room. They'll send you down to get something to eat, and you'll get started in a few days."

Jace paused as he opened the door. "What's the food like here? That Alliance stuff was pretty bland."

The doctor laughed. "It's not bad. Some of it's farmed and grown here. And don't worry, it won't kill you."

"Good to know," Jace responded as he closed the door behind him.

* * *

The hallway was dimly lit the entire way down to the commissary; in fact, the commissary was very dark. Jace remained cautious as his eyes adjusted to the light. He scanned the room, seeing what looked like shelves, but was only able to make out shades of gray and black.

"Don't tell me you're closed for the day. You got a customer still waiting," Jace joked in the darkness.

"Hold on. You damn people keep messing with my visual spectrum, turning on those lights. Ever try dwelling in a dark tunnel?" was a response from the darkness. Jace caught a glimpse of large eyes reflecting up at him.

"You crawling on the floor, or are you really that short?" Jace joked.

"You have to be the Terran," was the response before the light slowly became brighter.

Behind the counter, Jace saw a short, round man staring back at him with dark, round glasses almost the size of his hand. Jace pointed at the man's face. "You weren't wearing those a moment ago."

The man huffed. "You could see me in the dark?"

Jace shook his head. "Only a little, but I can tell the difference between eyes and glass."

The man stood on the stool behind the counter. "You've got pretty good vision for a Terran."

Jace smiled. "Always had good night vision. Wound up wearing sunglasses on really bright days."

The man looked him over. "Hmm, you probably have an extended visual range. May have to get you a visor when working near the extractors." He paused to hop onto the shelf and climbed quickly up the framework. "You look to be about four hundred semlins tall."

"If you say so," Jace responded. He still didn't know the man's name. Jace even searched for a nametag, which seemed conveniently absent.

Within moments, the man returned with a few bags of clothing and other goods. Jace could see the same light blue-gray color from each bag. There were a few pairs of overalls, pants, shirts, and they all looked to be the same color. The man placed them on the table and wrote in what looked like a logbook on the counter.

"I'm surprised you don't use one of those info pads," Jace joked.

His words brought a glare of annoyance from the man across the counter. "It *is* one of those info pads," he retorted, and as he tapped the page, it became several characters on the opposing page. Jace raised his eyebrows, somewhat impressed.

"You know, what the hell is a semlin?" Jace asked, trying to make conversation.

The man continued his recordkeeping. "It's a unit of measure out here, sort of a standard. In terms you'll understand—" the man looked up at Jace again, "—okay, maybe you won't. It's about a 182 centimeters."

Jace thought for a moment. "I'm about six-one. So yeah, okay."

The man looked directly at Jace. "I'm impressed, you converted that fairly quickly. You don't have an implant, do you?"

Jace shook his head. "Nah, pretty common conversion where I'm from."

The small, round man shook his head. "You're not as dumb as you look, Terran. You should watch yourself."

The next several minutes passed as the man brought additional items to the counter, logging each one in as he did. Jace found out that Arren Yuonto was the clerk's name, and he had been there since the compound was turned into a mining center. His race was known as the Lagt. They were miners long before the Alliance asked them to help. They usually ran the crews when underground. It only took a few minutes more before Jace had a stack of supplies standing tall before him.

"Am I really going to need all of this?" Jace joked.

Arren smiled. "Trust me, mining's dirty work. You'll thank me for this later. So, grab your stuff, and we'll get you a room," Arren said, hopping from the counter and waddling across the floor.

They entered the darkness again, and Jace was having trouble getting his bearings. Then he paused. "Arren, I know you're behind me. You like taking people through dark alleys or something?" Jace then placed his hand down and pushed Arren aside just on his right.

"Good, good, excellent dark peripheral vision. You'll do fine down in the shafts," Arren replied.

"Not sure I like the sound of that."

Arren snapped his fingers, and the hallway lit dimly. "Just getting a feel for you, Terran. I'm going to recommend that you get a filter for your suit visor. Sometimes when the reactors start, there is a bright glow. Can't stand it myself."

Jace nodded, and as they headed down a couple of flights of stairs, became curious. "Hey, Arren, how come the radiation isn't affecting anyone in the compound?"

Arren looked back at him before touching his palm to the frame next to a door. "You are a curious one, Terran. Most beings would be terrified of what was happening. There must be something wrong with you. Now touch your hand to the frame. And to answer your question, the whole place is shielded."

Jace took a breath, balancing the load of things before clumsily placing his hand to the frame. Moments later, he heard, "Occupant code accepted." They walked in, and Arren turned on the lights.

Even Jace had a problem with the intensity. "That's a bit bright."

Arren nodded and showed the controls for the cabin to Jace. "Light, temperature, oxygen, humidity, etc. Full controls of the environmental system for your room." Arren then pointed to the bed behind the wall. "Bed, storage, facilities. All the comforts of home."

Jace looked up, making Arren laugh. "You people and your sky. You keep looking for it, even when it's not there. I can't stand being out in the open."

"Well, Arren, to each their own," Jace said as he threw the pile of things on the bed.

Jace then looked at the large clock on the wall, the display just above a small viewing screen. Arren saw him staring and said, "You'll get used to it."

Jace then looked around. "Actually, this is better than where I was staying after the Daak attacked."

The smile faded from Arren's face. "Didn't realize you were a refugee."

Jace nodded. "Yeah, well, at least I'm alive."

Arren nodded. "You've got strength, Terran. Come on, let's get you some food."

Jace agreed and followed Arren as he led the way.

"So, Arren, what's next? Never been to prison off-world before."

The small, greenish-brown-skinned man scoffed. "Well, today you get some food. Tomorrow, you go through orientation. Don't worry, it's quick. You'll have most of the day to explore if you like."

Jace laughed. "Sounds like fun. Can't wait."

Arren turned to look at Jace. "Ah, sarcasm, a wonderful talent you seem to be mastering."

Jace laughed at his joke and then said, "I guess I better enjoy the time while I can. They asked me to test one of the new suits. We'll see how long that lasts."

Arren stopped. "You're assigned to testing the glyph model?"

Jace shrugged his shoulders. "I guess."

Arren shook his head. "You're either braver or stupider than you look."

Jace asked, "Why's that?"

Arren shook his head. "I'm not talking about testing the suit. I can't wait to see what Eis does to you when it gets ruined."

"Ice? Who's Ice?" Jace asked.

Arren stopped and motioned for him to lean down. "We call her Ice. Her name sounds like the cold stuff, but it's spelled differently. She's the one who has been making improvements to the resistance suits; she runs the crew assignments. I think she cares more about the suits than the people they protect. Oh, and she also heads the bar."

Jace rolled his eyes. "Great, can't wait to meet her."

"She's a piece of work, that one." Arren leaned back, whispering, "They say she's a starborn."

"Oh, is she?" Jace mocked.

"Yeah, and I would like to see how you handle her, Terran; she's a tough one."

"Why would you want that?" Jace asked as the hallway opened to the massive mess area.

"Probably place a few bets on you, just to the pass the time," Arren said as he turned to enter the mess hall.

Jace smelled the aroma of food wafting through the air, and honestly, he would eat anything right now. The ship rations were filling but completely tasteless. Jace looked around to see his fellow shipmates all sitting at different tables but staying with their own kind.

"So, Arren, how's this work?"

Arren pointed toward the display. "Place your hand on there, and it figures out what nutrients you need. After that, condiments are there. Use as much as you like."

"Food's really that bad, huh?" Jace replied.

"Actually, no, most people just like the condiments because they're fresh."

Jace put his hand on the screen, and a few selections came up. The dispenser spit out his tray. Jace jerked his head back as he smelled it. "Yum, just like home."

Arren laughed. "Eat up, Terran. I'm going to place a bet. Don't disappoint me tomorrow."

Jace watched as the Gel looked toward him before mumbling at Arren, "You're going to get me killed, you little shit."

Jace sat near the remaining Gilesian and watched them move away as the Gel turned, their eyes focused on him. Jace looked around before shaking his head. "This wasn't the brightest idea you've had, Jace. Let's see what tomorrow brings."

His statement made the man nearest to him ask, "Are you talking to yourself?"

Jace nodded, taking a forkful of food. "Yep." Jace took another bite and said, "Hey, this stuff's not half bad!"

Chapter 7

First Day Fun

Jace groaned, hearing the loud alarm blaring over the speakers in his room. His drowsiness was making the instructions it gave challenging to understand. He was supposed to meet with the rest of his workmates in the third-floor gathering room. It instructed him to meet at eight forty-five. Jace's eyes tried burning through the large numbers staring back at him, showing only six forty-five.

"Someone's got a sense of humor," Jace mumbled as he sat on the edge of the bed. His mind was reeling with everything that had happened to him in the last few months. Everything felt as if this was some bad dream he couldn't wake up from. But as he stared up at the clock, seeing the minutes creep by, he finally knew this was real.

"Not the best idea, Jace. Gotta keep things together. You'll get out of here eventually."

He showered, putting on the clothing he was given, and was amazed it fit.

"Well, Arren, it looks like you've got a good eye for fashion." He looked in the mirror at the shirt. "I hear postapocalyptic gray is all the rage nowadays anyway."

Jace was surprised at how fast the time went and found himself heading to the meeting room. When he arrived, there were a few like himself sitting toward the side of the room—several guards in front, some doing paperwork.

Jace walked toward the others, only to be stopped by the menacing stares back toward him.

"Hey, nothing personal, guys, just wanted to talk. See what you thought of this place."

Jace knew how things worked back on Earth, and to him, this was no different. He knew he couldn't survive alone and needed allies. But right now, everyone seemed to be keeping to themselves. He tried chatting up the guards, who seemed uninterested in speaking with a worker. But Jace knew they all knew the same thing: even though he was there voluntarily, this was still a prison.

Jace turned to see some Gel walking in. One of them sprinted straight for him. Jace stood his ground. If this alien wanted a fight, he was going to give it to him. Just as the Gel was about to reach him, Jace doubled over in severe pain in his head, making him fall sideways. But unlike outside, where it stopped after a few seconds, this continued. Jace's eyes were wide as he sat up, pounding the floor with his fist to distract from it. When he saw the Gel and others on the floor writhing like him, he understood what was happening.

"There will be no fighting in this facility," were the following words that all of them heard through their translators as the pain subsided.

It took a few moments for everyone to regain their balance, and Jace stood, walking by the Gel who had rushed toward him earlier. Jace only stopped when he heard, "I was beginning to think I'd have to teach you another lesson, Terran." Jace turned to see Bosh standing in the front of the room.

The imposing man of almost eight feet tall walked toward him. "Why didn't you attack the Gel while he was down?"

Jace looked the man in the eyes. "I've got no reason to fight them. I don't know what their problem with me is."

Bosh smiled back at him. "You really don't know, do you?" Jace shook his head in response. "The Gel are known to be the original inhabitants of your home planet, Earth. They were pushed out after another race arrived."

Jace looked at the Gel. "So? *I* haven't done anything to them."

Bosh looked around. "Everyone, sit. It's your first day on the job." Bosh turned, heading to the front of the room. "And you're all going to work as a team. I don't like people killed on my watch."

Jace sat in the nearest chair and looked around before facing the front of the room. He watched as the guards pulled one of the Gel and sat her down next to Jace. He was surprised when the guards also sat a Gilesian on his other side. The rest were allowed to sit where they pleased.

Jace looked at the Gel woman, who snarled back at him before staring forward. The other man glared with contempt toward Jace before he did the same as the Gel. When Jace looked ahead, he could see Bosh staring back at them in silence, an expression of study in his eyes as he sat behind the desk. Jace then looked at the other two and back toward Bosh before muttering, "Okay, why are the three of us together? What's so special about this setup?"

His statement brought another glare from both the Gel and the other man seated next to him before he heard Bosh speak.

"You're a smart one, Terran. I picked each one of you for a reason. You, because you're the only Terran here at the moment. But, the others, well ..."

Jace turned to look at the others seated next to him, then smiled. "Ah, that makes sense."

The Gel woman stood in anger, making Bosh flinch, touching his medals, and she was subdued by her implant. The Gilesian looked around the room. Jace could see the woman trying to stand and offered his hand to help her up. She swatted it away immediately then sat in the chair, making sure to knock into Jace as she did.

"If you're finally done acting like savages, I would like to continue," Bosh said.

Within seconds, one of the guards handed them all a binder with information, making Jace joke, "Just like my last job, but I think it might be less paperwork."

Bosh laughed and replied, "It probably is. Your people are known for such extraneous and frivolous actions."

Jace nodded. "Not going to argue with you there."

Bosh stood, then walked over to stand in front of Jace. "If you think you can gain favor by attempting to humor me, you are deftly incorrect."

Jace looked down at the book before looking up. "Nope, just agreeing with you on a fact. Not exactly a fan of my own people at the moment."

The Gel woman looked at Jace with contempt. "You hate your own race?"

Jace looked at her. "No, I'm just not a fan of them at the moment."

She angrily asked why.

Jace coldly told her, "They left me to die, and then the Daak did the same. So …" Jace paused, looking at Bosh, having suddenly realized something. "I see, she's their leader, and he's theirs."

The Gel looked at Jace with surprise, as did the Gilesian.

Bosh smiled. "On your left is Kasmae of the Gel Accordance. On your right is Helmen Yokesy, leader of the Light of Errata. And you are correct."

Kasmae stood. "I will not sit next to this Terran."

Bosh stared back at her with cold eyes. "Yes, you will, and you will all work with each other."

Kasmae protested. "I will not."

Bosh turned, touching his medals again, and Kasmae fell in agony. Bosh walked over and pulled her from the ground, throwing her in the chair. "You all chose to be here instead of in a cell. And you will work together to help others by producing the number of crystals needed to keep ships operating and to provide power for new ones."

Kasmae closed her eyes, feeling the pain subsiding. When they opened, Jace could see a hint of fear hiding inside them.

"You will work as a team; you will work as needed. This is by no means a slave-labor camp. Time off will be allowed. But you will have to serve your sentences, and you will work together. Now, if you'll all open to the first page, let's begin."

Jace sat for several minutes as Bosh read and explained what was in the booklet before them. When Jace heard how they were to be a team for the fifteenth time, he joked, "I was wrong. This is worse than the teambuilding exercises back home."

He heard what sounded like a slight humorous snort from Kasmae, and Jace turned toward her.

"Was that a laugh? I was making a joke."

The Gel woman only turned her eyes toward him. "I have no love for this either, Terran. I only wish it to end."

Jace whispered, "I'm with you on that."

Another hour went by, and Jace felt his throat becoming dry. He turned to see Kasmae starting to waver, making him ask if she was all right.

"I am dehydrated, Terran. I wish this to end so I may get water," she whispered in response.

Jace nodded. "Yeah, I'm thirsty too. You know, my people did something like this, denying water and food to make people suggestible," Jace whispered.

Kasmae looked at him. "Your people are monsters?" Her statement got the attention of Bosh.

"You wish to add to the orientation, Kasmae?" Bosh said.

The Gel was about to stand when Jace interrupted. "We were discussing the possibility of getting some water, or perhaps a short break. If that's all right with you, Captain? I'm sure many of the others are thinking the same."

The Gel glared toward Jace for a moment but realized what he had said. He was not denying her anything but instead offering a solution. She sat back and stared at Bosh for a moment.

Bosh looked at Jace, then at the others beside him, before looking around the room. "I would agree. We only have a few pages to go, and you may have the rest of the day and the next two days before the assignments begin." He returned his stare to Jace and watched as Jace looked at the two next to him. "Well, if the others agree, we should continue, don't you think?"

Kasmae nodded and then Helman, so Bosh continued.

Bosh was a man of his word, finishing in only a few minutes. He then reminded them that protective suits were to be assigned before the first day. Everyone had the remainder of the day exploring the compound and getting to know their surroundings, reminding them that no aggression would be tolerated. And as the rest of the others rushed out of the room, Bosh called out to Jace, "Terran, I want you to stay behind for a moment."

Jace joked, "Uh-oh, the principal wants to see me again."

The Gel looked at him with confusion, making Jace say, "Yeah, jokes don't work when no one knows what you're talking about."

Jace approached Bosh, who looked with concern down at the table. "You found a commonality with the Gel. Not many Terrans can do that."

"Commonality, how the hell did you find …" Jace stopped himself and tapped just to the front of his ear. "The translators. You can control them, and you listen as well?"

His remark made Bosh smile. "You're not a dumb Terran. Any normal being would have tried to kill someone to become feared by now. You, instead, are attempting to find allies."

Jace smiled. "Well, I'm just a different type of Terran. So, we're all bugged?"

Bosh sat back. "I already know what you are, and honestly, you are more valuable to me than them. But to answer your question, no. Hers is because their military counsel put it in. Sad to say, yours is a much simpler model."

Jace immediately thought, *That doesn't sound good. If it's simpler, how are you causing the pain?*

Bosh continued. "Today, I want you to meet with Eislie and get familiar with the new glyph suit. We have a situation, and we need to retrieve some valuable hardware."

Jace felt a weight on his shoulders. "So, no day off?" He looked at the captain with puppy dog eyes.

The captain laughed. "No, but you will right after. There is some mining hardware that had a reactor breach. It is blocking one of the richest veins of spide that we've found."

Jace looked at him. "I don't know how to drive anything here yet."

Bosh replied, "You don't have to. I just need you to get the reactor under control. Besides, I'm not sending you down alone."

Chapter 8

New Suit

Jace left the meeting hall and headed straight to the staging area. When he arrived, he could hear a woman yelling. "Butee, get away from me! I told you to stop bothering me!"

Jace walked a little faster to see what was going on. He could see a small, thin man; his face was elongated, and he was pushing on the shoulder of a woman trying to weld something on one of the suits. Jace realized that the thin man was tormenting her. Jace felt anger building and found it reckless, so he hurried over to see what was going on.

"Hey, Bosh sent me down. What's a guy gotta do to get a suit around here?" His words startled the man harassing her. But Jace was surprised when the man started circling him.

"Oh, look, a Terran. I've got money on the Gel against you, you know," Butee said. Jace feigned looking around, as if unable to see the man, but used his arm to throw the thin man several feet away. "Oh, sorry, I have trouble seeing in low light. Please forgive me," Jace said mockingly.

The thin man stood, brushing himself off, and said nothing as he walked away.

The woman turned to Jace, saying, "He's going to try and kill you, you know," before she started welding again, making Jace block the light with his arm.

He only replied, "Yeah, he's gonna have to get in line."

The woman finished her work and stood, looking at Jace. "So, you're the Terran," she deduced, making Jace nod.

She flipped up her face shield, and the light blue of her eyes struck Jace. When she took off her helmet, he saw the long, blonde hair she had fall to her shoulders and found himself saying, "Wow, wish I would have found someone like you back on Earth."

The woman sighed, looking at him with disgust. "What does Bosh want now?"

Jace smiled. "He sent me down to talk to Eislie about a glyph suit."

Her demeanor became defensive. "Why?"

Jace told her that he was supposed to get some hardware from one of the shafts and that he was supposed to disable a reactor so they could cool the area.

"I'm Eislie. I told Bosh the suits aren't ready to use. The shield circuits are still fluxing. Besides, I was going to do the job alone. I told him that."

Jace continued. "Look, he said I'd have help. Maybe he's sending us both down."

Eislie threw her welding mask on the table with a loud bang.

"The suit circuits aren't working up to specs yet. I have no idea who tested these before they came out here, but they don't work to the range they claim."

Jace could feel a genuine concern in her response. She acted worried about what might happen. He was going to tell her that it didn't matter to him but instead said, "Hey, I used a suit similar to this to replace an engine crystal. I'm sure it'll work."

She immediately started asking him questions about the coil windings, was the driver circuit inverted, and a whole barrage of questions that didn't make sense to him. He didn't know how to answer, but he did say, "I'll set it up the same way, but I don't know how to answer your questions."

Right after that, she grabbed his arm, dragging him back to the suit room. She immediately ordered him to get into the suit and set it up like from the ship. He was honest with her and said that was weeks ago. She only told him, "It doesn't matter. If you get close, I'll be able to figure it out from there."

No sooner did he get the legs on than she hoisted the top of the suit over his head. When she lowered the section down, she almost trapped his hand in the seam. After it clicked, Jace tried remembering how he grabbed the controls on the front. He placed his hand and looked down. "I can't see the controls. Are all the lights orange?"

Eislie shook her head. "Were they all orange?"

Jace nodded.

Eislie tapped the controls, causing them all to glow orange. She then looked up. "Forgot the helmet."

She went to turn the controls off when Jace stopped her. "No, the helmet wasn't on when the lights were orange."

She stepped back. "So, you put the helmet on after the controls were locked? I didn't know it would work that way. You're sure the lights were all orange?"

Jace nodded. "That's what they told me after the investigation. I was sort of busy trying to fly a ship away from the Daak."

He watched the woman smile. "Wonderful. I'm planning on going down at about," she paused, "twenty-eight hundred tomorrow. Come and get suited up around twenty-six hundred."

Jace nodded, and after talking with Eislie a few more minutes and getting fitted for a helmet, she sent him on his way.

She watched Jace leave and then said, "I'll have to remind Bosh I'm going down at twenty-five hundred."

* * *

Jace groaned, hearing the alarm of the room blaring louder than usual. He had arrived back at his room a few hours ago, having been out exploring the base until late. A typical day on Charon was thirty-one hours Earth time. The mild hangover from drinking last night wasn't helping.

Jace reached over to use the remote to shut off the alarm but found it wouldn't stop.

"All right, I'm up!" Jace yelled, looking at the clock on the wall. "Friggin hate thirty-hour days."

Just after he spoke, he heard Bosh's voice over the speaker. "Jace Tucker, report to the staging area."

"What the fuck are you talking about? It's supposed to be at twenty-eight hundred!" Jace yelled back.

"You were misinformed. We need you to get down here as soon as possible," Bosh replied.

Jace sighed. "All right, give me a few minutes. I'll be down."

Jace showered and dressed as fast as he could. It took about twenty minutes to make it down to the staging area. He could see Eislie sitting with two guards next to her. She turned away when the captain looked directly at her.

"Okay, Bosh, I'm here. Whaddaya have me doing today?"

Bosh looked at Eislie, who turned away further from his stare. Then Jace watched as the captain was about to touch the small patch that looked like the ribbons on his uniform, his actions making Jace think, *maybe those aren't ribbons.* He had seen the captain do that earlier when in the training room. He then told Bosh, "You know I can't lie to you, Bosh. It may have been twenty-five hundred. To be honest, I was looking more at her than really listening."

His last statement caused Bosh to chuckle and shake his head. Then Jace heard from behind him, "Terrans, always thinking with other body parts."

Jace turned to see Arren standing there holding a helmet and said, "Well, I'm here. I guess you were waiting for me?"

Arren handed Jace the helmet, telling him he had installed a shading visor in case the reactor was too hot. Jace thanked him, and Bosh ordered him to suit up.

It wasn't long before he was ready. The suit was pretty simple to get on, nothing like on the ship. Jace was about to put on his helmet when Eislie stopped him.

"These suits have limited power; Bosh, we need to get additional cells for these to use long term in the mine."

Bosh looked at her, then to Arren. "Were they ordered?"

Arren nodded.

"How long till power runs out, Commander?" Bosh asked Eislie.

"About four standard hours," she replied.

Bosh grimaced. "That's not a lot of time. But we need to get production going."

Jace was astonished at Bosh's planning. He seemed to know everything, down to the smallest detail. But when he said that they would have to bring up the line to send down the extractor, Jace had to step in. "Can't we send two lines down at the same time?"

Bosh looked at him curiously.

Jace told him that if they sent down a second line and something happened, they wouldn't have to wait till the line came down again. The base commander nodded, telling him, "That's a good idea."

As Bosh continued, Jace looked over at Eislie, who after a moment looked back at him before mouthing, "That is a good idea." Jace returned to listening to Bosh. Arren rigged a second winch, and within minutes, they were ready to head down.

The lines were set over the shaft, the rig floating with the line slack. "After you two get on, we'll turn off the mag-grav."

Jace and Eislie put on their helmets, and Eislie tapped hers.

"Comm test, you hear me?" Arren said.

Both of them responded in the affirmative as Arren confirmed that things were working. They heard the order to disengage the grav rig, and they felt the total weight of the suits as they held on to the lines. As Bosh gave the order to start lowering, Jace heard, "Start the timer."

Jace looked around as the ground rose, enveloping his view. He noticed the light from his suit made the stone surrounding them glisten. Eislie, however, didn't move as much.

"You all right?" she asked.

Jace looked at her. "Yeah, first time down a mine shaft. What about you?"

Eislie shook her head. "Too many to count. Why, you scared?"

Her tone was demeaning, but Jace was fast with a response. "Yeah, would you hold my hand while we go down? You know, for emotional support."

Eislie leaned her head back in annoyance, but both of them looked up, hearing Arren laughing loudly. And then Arren's voice came over the comm, saying, "I like you, Terran. You got guts, messing with her."

Eislie stared at Jace, tilting her head with disdain. Jace looked back. "Just nervous. Let's just get this done and back up top, all right?"

Eislie's demeanor changed hearing that, her reply more serious. "Yeah, you're right. Let's get this over with."

Several minutes passed. Arren checked in, and they responded with suit status and conditions. When they hit bottom, Arren was preparing the second line to send down the extractor. Eislie pulled Jace around and started pushing buttons on the front of his suit.

"What was that all about?" Jace asked.

"The spide radiation is pretty high right now. I was just checking your suit," she replied, suddenly seeming to become concerned.

She then stopped. "Arren, the radiation is about 130 percent above lethal, and we're not even close to the rig."

"How are the suits holding up?" Arren asked.

"Good, no problems yet. But we should probably get going and stabilize the rig. Send down the extractor as soon as you can. At this radiation level, it's going to chew up our power cells."

"Confirmed, Eis. I'll get the damn thing loaded. You work on stabilizing the rig," Arren said.

Eislie acknowledged him and motioned for Jace to follow.

As they walked, the sides of the tunnel became smooth, except for several archlike areas along the sides. When Jace asked what they were, she told him about the mining lasers and that the arches were safety shafts, just in case they needed to get a more oversized extractor down the tunnel. She then asked him to read out the radiation count. It was still under 200 percent.

A little further down the tunnel, Eislie stopped. "Arren, can you hear me? Arren?"

Jace became concerned and asked, "What's wrong?"

She only held her hand up before saying, "You little slac, can you hear me? I'm going to kick your ass when I get back up there. And steal supplies, like I did last time."

Jace looked at her. "Okay, now I have to know what's going on. Why are you mad at Arren?"

Eislie looked at him, motioning for him not to speak. They waited a few seconds before she said, "Good, they can't hear us."

Jace looked at her. "Too far down?" he asked, making her shake her head.

"No, radiation's too high. Are you even looking at your indicator?" But her transmission started to include static.

He looked down and saw the indicator reading 277 percent. "Damn, it is hot down here."

She looked at him, tapping her helmet. "I'm starting to hear static." Jace told her he was as well. "I don't know if we're going to be able to get to the rig; we're getting close to exceeding the max specs for the suits."

Jace nodded but then said, "If it's not far, we can still make it."

Eislie looked at him. She seemed to be deciding whether to continue or not. When Jace looked back at her, she said, "Yeah, let's go."

Within a minute, they could see a bright glow from just ahead. When the two arrived, Jace could see the rig. The radiant light from the reactor was causing him to shield his eyes. They could both see the crystal that had fallen from the tunnel roof, piercing into the power system. Jace tapped his helmet, making the visor come down. Eislie did the same. "Arren wasn't kidding. That is bright."

Eislie stared at her indicator. "We're at 450 right now. How's your suit power level?"

Jace looked at it, telling her it was already down to 63 percent.

She turned to look at him, her transmission filled with static. "I'm at sixty-five. We have to get this shut down fast." He nodded and watched her eyes focus on something behind him. Jace went to turn, but Eislie grabbed him. "Don't look."

Jace freed himself and turned to see the suits left behind from the original crew. He knelt and looked inside the helmet, seeing nothing but dust. He stood. "I guess we're not just here for the rig, are we?"

He watched Eislie shake her head slowly.

"Then let's make this quick," Jace said with a somber tone.

After trying for several minutes, the reactor was still too hot to shut down. A second crystal had fallen onto the rig, piercing the reactor shell and lodging itself against the main crystal, causing the overload. When Eislie tried using the tools, they merely snapped. One recoiled so badly that it struck her arm hard. Jace asked if she was all right and could see the ring of the glove dented. Eislie held her hand and said she was okay, but Jace could see she was in pain.

"It's too hot down here. We have to head back up. My suit's already down to 35 percent," Eislie said, almost sounding defeated. She turned toward Jace. "How did you get the crystal on the ship back into the reactor?"

Jace was about to show her, but the reactor's light was making it difficult to see. When he moved close to touching it, he felt a tingling in his hands. Jace looked around and rushed over to one of the other miners' suits and removed the gloves.

"What are you doing? Don't you have any respect?" she yelled at him.

Jace replied, "He's not going to need them right now, and I don't want to kill myself, okay?"

He then grabbed the second crystal with the gloves protecting his own. Jace then grunted as he wrestled the crystal from the hole in the reactor. He almost fell back when it worked loose.

Within seconds, Eislie noticed the radiation going down. "It's already at 375."

Jace placed the crystal down and walked away, still holding the gloves, but as he turned, they started to crumble.

Seeing this, Eislie yelled, "No!" and rushed to grab Jace's hands. She seemed confused when she only saw some cracking on the palms of his suit.

"What's your indicator say?"

Jace looked. "Three twenty-three. Suit integrity is still showing 100 percent."

His words seemed to calm her, but she still held on to his hands. All he heard her say was, "That was stupid," her words filled with regretful sadness.

Jace nodded. "Yeah, but it worked." He paused, but she was still holding on to his hands. "Thanks for being concerned."

She looked up at him. "Why did you lie to Bosh about what I told you?"

Jace looked away. "Something tells me Bosh isn't the nice guy he's leading us to believe he is. It's just a feeling."

Eislie replied, "You're right. He's not. I owe you one."

Jace turned, pulling his hands from hers. "Yeah, well, buy me a drink, and we'll call it even." He then picked up a piece left from the second set of gloves before dusting off his hands. "What about them?"

"After the extractor's come through, we'll come and get them. Right now, my suit power is getting low. We should probably head back." Jace looked at the indicator on his suit and agreed.

Most of the way back, both remained silent. When they neared the end of the tunnel, they could see the extractor.

Eislie tapped her comm. "Arren, did you have to put the damn thing in the middle of the tunnel?"

"Relax, Eis, just use the arches when it drives by," Arren replied.

"Yeah, well, we still have to decon here, and both our suits are running low on power. Mine is at 19 percent. Jace, what's your level?" Eislie asked.

He looked at the indicator and said, "Eleven. Shit, hurry up with that thing."

He then heard Arren. "Eis, Jace, when the extractor drives by, use the side panels. That should let you guys cool off."

"Acknowledged, send it down. We'll let you know when to stop," Eislie replied.

Within seconds, the extractor lumbered down the tunnel. Eislie and Jace squeezed into one of the arches as the extractor rolled toward them. When Eislie told them to stop, it did so quickly. The decon was fast and straightforward. They had to place their hands on the extractor plate, allowing the field to connect to the suits. A few seconds later, the radiation was gone. When Eislie told them they could continue, the machine rolled away. On the trip up, Eislie told Jace, "They're going to want to know why the power usage was different."

Jace replied, "Easy, I had to grab the crystal with the other gloves momentarily, so it didn't fall back into the reactor, remember?"

Jace briefly smiled as he watched Eislie nod in agreement.

* * *

When they arrived topside, Bosh asked for a status report from both of them as they removed their helmets. Eislie told them the readings and kept squeezing her left hand.

When Arren looked at it, he noticed the wrist linkage was damaged. "Get the glove off, and we'll take a look." He then pointed at Jace as he worked to remove the glove from Eislie's arm. "You, any damage to the suit?"

Jace held up his hands. "Unfortunately."

"Sweet darkness of Talin, your suit started to deteriorate!" Arren exclaimed.

Jace explained that the tools started to fail, and to stop the crystal from falling back again, he used other miners' gloves to grab and move it. "Thankfully, it wasn't for long."

As Arren worked Eislie's glove free, a few drops of blood fell to the ground. "Blessed Talin, you too?"

Eislie pulled her sleeve back a little. "It's just a cut. It's not even bleeding anymore."

"That's not a cut, girl, that almost made it to the vessels. You're lucky you didn't bleed out," Arren chastised her and was about to do the same to Jace but instead resisted when Bosh stepped forward. "What was the max reading on the suits?"

Eislie looked at him. "About four fifty." Arren took the data from the suits and confirmed the readings.

Bosh then took a deep breath and smiled. "Good work, you two. An excellent test of the glyph suits."

Eislie and Jace looked at each other before Jace said, "What about the others down there?"

Bosh stood tall, but Arren answered, "After the extractor's done, we'll send someone down to get them." A few seconds later, Arren added, "As crew chief, I'm recommending them both sent to medical to get evaluated. And I won't accept them on a new job for at least two days."

His words didn't go over well with Bosh, who reluctantly agreed. He then told Eislie that they needed to upgrade the rest of the suits with the glyph shielding and systems.

"But Arren just ordered two days off!" Eislie protested.

Bosh smiled. "You're not going down in the mines, Commander. But, since you are injured, wait till tomorrow to start the upgrades."

His remark brought a frustrated grunt from her as she turned to watch Arren finish bandaging her wound.

Chapter 9

Med Bay

After the glyph suits were stowed, guards escorted Jace and Eislie to the med bay. Arren had bandaged Eislie's wrist with the precision of an experienced field medic. He also included a list of possible injuries to be scanned for by the doctor.

When they arrived, Tulo immediately took Eislie to treat her more severe injury, handing Jace over to his assistant, Kala. She was Oppan, like the doctor, with the slight addition of green coloring, a small cluster of subtle, green-gray stripes across her face a dead giveaway. Jace looked at her, seeing the pattern flow up into her hair and fall like a hidden mane down her neck. Jace smiled at her as she worked. Kala seemed hesitant working alone with Jace as she read the request made by Arren.

"What's wrong?" Jace asked. Kala only briefly turned, a hint of fear in her stare.

When she returned to him, Kala asked Jace to move his fingers one at a time, slowly, then quickly. All the time, she was using a similar medical scanner to what the doctor had used earlier. Kala was diligent but kept her distance. She asked him to breathe deeply and again scanned his chest and then his hands, but her reaction to the readings seemed to puzzle her.

"What's up?" Jace asked, making Kala shake her head.

She was quiet as she excused herself. "I have to check with the doctor. The readings don't make any sense. Your cellular metabolism is more active than it should be. The report says you've been awake for only a couple of hours, is that correct?"

Jace looked at the clock, which read twenty-nine forty-one. "Yeah, they woke me up a few hours early." Jace paused. "I'm not even tired. Must be the adrenaline."

Kala looked at him and took another reading. "No, your adrenaline readings are normal. Let me check your biofield."

"My what?" Jace asked.

"Your biofield, the field that you radiate. It's sometimes affected by spide radiation." She then grabbed another device and scanned him. When Jace looked over, he could see a field surround an outline of his body. It seemed to be moving.

"So, your people read auras?" Jace joked.

Kala looked at him sternly. "Your people are so backward with superstition. You don't even realize that the people who settled your world knew how to do this."

Jace leaned back as she chastised him, saying, "Sorry, this is all still new to me. Do what you have to do."

She then turned the screen so he could see as she explained the field. "Field's got good strength. You're probably resistant to spide radiation, from what I can tell." She then looked at the screen again. "You seem to have a resonance factor, though."

"A what?" Jace laughed.

Kala huffed in annoyance toward him. "Your biofield has a resonance. Most Terrans and other beings have a variance-type field."

Jace looked blankly at her.

The woman then tapped the display and showed him another biofield. "You see the variances? The spikes both inward and outward? Your field is different; it is smooth and reinforced. And I'm pretty sure that's partly why you are resistant to the radiation. I'll inform the doctor."

Jace grabbed her arm. "You don't have to. He already knows."

Kala's eyes were wide with fear as Jace grabbed her arm, but when she noticed he wasn't hurting her, she relaxed. Jace quickly pulled his hand away. "Sorry, didn't mean to startle you."

Kala looked at him. "You're not a typical Terran. You act different, and your biofield is unusual." She then seemed to be trying to remember something but instead said, "I've seen something like this before." He watched her eyes grow wide and then turn to look in the direction of where Tulo was treating Eislie. Kala shook her head. "Never mind. You're good to go. Chief's and doctors' orders, you have two days off." She then looked up at him before pulling the pad to her chest and pointing toward the door.

Jace hopped from the table. "That's it?"

Kala nodded. "Yes, go get some rest."

As he walked away, Jace looked to where Eislie was, and he chuckled hearing her complaining that she was okay to the doctor.

Kala shook her head. "Not her first time here. She'll be fine. Go get some rest." Jace shook his head, smiling as he closed the door behind him.

Kala walked over to see the doctor. "Doctor Tulo, I have some readings I need you to confirm."

Tulo was concentrating on Eislie's wrist, using a device to repair the gash on it. "Everything all right, Kala?"

The assistant shook her head. "I need to confirm these readings."

Tulo straightened up, looking at Eislie. "Keep still. That's a fairly deep laceration. You should have taken care of it before you went down."

Eislie then said, "I did this while we were down there."

Tulo put his hands up. "Whatever, just remain still. The regen will be done in a few minutes." He then walked out with Kala, who handed him the pad.

"His readings show a resonant field, and the metabolism readings don't make sense," she told him. As the doctor reviewed the information, he sighed and opened the door to ask Eislie a question.

"How long ago did you say you got that injury?" Kala could hear her say, "About an hour ago."

Tulo then nodded. "Okay, I'll be back in a few minutes. Don't move too much, or you'll wind up with a scar." The doctor picked up a sample slide from the table, closed the door, and again looked at the pad.

Kala watched as he looked at the slide and then shook his head, sighing heavily as he leaned against the wall.

"What is it, Doctor?"

"The sample in the suit didn't make it. It's dust," was Tulo's reply. "The suits weren't as protective as we'd hoped. They both have a resistance that saved them."

Tulo laughed as he said, "Her injury looks to have been healing for a few hours already as well."

Kala scoffed. "That's impossible. They don't have a tissue-repair system down there. The radiation wouldn't allow it to work."

Tulo handed her the pad. "You've seen similar biofield readings before, haven't you?"

Kala nodded. "You suspect he's a starborn?"

The doctor chuckled. "I already know what he is. Amaian informed me when he arrived."

Kala smiled. "So, we don't have to worry about spide effects for him then?"

The doctor dragged his hands down the back of his neck, making Kala ask, "What's wrong?"

"How is your learning going with the starborn physiology?" Tulo asked.

"I know some, but I have to return to my studies at Covenant after my tour. Besides, he's Terran. Why?"

Tulo looked to the door Eislie was behind and again gave a subtle chuckle.

Kala stared at him but smiled when he turned around, saying, "She healed faster after her injury, and he has a reset metabolic rate. What does that tell you?"

Kala shook her head, not understanding the question.

Tulo took the pad from her. "There are a few things both of them had in common today. I'm surprised you don't see it. One was that they were fairly close to each other the entire time," he explained, making Kala look at him for clarification.

Tulo put his hand on the door and said, "My best guess is that they are biofield compatible. That means they would reinforce each other systemically. A sort of symbiosis, if you will."

Kala shook her head. "I don't understand."

Tulo turned to look back at her. "Our people had been dying off. Remember our history. We made medical advancements beyond most races to save ourselves but were unable."

Kala looked at him. "That's first-year Covenant history. Every medical student knows that. Biofield interaction is what saved our people."

Tulo smiled. "It also initially wasn't our discovery."

The doctor smiled; his memories of his time at Covenant were still fresh. The organization had been created to save their people from genetic extinction. Those thoughts also reminded him why they now served to help others around the galaxy.

Kala went to disagree but remembered what she had said to Jace as the doctor continued. "We agreed to take in starborn refugees only a few years earlier. We were a dying people and had hoped to pass the planet on to those who needed it. We only discovered biofield interactions and regenerative fields after noticing that certain individuals among them would recover faster when closer to each other. It was something we hadn't considered."

Tulo could see the look in her eyes as she had a realization. "Then that means that they—"

He held his hand up to stop her. "Yeah, the two of them would probably benefit from being near each other. But let's keep that to ourselves for now. All right, Kala?"

His assistant agreed as Tulo walked back into her room. "Okay, Eis, let's see how that injury is doing."

Chapter 10

Day Off

Jace was heading back to his apartment when Hemlen and a few other Gilesian stopped him. The few moments of silence only broke when Jace asked, "To what do I owe this audience?"

Hemlen looked menacingly toward Jace. "How do you get out of work detail for the next few days?"

Jace simply replied, "Because I've already been down in the mines. They had me testing the new suit type."

Hemlen smiled. "So, you chose to be a lab rat?"

Jace looked straight back at him. "Glad to hear you know what a rat is. But no, it really wasn't my choice."

The tall, light-skinned man gave an uneasy smile that sent chills down Jace's neck. "Good, we don't have to kill you. The captain will take care of that for us."

Jace stepped back in surprise. "Why would you want to kill me? I'm such a nice guy."

Hemlen pushed him aside and continued walking. "The Gel want you dead, Terran. I only wanted to find out if you were working with Bosh."

Jace felt very uneasy, as everyone seemed to want to kill him. As he placed his hand on the doorframe to his room, he briefly paused, staring inside before he entered.

* * *

Several hours passed. Jace had taken a short nap. He'd only been on the planet for five days, and everyone was an enemy. As he stretched, he looked up to see seven twenty-one on the clock. "You know, I could use a drink."

Jace changed into fresh clothes and set the others aside for cleaning. Thankfully, the room had everything he could need. Jace peered out the door and looked both ways, just in case someone was lying in wait. He muttered, "Coast looks clear," and headed down to the bar.

It wasn't his first time there. The first day, he wound up with a hangover from drinking too much. The bartender robot, Trumbo, had made some very interesting drinks. Most of them with a lot of alcohol. When he entered now, the place was empty. He only noticed two Gilesian who were not working the mines that shift. He attempted to say hello but was chased off by their scowls.

"Tough crowd," Jace mumbled as he sat at the bar. Trumbo slid over, asking what he wanted. Jace was about to tell him when Eislie came around from the back. "Trumbo, put more flock on order. The Gel seem to be going through it faster than usual; and that Earth-style whiskey as well. Do we have any more of the sweet balancers?" she asked the robot, but then mouthed a hi to Jace. He returned the gesture.

The robot acknowledged the orders and said, "I need to get his order."

Eislie told him, "Don't worry about it. I've got him."

Jace watched the robot slide down the other end of the bar.

He watched as she reached to count the bottles on the wall. "I thought you had time off as well?"

Eislie replied, "I do. I manage the bar on my time. I don't work the staging area or go down in the mines that often, only when something breaks."

Jace smiled, joking there's probably more money in the bar anyway. Eislie agreed and checked the inventory. She didn't seem to mind as Jace watched. She did stop when he asked, "How's your wrist?"

Eislie pulled her sleeve back. "Good as new." She looked at him. "I still owe you a drink, don't I? What'll you have?"

Jace responded, "Bartender choice."

She grabbed a bottle and poured him a glass before joking, "You don't want to say that too often out here. You might not like what you get. But I'm thinking whiskey."

Jace agreed, and Eislie pulled out another shot glass. When Jace asked, "You joining me?" she had already placed another right beside his and started pouring. Jace held up the glass and stated, "For surviving this time." Eislie did the same, and they toasted. Jace drank the shot; it was pretty good, not like he had the other day.

At that moment, Butee showed up to harass Eislie. "So, the tall light-hair is tending bar in a room all by herself. Bet you thought it was funny with that Terran walking into me earlier."

Jace startled him when he spoke. "I did say I was sorry; I tend to be terribly clumsy around people. Here, let's shake hands, and I'll introduce myself again," Jace said, but instead reached out with the drink in his hand, spilling it on the man's pants.

"Oh, I've done it again. I'm so, so sorry. I'm just so clumsy." Jace grabbed a tiny napkin and handed it to Butee. "I'm really sorry. What was your name again?"

The man replied, "It's B-u-t-e-e, you moron. It's pronounced Bah-tee."

Jace feigned looking flustered, then said, "Oh, we have a word like that on my world as well, but I could never remember if it's pronounced Butte or butt. I was always bad at that." Jace resisted laughing.

"You Terrans are so stupid. Ah, this is going to stain. I have to change," Butee complained as he walked away.

Eislie stood with a smile on her face. "That wasn't a nice thing to do, you know."

Jace smiled back. "Yeah, I know, but then why are we both smiling?"

She laughed as she poured him another round.

They both had several shots, and Eislie was staring out into the empty room. They talked about how few people were there and how strangely quiet it was while everyone was down in the mines. When he asked why she was there, he was surprised at how willingly she shared.

"I used to work as a maintenance engineer on a freighter. But I'm here because I stole a ship."

Jace responded, "Really? Me too, except for the engineer part. Small universe."

She laughed at his response before saying, "Yeah, but did you crash it into a military vessel?"

Jace cringed. "Oh, no, sorry, you got me beat on that one." Again making her laugh.

They were at the bar for some time, drinking and talking. Jace noticed it felt pretty good being there with her. When he looked at the bottle, it was almost finished. "Shit, how much have we had to drink?"

Eislie grabbed the bottle to inspect it. "Yeah, we should probably stop."

Jace laughed. "Weird, I don't feel a thing. You sure this is real?"

Annoyed, Eislie poured another round but then used a plasma torch to light it, the bright-blue flames creating shadows from the rim of the glass. "Yep, it's real." She handed him a glass and, after blowing out the fire, drank it down.

"Probably feel it in the morning. But it was fun letting you buy the drinks," Jace told her. He leaned back. "Your time here is probably up soon?" Jace watched as the smile ran from her face. He watched her eyes focus off into the darkness of the room.

It took several seconds before she said, "My time was up one and a half cycles ago."

Jace had a very uneasy feeling. At that moment, she had just confirmed what he suspected when he arrived. There was no way he'd be leaving here anytime soon.

* * *

A few days passed, and Jace was back on the work crew. He had noticed there were several times Bosh was searching for Eislie. She usually only showed up when she was scheduled at the staging area and usually when the bar was open. Although when Bosh had asked Trumbo where she was, the robot only answered, "You do not have authorization."

When she returned, Jace asked her where she had been hiding. Eislie told him she wanted to be outside in the sun. After that, they'd meet at the bar and spend some time outside in the light together.

She was amazed at how fast Jace learned the engineering of the reactors and how engines worked. Arren was as well, even likening it to being instinctual.

* * *

Weeks passed, and Jace was more than halfway through his sentence when he heard that they had some new "volunteers" arriving. They were also sending Jartal to his trial on Gilese. Jace overheard that Eislie volunteered to escort him but was turned down by Bosh. When she protested, Bosh had her locked in solitary to cool down. That thought turned Jace's stomach. He knew she was supposed to have been sent home already, and he began to wonder when Bosh would start focusing on him. Unfortunately, he didn't have to wait long.

Jace was outside walking along the fence when he came across various old ships in different stages of disassembly. One in particular caught his eye, and he tried to open it, quickly realizing he needed power to open the doors. As he was walking back, he came across several raza approaching the outside fence. Jace could feel their stares, seeing the dark red of their eyes, and their nails seemed to spark as they clawed at the fence. "Yeah, I'm getting away from those things." As Jace was walking away, Butee arrived with some guards. Seeing Jace gave the small gray-skin an opportunity.

"Trying to escape, Tucker?" Butee accusingly smirked.

Jace looked back. "Nope, just amazed at the damage those raza can do."

The small gray man looked at the fence. "Looks like you were trying to cut the fence to me. I'd say you were endangering us all."

Jace looked at him. "Not me. Those cuts are on the outside fence. The repair bots will handle it." Then, behind him, he heard the sound of cutters clipping the wiring. Jace turned to see Butee cutting the inside fence. "You little shit."

"I think we have an attempted escape. Let's take him to Bosh." Butee smiled as the two guards hit Jace with an electric rod and he was out cold.

Jace was shaken to consciousness and could see Bosh leaning on the desk behind him. Jace looked around before asking, "Where is this place?"

"Detention level. I don't think you've been here before," Bosh chirped.

Jace shook his head.

"Butee says you were trying to escape."

Jace looked at him. "That's bullshit, and you know it."

"He showed me the proof. Why would he lie to me?" Bosh smiled back at Jace.

"I've got a month left on my sentence. Why would I try to escape?" Jace asked.

"A prisoner will do anything to get out of here early. Even those like you. Do you know what the punishment is for attempting to escape?" Bosh asked.

Whether it was the adrenaline or the fuzziness of the shock stick, Jace replied with a smile, "A cake and some ice cream."

Bosh laughed. "I like you, Terran. You've faced some tough things here. But I'm going to tell you what the punishment is. And it's not cake or ice cream."

Jace prepared himself; he already knew what had happened with Eislie, and he suspected it was going to happen with him as well.

"I'm adding another planetary cycle to your sentence," Bosh told him, causing Jace to laugh.

"You find that funny, Terran? How about one and a half cycles?" Bosh smiled as Jace stopped laughing.

"You know, Bosh, you could just ask me to stay. It's not like I have anywhere to go," Jace told him.

The captain leaned down, his face uncomfortably close to Jace as he said, "Then you'd have the option to say no."

Jace laughed again.

"You see, Butee? He thinks this is funny. And he seems sort of violent to me as well. Don't you think?" Bosh paused before saying, "Give him a week in solitary."

Jace fought to free himself from the guards but was again hit with the shock stick. But just before he passed out, he overheard Bosh say, "Send a message to Radit. He'll have his crystals on time."

The cell they put Jace in was dark. The temperature was cool but tolerable. He was sure it would have been uncomfortable for others used to warmer climates. At least they fed him, although he never knew when they'd show up. There was no set schedule.

Jace's mind wandered, and it kept coming back to that ship he'd found. He remembered its design and the markings on the door. To

90

pass the time, Jace thought about the work he had been doing. The ship needs power. I can't bring one up from a driller. Too large. Jace went back and forth in his mind. *What* if I make the reactor smaller?

Jace had a subdued smile on his face as he worked out how to miniaturize one of the reactors. In his mind, he drew up a picture, making everything fit that he could. Back on Earth, he had done similar exercises, but those were primarily for breaking into things. The quiet darkness gave him an opportunity, and over the rest of his time, Jace found a solution.

The week went by quickly, and Jace covered his eyes as they brought him to the med bay. It was policy to have any volunteer who was serving solitary be evaluated before returning to work. The guards remained as Tulo placed an injector on his arm, but Jace didn't feel a pinch.

"There, he's sedated. You two can go. I'll release him to Arren and send him down after he's been checked out."

Jace realized what the doctor had done and understood, even moving his head slowly to look around the room. After the guards left, the doctor placed a device over Jace's chest.

"Breathe in, and exhale." The doctor pulled it away. "Everything looks good so far, but I'm going to recommend a couple of days of medical rest for you anyway. Same sedation, of course." The doctor gave a wink.

Jace nodded. "Okay, Doc, you're the expert."

The doctor placed another device on Jace's forehead and whispered, "Welcome back. It looks like you and the girl have more in common now."

Jace smiled and chuckled, "I was wondering how long it was going to take him to do this," Jace said, referring to Bosh.

Tulo looked him over. "Yeah, I'm keeping you for a couple of days; get your strength back."

That night, Jace slept in the medical bed. He was amazed at how comfortable it felt compared to the metal floor. Kala had just taken away what was left of the food, and Jace looked up to see Eislie standing in the doorway.

"I see you spent a day in solitary. It's not much fun, is it? I told you Bosh was not a nice captain," she scolded him.

Jace laughed. "Yeah, when I heard what happened to you, I was wondering how long it was going to take as well. Oh, and it wasn't a day; it was a week."

"A week? No way, this was the first offense," Eislie said to him.

Jace became serious. "Yes, a week, and one and a half cycles."

Eislie looked horrified. "He can't do that! You have to contest it."

Jace agreed but reminded her of what happened when she tried. He then said, "Look, after I get back to work, we'll talk, okay?"

Eislie looked at him. "I can't believe you're giving up."

All Jace said was, "We'll talk later."

Chapter 11

The Plan

As Jace was leaving his doctor-mandated medical rest, there was a sudden flurry of activity. When he asked what happened, Tulo said, "Some raza got inside the fence. Some of the Gel tried escaping."

Jace scoffed at the doctor. He had worked with the Gel, and they did not attempt to run when the raza were around. They may not have liked Terrans, but the Gel seemed honorable and took pride in the work they accomplished. He had noticed that when they were outside, the raza appeared to be afraid of them. Something didn't seem right, and to Jace, this had the markings of Butee all over it. But for the moment, he needed to get back to work.

While he was resting, Kala had brought several books that he requested and others Arren recommended, including engine and reactor design. He remembered the almost-intact ship and did some additional research. He found it was an old Takloh vessel. They used a form of radium and other radioactive-material reactors for their ships. Jace was wondering if maybe he could retrofit it with a spide reactor.

In his research, he found that the Takloh had used extremely dense alloys on the hull, strong enough to withstand even a star's pressures. In combination with the magnetic shielding, they could mine gas from the stars themselves. He also found out that their own experimentation with genetics is what killed them off, even joking, "They perfected themselves out of existence." When Jace had time, he mentioned it to the doctor and found out that Tulo's people almost had a similar outcome.

When Jace returned to work, he kept a low profile. He continued to research reactor and engine designs and worked on getting machine shop time when he could, although he did make time to meet with Eislie at the bar. She was usually too busy, or he was. However, Eislie became suspicious of why Jace hadn't been around and asked Arren if he had seen him. She became curious when the old miner mentioned he was down in the machine shop. She seemed annoyed, having just come from the staging bay nearby. Her frustration toward Jace made Arren laugh.

The next day, she heard someone in the work area and decided to take a look. She could see a man welding what looked like the manifold for a spide reactor at one of the stations. However, when she approached, he stopped and covered the device.

"I haven't seen you in a while. I was beginning to wonder if Bosh put you in solitary again."

Jace lifted his face shield. He noticed it wasn't her usual tone.

"Hey, Eis. Sorry, been busy the last few weeks. Had a project I was working on."

She scoffed. "Something Bosh wants, right?"

Jace looked at the covered item. "No. I had an idea on an upgrade for the spide reactor on the … diggers."

She wondered why he hesitated and then grabbed the cloth, pulling it away. She was surprised to see what looked like a modified containment chamber for a spide reactor on the table.

"You weren't joking."

Jace shook his head. "I have an idea. This will hopefully make things easier for us."

She smiled and moved closer. "I'm off work now. I didn't see you on the schedule. You want to spend some time together?"

Jace screamed *yes!* in his mind. But as he took off his mask and placed it down on the table, the sound of it rattling against the reactor distracted him.

Eislie reached out and grabbed his hand. "Come on. You can finish with that later."

Her grasp felt warm; the last few months made him realize how alone he really was. Jace had buried himself in work and avoiding pissing off Bosh, and here was a woman he could have only dreamed of, asking if he had time for her.

Jace seemed distracted, and Eislie noticed that when she asked, "What's wrong? Don't you have time off?"

He hesitated, telling her, "Yes, I do, but …" He paused. "Sorry, I've got something planned. Can I meet you in a couple of hours?"

His question didn't cause the reaction he had expected. Eislie looked dejected when he said that. Quickly he moved closer, grabbing her hand, holding it with his other hand.

"I do want to, I really do. But I need to see if this works."

Eislie was angry for a moment, then thought, Why is he focusing on the modified reactor?

She had known how to fix them since she was on her first ship. Even though she was a researcher, she learned about how the engines worked. And this was not like anything she had seen, even with the diggers' and extractors' new designs. Then what he said sank in. This will hopefully make things easier for us.

"Do you need help with what you're doing? Maybe I can go with you?" She bit her lip as she smiled.

Jace's heart soared, and he nodded. "Okay, let me finish up and do a quick test."

Eislie nodded and watched as he finished. Jace then pulled out a small, shielded box from beneath the bench. She was just about to ask what it was when he opened it, quickly shoving a small spide crystal into the chamber.

"If Bosh finds out you took crystals, he'll kill you!" she whispered.

Jace nodded. He knew no one was supposed to move the crystals beyond the safety points from the mine, but he needed this to make things work. To him, that was a risk he was willing to take.

"Are you crazy? You can't take spide past the safety shields. It's dangerous," she warned him.

Jace nodded. "Yeah, for them. Not us."

"What are you talking about? You'll get yourself killed. Give me that thing." Eislie reached over, and Jace grabbed hold of her before she pulled it off the table. She struggled as he held her tight but was surprised when she stopped resisting and looked him right in the eyes. Within a moment, she placed her forehead against his, and he felt her body relax. But his surprise subsided quickly, feeling her leaning against him. There was a feeling of bliss that enveloped him. But that faded as Eislie pushed away from him, running her hands down her face. She then looked at the reactor chamber. "We have to get rid of that thing. If Bosh finds out, he'll kill you and probably ..." Eislie paused. "Give me that thing before you kill yourself."

Eislie felt Jace's hold on her again, and she mildly resisted, warning him, "Look, I don't want you hurt, okay?"

Jace laughed. "I held that thing with my hand, Eis. How is it going to hurt me?"

She looked at him in disbelief before realizing what he said. She knew she was resistant to the radiation, but Bosh hadn't told her that Jace was. "What do you mean, held it?"

Jace showed her his hand that he used to put the crystal in the chamber with and laughed. "The radiation doesn't affect me either."

Eislie looked around, confused, before looking toward him. "What do you mean? I know Terrans have some resistance, but it usually kills them."

Jace leaned in to say, "I'm like you."

Eislie pushed away. "Wait, what do you mean? You're not from Gilese."

Jace shook his head. "No, but we have a lot more in common than you realize."

Eislie was trying to wrap her head around what he was telling her when she had a realization. "Resistant to spide radiation; Bosh is keeping you here. You can't be." Eislie moved toward him, a large grin on her face as she whispered, "You're a starborn?"

Jace nodded. It felt strange hearing her say it. He didn't know whether it was the realization that he was just like someone else in the universe or that when he looked at the subtle smile she still had, it made him feel happy.

Eislie looked at him before laughing nervously. "That explains why when I'm around you, I feel like ..." She stopped, then looked embarrassed. "Uh, never mind."

Jace almost felt slighted and asked, "Never mind what?"

Eislie moved in close. "Look, relationships between volunteers are frowned upon, okay? They sometimes remove the, um, *desire*, if they find out. If you know what I mean."

It took a moment before Jace's eyes widened, making Eislie laugh when he said, "Yeah, don't want to get neutered on some alien world. Got it."

When they finished, Jace asked her if she still wanted to help. When she said yes, all Jace said was, "Good. Now I have to get *that* outside." Jace pointed to the reactor.

Eislie thought for a moment before putting it into a utility pack. "We can use the lift behind the bar."

When Jace asked what she was talking about, Eislie told him that she used it to bypass Butee when she wanted to go outside. They were both sure it was monitored; however, the lift was almost never guarded. But Eislie suggested, "Then let's do some drinking outside. Who's going to notice two people going out there for a drink?" She held the pack up and handed it to Jace, who smiled.

"That's not a bad idea."

* * *

Jace followed her, and she pulled him into the back of the bar, grabbing random bottles of the cheapest liquor she had, placing them in the pack. She made sure it was all around the reactor chamber and explained that if they were caught, they'd claim they thought the heat would make the liquor taste better.

He gave an evil laugh, saying, "Or if they don't believe us, we can always open the reactor and show them."

"That's a horrible thing to do. It'd kill them."

Jace nodded. "Yeah, them, but not us."

Eislie looked deep into his eyes. She had considered doing what he was suggesting to Bosh when he was near one of the diggers, but the captain always stayed just inside the safety shields. And now she found out that someone else like her was suggesting the very same thing. An uneasy feeling grew in her stomach, but she knew he was right. If they had to escape, then maybe it was something they needed to do.

"All right, but only if we really need to."

Jace nodded, and she showed him to the lift area. They both climbed on the grate and headed outside. Thankfully, they hadn't met anyone, but they knew they were probably being watched.

When they reached the top, they headed toward the shipyard and sat on the nearest ship, both taking a bottle and taking a drink.

One of the guards walked by, and Eislie sounded drunk as she offered the guard a drink. The guard refused, saying he only drinks on his days off, and after looking at the bottle, remarked, "That stuff will kill you."

After they were alone, seeing no guards, Eislie asked, "What now?"

Jace smiled. "Now I show you what this is for."

The darkness had fully covered the base, and Jace and Eislie weaved in and out of the ships, sounding drunk. Then Jace stopped at one ship and knelt to plug in the cable from the small reactor. Eislie paused, and both gasped as the display on the outside of the ship lit.

"Oh my gosh, it works!" Eislie was quietly elated.

Jace nodded. "Yeah, let's see if we can get in."

He used the controls, and the door started to open. Jace tried to do so quietly, but when there was a loud clang from the door unsticking itself, they both jumped. They knew that that kind of sound would probably bring the guards. But Jace was quick and yelled, "Shit! I dropped the bottle! It smashed all over the ship. Give me another one!"

Eislie caught on. "Don't break this one; we only have three left!" She then started laughing loudly. They both listened in the silence for any footsteps in the gravel of the shipyard. Hearing none, they continued.

The door to the ship had fully opened, and some of the systems inside were coming online. Jace told Eislie to watch the door and quickly entered, connecting the reactor inside the ship.

"This is a Takloh ship. They built them like defenders," Eislie said.

Jace finished quickly and met Eislie at the door. "What did you do?" Eislie asked.

He tapped the panel, and the lights all went dark. "I hooked up the reactor inside. There's a bypass. I turned it on so we can open the door from here."

When Eislie asked how he knew how to do that, all Jace said was, "What d'ya think I was reading all those manuals for, this place?"

They both grabbed another bottle from the pack and drank. As they walked back, leaning on each other, seemingly drunk, Jace whispered, "We're going to need more spide if we want to get out of here," making Eislie nod in agreement.

Chapter 12

Ship's Control

Over the next several weeks, Jace had amassed a tidy cache of spide and placed it on the ship. He had taken measurements from the engines and systems without really powering them up till he was sure no one was aware of the work he was doing. Jace continued to focus on the project for several more weeks. Eislie usually found him in the machine shop or outside when he wasn't working.

Eislie found herself joking with Jace more when he was at the bar. Being together with him made her feel stronger, happier. But as the days passed, she dreaded what was going to happen.

It wasn't long before Bosh again put her in isolation, as he had done to Jace. The captain didn't really need a reason, and he found out from Trumbo that Eislie had again requested to be on the cargo detail. When she returned from isolation, the doctor recommended that she stay in the med bay for a few days. But even sleep wasn't enough to settle her mind, and her patience was wearing thin. She needed to know how things were going with Jace and the ship.

"Kala, have you seen Jace?" she asked.

The woman nodded. "Yes, he was just in with the doctor. He came to check on you, but you were sleeping." Kala then looked strangely toward her. "He was asking for a med pack, something

99

bigger than you'd have on one of the tunnelers."

Eislie's eyes widened. "Why would he want a med pack? That doesn't make any sense," she replied, making Kala shrug. Both knew that it was nothing more than bandages, anesthetic, and some relaxants in a standard pack.

Eislie decided to see if Tulo had any insight, but when asked, he told Eislie that he gave Jace a recovery pack, along with a few extras. He didn't ask questions. Knowing what she did about the ship, she knew she had to find Jace.

* * *

In the junkyard, Jace had rigged another power cell to open the door and had just installed the recently modified reactor he'd been working on for the past few weeks. He finished the last connection and was ready to push the button.

"Either I'm right and this thing powers up, or I won't know it if it worked," Jace joked, knowing he'd probably be dead if the ship exploded. He loaded the rest of the crystals into the reactor, which started to cause a small overload before he hit the button to start. Jace's face lit up, amazed as the reactor powered on.

"Ten percent, thirty, eighty. Shit, that's rising fast." He was able to breathe again as the reactor topped at ninety-eight. It looks like I've got some tweaking to do.

Jace sat down hard, and the chair creaked and wheezed as it settled. He pressed the controls to start the ship's computer. It took a few seconds, but Jace was startled when he heard a voice in a language he initially didn't understand blaring all around. He held the spot just before his ear, and his translator scanned the speech. When he heard, "Takloh detected," he was able to understand the computer.

"Intruder alert! Vacate this ship or I will be forced to eliminate you!" the voice of the computer repeated.

"You know the people who built you are dead, right?" Jace responded.

"Language unknown, searching for a match." The computer again spoke.

A few seconds passed, and Jace heard in his language, "You will be terminated, intruder." Jace heard several clicking sounds as valves were opened and closed. "Atmosphere detected. Unable to activate decompression." Then Jace heard, "Overloading reactor." The computer paused. "Reactor controls are offline."

There was silence for a few seconds before Jace asked, "Are you done trying to kill me?"

The computer responded, "The power system you are using is unfamiliar to me. What type is it?"

"It's a spide reactor," Jace said.

"Impossible. Spide reactors are incompatible with this ship's power system."

"No, it's not. This is a prototype," Jace replied.

Several seconds went by before the computer asked where the crew was, saying, "I calculate the galactic time base to be approximal fifty planetary cycles from my last operation."

Jace leaned back in the chair. "That sounds about right."

"Where is the crew?" The computer insisted on a response.

Jace took a breath. "They have been gone over fifty-seven of your cycles. I'm sorry."

"That is impossible. The Takloh Empire is forever. Attempting to return."

Jace heard several small pops and arcing beneath the ship.

"Drive systems malfunctioning and offline."

"Yeah, I haven't gotten to them yet. But I'm working on it," Jace replied. "Right now, I need you to tell me if the reactor is functioning normally and if there are any power fluctuations."

The computer remained silent. "Running diagnostics. New sensors detected, integrating."

Several minutes went by before the ship returned any report. It seemed the drive system was incompatible with the new reactor power and was now disconnected. Life support was functioning, and the medical bay was active. Crew cabins and facilities also had power. But Jace didn't know how, since the power plant was different. When the computer told him the mag shields were active and functioning, Jace realized why. The internal power system must be an oscillation type. The base systems in all the manuals were about the same. It seems even after tens of thousands of years, electricity was the same everywhere.

The drive systems now, however, were of a flux type of power. The original drives on this ship used something similar to standard electricity. But now, the reactor used dimensional flux to power the drives directly for efficiency. It seemed all Jace had to do was figure out how to convert the grav and tunnel drives to the new power source.

"Thanks, ah … what do I call you?" Jace said.

The computer repeated a string of words that sounded to Jace like. "Etractionie Duquetional."

"What was that?" Jace asked, trying to understand.

The computer repeated the words. Jace could make out what sounded like *E, whether hell and D quick*. But the words didn't make sense, so he said. "*E* and *D*? Uh, I'll just call you Ed."

The computer paused for a moment. "Ed is acceptable. You are Terran, are you not?"

"Yeah, how'd you know that?" Jace asked.

The computer responded, "I have accessed this facility's computer systems through an open port."

"Whoa, stop. This is a prison. You want to get us both killed? Stop what you're doing!" Jace yelled at the computer.

"I have confirmed your story, Terran, and have disconnected the link as requested. It seems as if I can no longer serve the Takloh Empire."

Jace sat up. "Look, I need your help. Would you work with me instead?"

Several seconds passed again before the computer replied, "But you are a criminal."

Jace agreed. "And did you see why I was sentenced?"

"It says that your sentence is over. You have returned to a neutral planet."

"Really? Wow, Bosh is good at covering up his lies. Now I definitely have to get off this planet," Jace muttered.

The computer then responded, "You are a prisoner, but without a crime, so you are being enslaved."

Jace nodded. "That's probably a good assessment."

"The Takloh never enslaved any race. They valued life."

"Sounds like they were a wise people. Even my people still do it," Jace joked.

"I was made to serve the Takloh Empire, but I will now serve you, Jace Tucker of Terra."

"Good to hear. I have to work on retrofitting some spide-compatible engines for you. It may take me a while. So, I hope you don't mind waiting."

The computer replied, "I have never used that configuration of engine. I had noticed ships outfitted with them traveled more quickly through hyperspace."

"Ha! You sound a little jealous," Jace remarked.

"It is not in my programming. But I am willing to serve."

"Thank you, Ed. Can you tell me if there are any weapons on this ship?" Jace asked.

"Negative. The drill and refiner ports are the major power usage for this vessel. No weapons were permitted when mining."

"Does the drill still work?" Jace asked.

"It appears to be intact. Auto-repair functions can repair its disuse degradation."

"What are refiner ports?" Jace asked.

"Refiner ports are used to extract gas from stellar bodies. They can also be used to expel waste from refined materials."

"Could they be modified to shoot a projectile?" Jace asked.

The computer thought. "It does that with slag from refining already."

"Could they be modified to throw it harder?" Jace asked.

The computer responded, "No weapons are allowed when mining."

"We're not mining, Ed; can they be made into weapons or not?"

Seconds later, the computer said, "It would take three standard days to modify the slag ports."

Jace stood. "Great, and then we'll have slag cannons. Are there any other modifications we can do?"

The computer replied that there weren't.

"Okay, Ed, sounds like a plan. But we have to keep the power low. I don't want them finding out you're active. They'd dismantle us both."

"Agreed. My system will remain in stealth power. When do you think you will have the new drive systems installed?"

"Easy, Ed, I have to figure out how to modify the ones I have here first. But I'll do it as fast as I am able," Jace promised. He left the computer to fix what it could using its automated systems, then went back to his room without incident.

* * *

The next day, he spoke with Arren as they waited for the rest of the crew to arrive. Jace was under one of the drillers, fixing the grav system. "This thing's a pain, you know that? How old is this rig?" Jace complained while Arren laughed between watching the diagnostics.

"You've surprised me, Jace. Your kind usually doesn't learn very fast. Especially when it comes to mechanics of grav systems."

Jace chuckled, then became distracted. Something about the driller looked familiar. He asked what Arren knew about the drive system on the driller.

"Oh, this thing has been around since before I got here," Arren told him.

Jace looked at the small, round man. "I have to ask. How long have you been here?"

The old miner gave him a discerning stare. "You've been very curious recently. Have you been reading those books I've lent you?"

Jace nodded.

Arren stroked his chin, or lack thereof, and spoke. "What's your real question?"

Jace looked at him. Arren seemed to actually care, but he couldn't risk asking outright about the drive system. "I was reading about the Takloh. This is one of theirs, isn't it?"

Arren leaned forward. "Yeah, this used to be a mining colony of theirs. I worked it for good pay. Took all the radium out of the planet." The miner paused. "They have a few ships still in the scrapyard. Too bad none of them fly."

"Yeah, too bad," Jace replied. "But if they used radium for power, then how did this thing get a drive system that works?"

Arren smiled. "You are curious. But to answer your question, it's got parts for a Beduvial hopper. I modified them myself."

Jace didn't know if he could trust Arren. So far, he had figured out how to get the tunnel drive connected but not active, and he had run into a block to retrofit the engines on the ship. But as the others showed up, all Arren said was, "We'll talk later, Terran. I might have something for you."

The rest of the shift went without a hitch.

It was only a few hours before they loaded additional crystals onto the containment shuttles. Bosh was so pleased that he gave everyone the rest of the day off. After finishing, Jace was joking with Eislie as Arren came up to them. "Hey, Jace, come over here. I want to show you something."

Jace followed, and Arren took him to a door that had not been opened for some time. "Forgive the dust; haven't been in here for a while."

Arren turned on the lights and jumped onto the table, reaching up to a small shelf just above the light on the wall. He pulled out a small stack of papers and handed them to Jace. When Jace looked at them, he could see the modifications Arren had done for the driller.

"That's what you're looking for, Terran. There's plenty of hopper grav systems out there to modify. I presume you've converted the tunnel drive connections already?" Arren then sat on the table, making it squeak.

Jace looked suspiciously toward him. "Why are you giving these to me?"

Arren smiled. "You're not a Terran, Jace. You and the female out there do not belong here."

"Never took you for a speciesist, Arren," Jace replied.

The old miner laughed. "I'm not. I know what Bosh is doing to both of you. And I've already confirmed with Tulo what you both are. And you don't belong here. Both of you belong out there." He then pointed to the ceiling.

"You still didn't answer my question," Jace said and watched the old man sigh.

"My people live about twelve hundred tetrels, about eight hundred of your years."

"Good for you. What is it, your birthday or something?"

The old miner nodded, making Jace feel guilty. "Really? Wow, happy birthday."

Arren smiled, thanking Jace.

"I've been working at this mine for 276 of those years. I worked for the Takloh and the Alliance. The Takloh were a noble race, if misguided." Arren paused as if reminiscing. "I'm eleven hundred and ninety-three tetrels today."

"Wow, congrats. I wish I lived that long. Have any regrets?"

The old miner nodded. "Yeah, I should have helped her escape when I found out what Bosh was doing. And now I find out that he's enslaving you as well."

Jace felt his heart become heavy.

Arren looked at Jace. "I can't be a part of enslaving beings just because of what they are. No matter how useful you can be." He looked toward the door. "Just say goodbye before you leave. I'll keep Bosh and the rest off you till you get out of here."

Jace was stunned by Arren's offer as he watched the old man jump off the table.

"Please tell her I'm sorry I didn't help her before. I've been trying to protect her, but you both need to find your people, and you can't do that working down in some mine." Arren paused. "If you need help with the modifications, let me know. I'll do my best to help with them. You understand, Terran?"

Jace nodded.

"Good. Please tell her I'm sorry I didn't help. I was a blind old man stuck digging holes in the ground. I didn't look up until it was too late."

Jace watched as Arren shuffled out of the room. He had a new respect for the old guy now. And Jace smiled, placing the papers inside his overalls as he followed after Arren.

Chapter 13

Pirates About

Jace met with Eislie and showed her the plans Arren had given him. Eislie was brought to tears after telling her what Arren said. She thought no one was on her side. She now understood why he never disciplined her for stealing supplies and that he was trying to protect her.

Over the next few weeks, Jace asked for Arren's help moving the drive pads. When the guards stopped them, all Arren told them was, "Need them to fix the damn driller again. We should get new ones," and they walked away. That night, Jace was able to install the new drives as Arren kept watch. When he finished, Jace found Arren staring out into the night sky.

"They are beautiful, aren't they," Jace said.

"I prefer the dirt above my head. But seeing this, I would agree." The old miner huffed. "How'd the drive system go in?"

Jace gave a thumbs-up.

"Good. You can test it in the next few days. Butee will be busy watching everyone else since Bosh will be off world. He's making a delivery."

"Sounds like a plan," Jace said as he wiped the sweat from his face before looking up at the dark sky. Jace had never piloted a ship and mentioned that to Arren, making the old man joke, "You'll learn. But talk to that female of yours."

"She's not my female." *You old fart.*

Arren laughed. "And you think I'm blind in the light, do you, Terran?" The miner laughed heartily before focusing on something over on the horizon. He removed his shaded glasses as if looking closely for something. "You see those dots moving over there?"

Jace saw what looked like a few meteorites hitting the atmosphere when Arren started running toward the compound door.

"Those aren't meteorites, kid. Those are pirates!" Arren hit the alarm, making Bosh and guards flood the yard.

"You catch the Terran trying to escape again, Arren?" Bosh then ordered Jace to be taken to confinement.

"No, you idiots, we were working on salvaging parts. We got incoming. Southwest, just over the ridge!" Arren pointed.

Bosh shook his head. "There's been no perimeter alert. What are you talking about?" Seconds later, one of the guards hit the alarm. "Get to the towers! We've got incoming, southwest ridge!"

Bosh raised his eyebrows as Arren glared at him. "Forgot how good your eyes were, old man." The commander took a deep breath before yelling, "Battle stations! Secure the compound! We lose no inventory tonight!"

Bosh turned to Arren. "Get him inside and secure with the others. It'll be safer."

Jace felt the old man pull him along with ease, even after he protested. All Arren said was, "Just keeping my promise, Terran."

Inside the compound, Jace arrived at the commissary. It was the deepest habitable area. It was also right next to the shielding generators, and Jace watched as they brought in everyone before closing the doors. The Gel huddled together. Jace noticed as one of them looked toward him, only to have a guard suddenly block his view. They could hear the explosions and weapons fire above. Jace looked up, inspecting the ceiling for a crack after the floor shook.

"Don't worry, Terran. We won't get buried in here," Arren said.

Jace nervously smiled and scanned the room. He could see several others thinking the same as he was.

Jace hadn't noticed one of the Gel until the man struck him from behind. He was stunned for a moment, but having had to fight back home to survive, he regained his footing. As the Gel swung again, Jace twisted, and as the attack missed, Jace made his move, throwing his weight into pushing the Gel away from him and over a table. His attacker was knocked senseless as his head hit the floor. Jace widened his stance as the others rushed toward him. He was ready for a fight, yelling, "Are you all stupid? There's a battle out there! What happens if they make it in here?"

His words made the Gel hesitate.

Jace looked around. "I have no idea why you hate me. I've done nothing to you. As for something in the past," Jace paused, "just get over it. It's not worth it."

He heard the Gel growl and was again ready to fight, but his vision was suddenly blocked by what looked like a massive gun pointing right at his nose. Jace slowly looked at the barrel and said, "That's a really big gun, you know that?" The woman holding the weapon scoffed and tapped his jaw with the top of the barrel, making Jace bite his tongue as his teeth clicked together. Jace put his hands up and backed away. He said nothing as the guard fanned around, pointing toward the Gel.

"The Terran is right. We can't have you fighting. If the pirates make it inside the compound, you'll all have to fight them anyway. They do not take prisoners."

Jace could feel something running from his mouth and the pain of his tongue. He wiped it away only to see the blood on his hand. He stepped back, his hands up, when they all heard a loud crash of metal from the wall behind them. One of the guards stepped closer as they heard a loud, metallic scraping sound. "They're in the old access shaft!" the guard yelled.

Jace remembered that the shaft exited behind the bar on the next level, and he joined the guards as they headed down to investigate. Jace heard the fighting, as several pirates had made it through the access shaft. He turned the corner and was met with several ricochets nearly grazing him. He could see the bar, and one of the pirates jumped over, pulling Eislie from behind the counter. The pirate tried holding her, but behind him, the robotic bartender came up, skewering him with its spindly arms. Eislie finished him off with the bottle she had broken on the bar.

The guards made short work of the remaining attackers, but they were surprised when one of the final pirates pulled the pack from his back, ripping a cord from it. The pirate dropped it and ran toward the access shaft as fast as he could. The guards chased him, but one stayed back to inspect what was left behind. Jace heard the woman's voice crack. "Spide device! Everyone out!"

Everyone rushed past Jace as he remained behind the corner. Eislie was still trapped behind the bar. Not seeing her, Jace decided to see if she was all right. As he turned the corner, one of the guards tried grabbing him but missed. The guard never stopped as they ran from the area. Jace could see Eislie running toward the pouch on the ground. She opened it to view the countdown on the device.

"Shit, this is going to kill everything down here." She looked over to see Jace staring back. "We'll never get this topside in time."

Jace looked at it. "Even if we did, it'd kill the guards up there. We'd still have the pirates to deal with."

A few moments went by, and they both looked toward the mine access. Jace grabbed the bag and headed toward the shield doors. "If we drop it down the shaft, the extractors and field should help!" Eislie yelled.

Jace was already working on the shaft entrance as Eislie worked to close the outside door. Eislie turned on all the extractors as he ran through, and Jace dropped the device down the shaft. He had just secured the inside door when the device detonated.

Alarms sounded as the extractors maxed out. Eislie had activated the full shield and backups. When she looked at the display, it no longer read a coherent number.

"It has to be over 900 percent in there right now." Concern was evident in her statement.

Looking across the entrance wall, they could see the shield's edge starting to fluoresce.

"That doesn't look good," Jace said. Eislie did her best to keep the extractors functioning, but they were beginning to overload.

"We're still at acceptable limits in here. We should be okay."

Jace turned to see guards looking at them through the base access door. When he walked up, they motioned for him to move away from the door. He tapped the comm. "You'll have to let us out. It's pretty hot in there right now."

The guard shook her head. "We follow protocol. The base is the main concern."

Jace pouted in a very sarcastic way and rejoined Eislie by the shield controls.

"They aren't going to let us out until that gets much lower," she said, pointing to the gauge.

"Yeah, I know." Jace looked back. "I wonder if that shield wall will hold the radiation?" Eislie turned to look and shook her head. "The outer shield isn't designed for that. This one is."

Jace chuckled. "We could always let the shield down."

Eislie paused and looked back as if considering his suggestion. "It's around six hundred now. We'd probably be okay. Some of the guards with the upgraded suits might survive." She sighed. "And we'd still have to deal with the pirates."

"Thought about that too. That's why I haven't turned it off. Although it would probably make it easier for us. Maybe get you home as well." Jace pointed to the emergency shutoff.

Eislie looked back and gave a slight laugh. "We could, couldn't we." She liked his suggestion of leaving and heading home. She had noticed his tone almost sounding like a promise.

As the extractors whirred, the radiation level continued to drop until the central alarm went silent. Jace and Eislie set the systems to finish, and both walked back to the entrance. Eislie tapped the comm. "It's at a hundred and forty in there right now. The extractors should have it covered in a few minutes."

The guard nodded and again repeated what she had told Jace, but as Eislie shook her head, she watched the guard say, "Thank you." Eislie turned, leaning against the wall as she slid down to sit on the floor. Jace joined her.

"The guard just thanked us," she told him, making Jace laugh.

"Finally, some gratitude. Now, if they'd just let us go."

Eislie laughed and hit him with her elbow. On the other side of the protective glass, neither of them heard one of the guards say, "Must've had some radiation exposure. They seem to be losing it."

The woman who thanked Eislie tapped the comm. "As soon as the level is safe, we'll get you out of there." She then turned to the other guards. "Alert medical and have them meet us over there." The guard pointed to the bar. "I want to move away from this as soon as we can."

When the radiation had fallen to reasonable levels, Jace and Eislie were taken to the med bay for evaluation, Tulo even joking, "I think you two like this place better than your own." Kala laughed as she took readings on Eislie.

It took time, but Bosh was informed about what the two of them had done. He immediately became angry that they endangered the output of the crystals. But when some of the guards spoke up on how they saved everyone, the captain realized the situation had to be handled with more subtlety. Or at least until he had some new guards brought in.

It took a few hours before Jace and Eislie were cleared, the guards crediting their survival to the work Eislie had done to upgrade the shield generators with Jace's help. The new praise didn't sit well with Bosh; Jace and Eislie were gaining support from both the prisoners and his staff. He made sure to get everyone working as they finished hunting down stragglers from the attack. Bosh had other concerns, however. He had a shipment of crystals to get out and away from the planet. He would have to deal with these two later.

Chapter 14

Raza Rumble

After the pirate attack, the entire compound was on edge. There wasn't much damage, and the episode didn't last long. It was more as if the pirates were testing the base's defenses. There were now more guards operating the towers and an increased number of plasma cannons to defend the facility. It became harder for Jace to work on the ship. Thankfully, Arren did his best to help Jace with the upgrades. He was amazed at how easy the retrofit of the Takloh ship was with his help.

"You know, Arren, they'll probably lock you up for helping me," Jace joked as he cinched down on the power connector.

"No, they'll probably shoot me." Arren looked at Jace, who responded with a look of concern. Arren, on the other hand, had a more philosophical response. "It doesn't matter; I'm doing the right thing. You kids need to get off this world anyway."

"Kids? Really, Arren?" Jace scoffed.

"You're children compared to me. Besides, I've seen worlds building up for war before."

Jace again looked concerned, making Arren laugh, but his cheerful response was cut short as he looked around the corner of the ship. "Get scarce, Jace. Now."

Jace did as the old man ordered and slid under the drive system; he waited a few seconds, listening, before darting under one of the other ships. When he stopped, he could hear Arren talking with Bosh.

"You've been taking one of our best miners, Arren. What are you using him for?" Bosh sounded a bit annoyed.

"Kid's good with hardware, Captain. I'm not as young as I used to be," was Arren's reply.

"We're on schedule. I don't want us falling behind. After that last attack, I want the shipment off world and delivered sooner than the timeline," Bosh told him.

Jace could hear Arren groan. "You'll have that ship to capacity tomorrow. If they don't attack again, you can send it then. But right now, the second digger is needing repair. You'll have to wait a day."

He could hear Bosh cursing the old man before he said, "Where's the Terran?"

Jace grabbed a coupler for the digger they extracted earlier and waited for Arren to call out, "Jace, get your ass over here!" Jace hit the ship next to him with the coupler and did some cursing of his own before rounding the corner rubbing his head.

"Damn, that's a hard hull. What d'ya want, old man?" Jace yelled.

Arren looked condescendingly toward him, but Jace could see Arren trying not to laugh. Bosh, on the other hand, seemed to be enjoying his artificial pain.

"Is that the coupler?" Arren asked.

Jace handed the part over, and Arren inspected it. He held it up to Bosh. "It's the right part. Told you the kid was useful." He then placed the coupler in the vehicle and ordered Jace to get in. "We need to get production going again." Jace feigned being annoyed, making Bosh smile.

After Jace entered the truck, Bosh said to Arren, "I want that shipment by tomorrow night. We need to get the whole lot of it off this planet. I don't want those pirates thinking we still have the stockpile here."

The old miner nodded and ordered Jace to head back to the staging area to install the replacement part. Jace looked back in the mirror to see Bosh smiling.

"That smirk on his face doesn't look good," Jace muttered.

Arren looked forward. "Never mind about the captain. He's got greed working on his mind. If it comes to it, I'll deal with him."

Jace looked over at Arren, and the old miner smiled. "I haven't been through seventy base captains for nothing. Accidents do happen. This is a mine, after all." His statement sent a chill through Jace as his thoughts filled with, Wonder how many captains Arren's dealt with personally.

* * *

Jace installed the new coupler, and they started digging again. It took several hours, but they filled the storage bins. Arren ordered it brought to the loading area, and he called Bosh to let him know things were ready to leave. The shipment was set to go that night, a day early, and Jace knew that Bosh would be on that ship. He needed to test the grav drive and see if the retrofit was working. Arren inspected his work, but they both knew it needed adjustment before a flight; still, Arren was pretty confident in Jace's abilities.

With all the activity getting the ship ready and the extra guards sent along to protect it, the compound was reasonably quiet, allowing Jace to work relatively unnoticed for the rest of the day. When night arrived, he was already on the ship, ready to test.

"Okay, Ed, let's run diagnostics. Can you see the drive now?"

The computer responded, "Running diagnostics. System confirmed. Do you wish to power up?"

"Go for it. Run at 2 percent. If we have that stable, then we'll know the resonators are working."

As the ship sent power to the drive, the ship shifted, making Jace hit the throttle down.

"The drive systems seem to be operating. Why did you shut the system down, Captain?"

"The ship shifted; we don't want to draw attention to us, remember? I just hope no one heard that."

"Sound readings indicate that there was a decibel level of seventy-three when the ship moved."

At that level, Jace knew someone was going to check. He had to think fast. Grabbing his tool set, Jace headed into the field of ships. Quickly, he dislodged one of the small carrier doors, and it made a loud bang. That drew the guards to his location and away from the ship.

They questioned him, and he told them that he was learning

about the strut systems and wanted to see how they worked. He didn't expect it to be so loud. The guards were even laughing until Butee showed up.

"Causing trouble again, Terran?" he whined, his thin face showing a smile.

Jace didn't like Butee, and he was sure the feeling was mutual. Jace explained that he was testing to see if the door's struts would hold the entire weight if he disconnected the alignment linkage. He gave some bullshit story about the tunneler door and how to make it close faster just in case there was a spide runaway. The small, gray-green man took him seriously.

"You mean you're trying to come up with something to help us? I thought you Terrans were all about anarchy."

Jace smiled. "Can't we be both?"

Butee looked at him with contempt. "Ugh, just don't get killed. Bosh still needs you." He then looked around and saw parts everywhere from the door crashing down. "Clean this slac up and go back inside when you're done."

Jace snapped his heels and saluted, making Butee look at him strangely. But the small man walked away with the guards, leaving Jace to clean up the mess he'd made.

"Well, it's your own fault, Jace. At least they didn't catch you." He lifted the door using all his strength. "Shit, this thing is heavy. Hopefully, I won't have to do this for much longer."

He cleaned up most of the mess, leaving a few parts lying around in case he had to cover with Butee again. When Jace returned to the ship, the computer had finished with the diagnostics.

"The modified engines have a higher efficiency than the previous. I recommend using approximately 40 percent offset power for the current systems due to the differential."

"So, you think the power system is too strong? I can adjust the level pass through," Jace replied.

"Negative. The entire system is more efficient. This ship will be able to travel much faster thanks to the upgrades."

Jace nodded. "Got it. I'm getting the feeling that you like the new upgrades."

The computer seemed to pause to think. "This ship has been out of service and without a crew for approximately fifty-seven-point-six standard years. The upgrades are welcome."

Jace began to wonder why the Takloh left the ship instead of returning to their world. When Jace asked, Ed's response was something he hadn't expected.

"I was ordered to shut down until a reclamation crew was dispatched."

"You mean they were scrapping you?" Jace asked.

"Affirmative. I was to be decommissioned and recycled."

"But they were going to put you on another ship or job, right?"

The computer paused before responding, "No."

Jace thought out loud. "Damn, they left you for dead. Been there, unfortunately."

As Jace continued his updates, the computer remained silent for most of the night. It took a while for Jace to discover something running in the background.

"What are you running, Ed?" Jace asked, half expecting the ship to close up and try to kill him again. The response was a bit more enlightening.

"I am updating star charts and locator beacon databases."

Jace looked concerned. "Remember, take it easy. We don't want them to discover you're up and running."

The computer reassured Jace that they would not be detected. He was mentioning something about an open port and continuous images of questionable content, making Jace laugh.

"You've got to be kidding. Someone is streaming interstellar porn?"

"I can identify the location," the computer said, and within seconds, a holographic rendering of the compound hovered before Jace.

"That is so cool. I didn't know you could do that, Ed."

"Holo-emissive systems are fully interactive. It is the only way to interface with biologicals."

"Ed, you're quick, for an artificial life form. Not downplaying that any. I really like the way you do things."

"I can access the image feed if you would like to know who is 'streaming' through the open port."

Jace immediately replied, "No, I don't want to see that. No, thank you, Ed, but again, no." Jace suddenly felt that Ed was messing with him for some reason.

The computer then asked if Jace had chosen a new name for the vessel. The computer told Jace that it was customary for his makers to rename a ship once the engines or reactor were replaced. He mentioned it was akin to changing a vessel's heart, and changing things made it a different ship.

"You know, Ed, I hadn't thought about that. I guess if we're going to fly together, it'll need a name. I'll have to see what Eis thinks," Jace said.

"I must inform you, Captain, that ship operations may only be discussed with active crew. Is Eislie Licessien to be considered crew?"

Jace leaned back in his chair. "Actually, I was hoping she'd be captain as well."

"You do not wish to be captain of this vessel?"

Jace replied quickly, "I do, Ed, but I was hoping she could be captain too."

The computer thought for a moment. "Up to three captains are allowed for a ship in service; that is acceptable for Takloh command structure."

"Really? That's awesome, Ed. Put her in as captain," Jace ordered. The computer complied, and on the display, Eislie's name appeared next to his.

Another hour went by, and Jace was tired and was getting ready to head back inside when he heard yelling from off near the main entrance. Curious, he decided to take a look and sneaked around to see what was happening. His heart fell seeing Eislie dangling in the claw of the crane they used to offload ships. He watched as she was struggling to free herself.

When Jace looked in the control tower, he could see Butee and heard over the loudspeaker, "Bosh doesn't need you anymore, slac. He's got that Terran under his thumb. And to prove it, I'm throwing you to the raza. It'll look like an accident, killed while you were trying to escape."

Jace watched as Butee moved Eislie over the fence. He could hear her screaming not to be dropped. When the arm stopped, Eislie yelped from the pain of being crushed by the jaws. Jace was already running toward her.

As the claws opened, Jace felt the world slow as he watched her fall toward the ground. It took moments for Jace to make the fence. He noticed some of the guards looking horrified at what Butte had done.

"Why didn't you stop him?" Jace yelled.

One guard stammered, "W-We didn't think he'd do it!"

Jace pulled at the fence as the raza started to circle Eislie. He tried climbing over but was pulled back by the guards.

"If you're not letting me get her, then you go out there and help her." As he fought the guards, several raza started clawing at the fence, making the guards back away.

"You're all fucking cowards. Give me a weapon and I'll get her," Jace demanded.

Butee spoke up. "Anyone giving him a weapon will be thrown in detention. It's illegal to give prisoners weapons."

Jace looked at Butee with angry disgust, but as no one stepped forward, he looked to the box of tools nearby. Jace grabbed a screwdriver and sledgehammer before jumping onto the crane arm still over the fence. He raced up and immediately jumped off the end, landing with a thud in the sand below. His sudden arrival startled the raza, and they scattered. He struggled to get up, limping toward Eislie. In his fall, he had dropped the screwdriver but still held the hammer.

When he reached Eislie, she was barely conscious. He yelled for her to wake, only to watch her lazily open her eyes before coughing up blood. Jace was more concerned about Eislie and hadn't noticed the raza again until one bit down on his shoulder. Jace was lucky. The creature appeared to be aiming for his throat.

Jace reached up, gouging the eye of the beast, making it let go. But his respite was short as Jace felt another sink its teeth into his arm. Jace still held the hammer in his free hand and raised it. He brought the steel head down, striking with enough force to cave in the creature's skull.

Jace stood, his eyes scanning all around at the raza circling. "C'mon, I didn't come out here to die. What about you, assholes?" Jace's voice was filled with anger and resolve, and with every attack the creatures gave, Jace returned with twice the deadly force. Within seconds, Jace was building a wall of dead raza around them! Jace continued and swiveled his head, looking for the next attack, but none came. Jace's head darted around as he felt Eislie grab onto his injured arm. He could see her eyes were wide and pleading. All he heard her weakly say was, "I want to go home."

Jace felt his eyes saturate, and he mumbled, "I know. I'll get you home."

With what strength he had left, he pulled Eislie over his shoulder, telling her to hold on. Just as he arrived at the gate, it was opening, with Tulo and armed guards escorting them in. The doctor grabbed Eislie, trying to stabilize her before rushing her off to the med bay. Jace watched as Tulo even pushed Butee aside as he tried to stop them.

When Butee approached Jace, the small man said, "You're lucky you're not dead. Bosh would have had a fit." Jace still held the hammer and was about to strike the guard but instead, Jace growled as he threw the hammer deep into the scrapyard. It took seconds before there was a loud, resonant sound as it struck something metallic. Jace's eyes silently stared at Butee as Kala returned to bring him to the med bay. As Jace was led away, he looked back to say, "Would somebody strike him, please? I don't want to add any more to my sentence."

Jace laughed as he watched one of the other guards punch the small, green-gray man with enough force to knock him to the ground. Jace could hear several guards yelling at Butee but didn't remember much after that as the blood loss took its toll on him.

Chapter 15

Med Bay Again

Jace woke suddenly, startling Kala, who was finishing her report. She watched as Jace grabbed at the wound on his shoulder, feeling the pain.

"Easy, the anti-infective has to kick in. I've sealed the wounds. They were pretty deep, and we've been sort of busy with our other patient," Kala told him with a genuine look of caring concern as she gently pushed him down to the bed.

Jace swallowed hard before asking, "How's Eis?"

Kala looked at him. "That's why we're busy. You both were in really rough shape when you came in."

Jace sat up to look around, but Kala again pushed him back down. "She's stable. The doctor's helping her right now. I just came over to get you started with the regen field."

Kala gently touched his face. "We'll let you know when she's awake. I'm going to sedate you now; you need to rest."

Jace felt his eyes fall heavy, the sedative taking effect quickly. Kala again touched his face, and a smile graced hers as she finished setting the regeneration field before going back to assist the doctor. She opened the curtain, hearing, "Sounds like he's awake."

Kala laughed. "Yeah, I don't know how he's even functioning. Those wounds were deep."

Tulo chuckled. "Terrans are strange. They have such a high pain tolerance. You could probably put their hand in a reactor, and they wouldn't scream if you wanted them to."

"That's a horrible thing to say, Doctor," Kala interjected.

"It's true. They can handle a lot." He then paused, his voice now concerned. "But I think he's reaching his limit."

The doctor pointed to some instruments, and Kala knew exactly which one he needed, handing it to him before asking, "How's she doing?"

Tulo sighed. "She's alive. It's going to take a few days in regen, but she'll make it." He turned to look back at Jace sleeping in the bed nearby. "I think we should move them closer; it should help them both." Kala nodded before leaving to push Jace's bed closer. She could see on the display as their fields started reaching out to each other.

"I've never actually seen that before," Kala said, her statement making Tulo smile.

"Well, when you get back to your studies, you will. It is unique to starborn physiology."

Kala smiled. "It's beautiful, in a way."

Tulo nodded. "You said that Butee grabbed her on purpose with the loader?"

Kala nodded. "Yes, the guards confirmed it. A few of them even attacked that slac afterward."

"Well, well, we have some guards with empathy. They'll be removed quickly," Tulo said regretfully.

Kala watched as the doctor examined Jace's wound while the regen field worked. "Kala, I'm filing a secured report. I suggest you do the same."

The doctor's assistant appeared concerned. "But I would have to send it through the main security office."

Tulo shook his head. "No, use the med system. It's separate. We use it between ships while in service. I've given you access. This can't go through this compound's security."

"But in our agreement, we use Alliance systems while we serve. It will void our service with Covenant," Kala protested.

The doctor nodded. "I know, and you've been an excellent assistant. They'll probably be reassigning us both after we do this. Whatever happens, please promise me you'll continue your studies."

Kala nodded. "What about you, Doctor?"

Tulo ran his hands down the back of his neck. "I've had enough of colony service. My future is up in the air on this one."

When Kala asked what he meant, all Tulo said was, "Sometimes, you know when it's time to move on." He turned to see the sadness in Kala's face, but he smiled. "Who knows? You may see me teaching at Covenant."

* * *

A few days passed before Bosh returned from his off-world dealings. Several guards had already submitted reports of recent events, and given the furor behind them, Bosh had to punish Butee for his actions. The small, gray-green-skinned man didn't go silently as they placed him into solitary. Bosh even made a speech about it being a dark day.

Jace was finally awake, and Tulo chastised him for his reckless actions before shaking Jace's hand and telling him, "You Terrans are crazy. I had to put two pints of synthesized plasma into you and four into her."

He told Jace about the report he sent off and expected to be relieved of duty before the next supply flight. He mentioned that Kala would probably be replaced as well. Jace thanked them both for their help, but he knew that both he and Eislie would have to get out of Bosh's reach soon.

Jace could not work on the ship and was hoping the guards had not discovered it active. But when he ran into Bosh, all Jace could do was stare at the captain. The captain tapped the ribbons on his chest, making Jace turn away. Jace's memory of the pain from his implant was still fresh from times before.

The following night, Jace headed out into the scrapyard as soon as he could to check on the ship. When he arrived at the ship, the hammer used to kill the raza was next to the door. He huffed, saying, "Wow, threw that pretty far," before opening the door to check in on Ed. He updated the ship's computer on what had happened, and it made a recommendation.

"Captain, I recommend ordering me to self-destruct if you and the other captain are killed." When Jace asked why, the computer replied, "Because I do not think anyone else will give me a chance to serve as I wish to serve."

Jace didn't like Ed's recommendation but ordered it anyway.

* * *

Over the next few days, Bosh stayed out of everyone's sight. He only showed himself when the guards delivered their daily reports. Jace visited Eislie several times while she was still recovering. And when Jace didn't show up for work, Bosh didn't argue when Arren told him that both Eislie and Jace were still not clear to return to work. No matter what it was. The old miner even threatened to hold production if he countermanded Arren's recommendation. The captain didn't like the options but conceded to Arren's suggestion.

Production continued. There was no activity from the pirates, allowing the guards to relax, which made Jace worried. Even he knew you let an enemy sweat, and as soon as they get comfortable, strike. When Jace spoke to Arren about the pirate attacks over the years, he mentioned his theory to the old man, making him laugh. "You might want to think about becoming a pirate, Terran. You'd probably be good at it."

Tulo cleared Jace to return to work. And with Eislie finally awake, Jace was in a good mood. There was a lot of activity as the crew went down to get the rest of the crystals from the diggers' last pass. Jace had taken one of the shifts that opened when some others were injured. The crew was mostly Gel, so Jace was taking a chance. Kasmae was with them when she saw Jace working alone. "Your people are a curse to that world," she muttered under her breath as she moved closer.

As she neared, she was startled when Jace turned to ask, "What do you want, Kasmae?"

She looked flustered, only able to blurt out that he was a bane on the planet she knew. Jace only smiled, saying, "Get over it."

The Gel leader became furious with him, her mind twisting words. Was this Terran trying to provoke her, she wondered, and put her helmet to his. "I hate your kind. I'm going to kill you."

Jace tapped her helmet. "Go ahead. Show me that you can stand life as a prisoner in a mine. Because that's what you'll get if you do, so it's your choice." He paused. "You know I was thrown off Earth, right? My people didn't want me because I was a burden. Or so they claimed. And truthfully, I've never even heard of your people till recently. So rather than hate me, educate me. Hell, you might even find me an ally."

Jace's voice filled with a growl that Kasmae reeled from. The man before her seemed resolved, stronger, and his confrontation and lack of fear confused her. The Gel leader went silent.

It took a few minutes before she could speak to him again. "How dare you speak to me like a child! We are a proud race."

Jace responded, his voice filled with an annoying frustration,

"Good, tell me more. I'd rather hear the story of your people than the constant pebbles tapping against my helmet."

Kasmae found his annoyance amusing and started to laugh. Jace turned to her. "Good, you have a sense of humor. Now we can talk."

Kasmae told him the story of her people back on Earth and Grotin, their new home world, how they were warlike and divided. The Gel split from the Ergo, a faction focused on genetic purity and clans. Jace made her laugh with disbelief when he said, "Looks like we aren't so different. There are a few of them back on Earth still. Must be something in the water."

But as she was laughing, Jace felt the ground shift and within seconds, could see one of the tunnelers breaching the roof just above Kasmae. Jace realized they were both at the end of a tunnel and instinctively, he pushed her out of the way. He felt the weight of the stone dirt as it piled on top of him as the digger continued down. The machine stopped, and Jace felt the hard metal of its frame pressing painfully into his side. He worked to extricate himself, but the tunnel around them destabilized and continued to collapse.

Then, Jace looked up. Panic filled him as the tunnel behind the Gel grew dark. Jace reached out as he continued to struggle as the rest of the tunnel collapsed. Kasmae stood, angry at him for pushing her down, but paused seeing him half-buried where she once stood. She watched as he wrestled himself from the stone before he grabbed his side in pain.

"Are you injured, Terran?"

Jace looked up with a smile. "Only my pride. That, and my side. I think I bruised something."

The Gel laughed. "You joke after saving me, Terran?"

Jace nodded. "Yeah, I was thinking of the irony as well."

His last statement triggered her to attack him. She felt he was insulting her. She was much stronger than him, and the force she used to slam him against the stone behind him damaged his oxygen feed. But when Jace yelled, "We're trapped, are you blind?" it caused her to spin and look behind her. She suddenly became animated, frantically looking for another way out. Jace was going to try and calm her when he heard the radiation alert go off on his suit.

"Kasmae, what's your suit reading for radiation?" Jace yelled.

The Gel looked at him blankly, making him ask if she could hear him. When she nodded, he repeated his question.

"One sixty-two. Wait, that can't be right," she said in disbelief.

Jace sighed. He had been working with Eislie on the suits, and they made them resistant to almost 500 percent, but the power cells went very quickly on anything over two hundred. However, Jace had another problem. Her attack had damaged the feed line for his oxygen supply. It was now leaking into the surrounding cabin. With the radiation climbing, he was wondering if he could withstand it at such high levels.

They called topside. Jace was surprised to hear they were still working as he listened to a very static-filled response. "We're trying to dig you out, but the radiation is making it difficult. What's your status?"

Arren sounded concerned when he heard the radiation level climbing. But when Jace said, "My oxygen supply's damaged," he knew they had to get them out of there.

As Jace sat feeling defeated, the ground around them moved as stones from above continued to fall. One large stone struck the front of Kasmae's helmet, causing a crack. Kasmae's suit increased its shielding to compensate for the damage. He could see the horror in her eyes, and Jace stepped forward to calm her.

"Kasmae, tell me about your people. Why do you hate Terrans so much?"

She paused, and her mind snapped back from the fear. She told how about one million Earth years ago, the Gel met the Lyri, and that they traded technology for learning about their people. Most Gel were peaceful and knew about genetics and cellular-enacted fusion, a biological technology that helped run the world they called Earth.

She told him about the Ergo and that they felt the Lyri were tainted and anyone who associated with them was unclean. The Ergo used their knowledge of genetics, integrating it with the Lyri technology, allowing them to leave for the stars.

Simultaneously, the Ergo searched for a new world, a pure world, while most Gel remained. Her people eventually followed the others, leaving for the stars. It took centuries, but they decided to turn back to Earth. But when the Gel returned, they found most of their kind had perished, and what remained of the Lyri had taken over.

When Jace asked if they knew what had happened, she only said, "What remained of our people were purged, and only a shadow of the Lyri now existed."

Communications from the suits were still functioning, and in the staging area, others were listening to their conversation.

After about an hour went by, the radiation again spiked, and Kasmae's suit gave a warning. She looked at the alert in horror, telling Jace, "My shield will not last long, Terran. And you have a damaged air supply. I can only hope to watch you suffocate before I burn."

"You're right. We have to get out of here," he said mockingly but paused when the low-oxygen alert on his suit flashed.

"Your shield is about to fail as well, Terran. I cannot blame you; you've fought well." She then looked at her display. The red warning light for the shield was now flashing dimly. "If only I had another power cell and a new helmet. This one is badly damaged."

Jace looked at her. "It's not my shield that's failing. You damaged my oxygen supply, remember?"

She looked at him with contempt, but a softness entered her tone. "Then you will suffocate before you burn."

Jace nodded. "You're right." He then adjusted his protection field. And since his oxygen supply was almost gone, he decided to help her. Thankfully, the helmets for the glyph suits were all the same. He hoped he could survive the radiation and was thinking about giving her his helmet.

"Kasmae, why were you sent here?" Jace asked with genuine concern.

She proudly sat up. "I stood up for my people and against those with wealth."

Jace nodded. "A noble cause."

"And you, Terran?"

"I'm here because I ran from my planet. Disease was spreading, and we were being hunted. I fought when I could; I helped others when I was able. I was defending against those who attacked my world." Jace chuckled. "I was brushed aside by my people. And when I helped Alliance personnel when they were attacked, I was tried for crimes against the Daak—before those very same people sentenced me for my good deed. The Alliance sent me here. I figured it was better than certain death. At least I got to see things out here that I would never have if I just let them send me back to Earth."

Kasmae shook her head, giving Jace a look of admiration. "You're not a coward for running. You chose a path of the unknown over the path of death they were choosing for you."

Jace nodded. "Didn't think I'd go like this, though. Talking to someone who considers me an enemy."

"Your people are. They removed us from that world you now call home," she responded quietly.

Jace laughed. "How long ago was that anyway, again?"

"Approximal one million of your years," she said with an angry snarl.

"One million years, one million years," Jace mockingly said.

* * *

In the staging area, Tulo remarked, "Is he trying to get her to kill him?"

Eislie arrived in the staging area, and she heard Tulo, the doctor's words making her decide to see what was happening. She moved cautiously, still feeling the results of her injuries as she moved beside Tulo. "No, he has a weird way with logic sometimes. It just pisses you off."

Tulo turned to look at Eislie. "You should be resting. You were seriously injured, Eis."

Eislie just shrugged him off.

* * *

Back in the cave, Jace continued. "One million years. Wow, it's amazing. In that time, your race has evolved. My race has evolved. We're not even the same beings anymore. Why the fuck are you still whining on about it? You've held on to that anger for one million years. Man, I thought *my* people were screwed up, but your people have issues. Think of all the energy wasted on nobodies like us."

Kasmae became enraged and went to strike Jace, who caught her blow and threw her to the side. "You're still willing to attack me. Why? We're both going to die."

She stood again, ready to attack, but stopped when her helmet alarm went off. "No, my shield!"

Jace removed his helmet and handed it to her. "Take mine. I'm out of air anyway."

From the speaker on the digger, they heard Arren yelling, "Jace, return your helmet onto the suit! You've broken your shield integrity!"

"No. My oxygen is gone. I'd rather face the radiation than suffocate. Her supply is still working, but her shield is failing. At least one of us can get out of here alive."

Kasmae looked confused. "But you are an enemy."

Jace shook his head. "No, I'm just a man. The enemy you think I am has been a ghost for almost a million years." He paused, handing her his helmet. "Take it. Your shield's about to fail."

She hurriedly put his helmet on, which restored her shield. Jace then took a spare power cell and handed it to her.

"How much longer you guys gonna wait to dig us out?" Jace yelled as he handed her the power cell.

Arren replied, "We're working as fast as we can. The whole tunnel collapsed up to the junction."

His words made Jace slump down onto the floor of the tunnel. "Shit, at least a few hours then." He looked around. "The CO_2 will probably get me before that."

Kasmae checked her suit's battery status. "No, Terran, the radiation will take us both before that."

About an hour went by. The power to her suit was blinking again. Jace's suit reserve was depleted, but he wasn't feeling any effects from the radiation. When the alarm sounded in Kasmae's suit, she went to remove her helmet to die quickly, but Jace stopped her.

"Why would you ruin a pretty face like that," Jace said.

Kasmae hissed at Jace, making him laugh. "You Terrans are strange and perverted, you know that?"

"If that's what you think I meant, then I'll give you that." She looked at him with confusion.

"What I meant was, you have a grace, a presence, a beauty that your people follow. I've noticed it; you shouldn't be so quick to throw that away. You should hold on to it, give them a little more time."

She sat beside him. "I think the atmosphere is making you delirious, Terran."

He looked at his wrist display. "Nah, still under 5 percent on the CO_2 and 15 percent oxygen. I'm good for a while."

"Then why did you say that? I think you are repulsive," Kasmae replied.

Jace smiled as he spoke. "Beauty is in the eye of the beholder. It's an old Earth saying."

The Gel looked at him strangely.

Jace sighed. "My people are sort of like yours, although probably more like you described the Ergo when it comes to our people. Always fighting or trying to destroy what doesn't please or look like us."

Kasmae nodded.

Jace continued. "I think my people realize that but don't know it. We could be in the heat of battle and pause to see the sun rising along the horizon or watch a bird land gently on a branch before us."

As Jace paused, they heard someone over the speaker on the digger. "Yep, he's losing it. Ten shills he dies in the cycle."

Jace laughed as Kasmae looked horrified toward the digger at the statement she heard.

"Why do you laugh, Terran?"

Scrounging on the floor, Jace picked up and handed her a sizeable bright crystal, a carbon diamond the size of a baseball, its cracks refracting the light from his suit into beautiful colors. Kasmae looked at the light all around them in wonder.

"Because after all the things I've seen, my world has seen, and us facing death, I'm still able to find something of beauty. Even you're enjoying it." Jace smiled as he looked to the ceiling of the tunnel.

Kasmae almost looked embarrassed.

"Ah, it's all right. I wasn't even looking for it; just started to zone out from boredom," Jace told her.

He handed it to her, along with his remaining power pack. "You're gonna need this soon."

She hesitated. "But you'll die."

Jace sighed when he looked at her. "I have a resistance to the radiation. I don't know how much I can take, but I figure I'll see how tough I really am."

The Gel looked at him with horror and pushed his hand away. Jace then took the spare power cell and jammed it into the plug on her suit. "Nope, you're not getting out of this that easy. I've heard you tell your people you want to go back; you should."

She looked at him for a moment as she realized this man was not her enemy but a fellow warrior.

"Five shill he fries!" Butee yelled, making Jace respond, "Put me in for five too. I recognize your voice, Butee. I'll happily take your money."

* * *

In the staging area, Tulo watched the video on the screen when Eislie turned and asked, "You think he'll make it?"

The doctor reminded her, "He's resistant, but the level is over seven hundred." He was surprised the suits hadn't deteriorated.

Then, behind them, Bosh said, "It's a good test," making everyone turn to hear him say, "What? It's good to know how much they'll handle, so more people don't die. Put me in for ten shills."

Eislie scoffed. "Make it fifty he lives, and I'll take that bet."

She then turned to the doctor. "Tell him the level. He should know. They both should."

Tulo nodded before hitting the transmission button. "I want to inform you both that the radiation level is now over 730 percent. Your suits aren't going to last much longer."

Jace sat up, yelling angrily, "Then fucking hurry up and get us out of here!"

"Why did you have me tell them? Now they're both pissed off," the doctor said to Eislie.

Eislie straightened, her body still unsteady from her recent injuries as she looked at him. "Yep, now he'll have a better chance of surviving."

Her statement made one of the Gel say, "I don't get Terrans."

Eislie glared at the Gel. "I'm Gilesian, not Terran."

They watched for a couple of hours and knew time was running out when the digger's controls and feed started to fade.

Kasmae's suit power was about to run out, and the CO_2 was getting high, making it hard for Jace to stay awake. The tunnel was also getting cold. Kasmae turned off her heaters to conserve power. She even resorted to sitting next to Jace for warmth.

"Jace, thank you for the power cell and helmet. You've shown me that not all your people are the ones we hate."

Jace looked up at the cavern ceiling. His suit power failed hours ago, and he wasn't feeling very well but was holding on.

He was about to say something but heard the alarm on Kasmae's suit go off. She rolled over and touched his face with her gloved hand. Jace watched as a pained look entered her eyes and she dragged her hand down his chest. Jace watched as the radiation turned the person before him, one who thought he was an enemy, to dust.

* * *

Back in the control room, Butte said, "Whoa, what's she doing? Gonna give us a show? I thought you Gel didn't like Terrans. Ha-ha!"

His words were met with silence from the room as the monitor for Kasmae's suit went black.

In the dim light of the digger, everyone watched as a tear ran down Jace's face as he fought back more. His following words stuttered as he fought back the tears. "S-sometimes, you shed a tear for your enemy because you realize at the moment they leave, they never were." His words made the eyes of everyone in the room well up, including Bosh.

134

Jace turned to the light on the digger as it flickered. "Let the Gel know she died fighting to the end." His statement made tears roll down almost everyone's faces as the video dimmed and the power failed on the digger.

No one spoke except for Butee, who said, "All touchy-feely now, are we?" his statement bringing an attack by the Gel in the room.

Eislie pushed Butee aside as she rushed toward the door, telling Bosh she was going down to get him. When he tried to stop her, the group of Gel growled. Eislie struggled to get her suit on and noticed one of the Gel walking toward her. The woman made a timid statement. "Bring her back as well."

Eislie nodded.

It took another hour as Eislie used one of the spare diggers to reach Jace's location. Tulo had warned her several times to watch the power on her suit. She would only tell him, "Confirmed," every time.

When she broke through to where Jace was, she hurriedly put a spare oxygen mask over his face. She could see his breathing was shallow. "Don't you die on me. You made a promise," Eislie said as she lifted and dragged him to the digger

As she placed him on the back of the machine, the impact made his eyes flutter. "Eis?" she heard, his speech groggy.

Eislie rushed over as he was trying to remove the mask and pressed it down on his face. "Keep it on. You're not dying on me."

Jace groaned. "I've got one hell of a headache."

Eislie smiled as she felt a tear roll down her face. She removed her glove, making the suit's alarm sound, and she touched his face.

Arren was about to order her to replace her glove when Jace's and her vitals jumped, making him ask, "What did she just do?"

Tulo sighed as he stood. "You want to tell them, Bosh, or should I?" He turned to see the captain staring sternly back at him.

The doctor took a breath. "You have to understand starborn physiology. She's not the only one here."

One of the Gel spoke up. "Starborn are planetless beings. The Duggor drove them out." The Gel pointed to the screen. "They are starborn?"

The doctor nodded.

The Gel walked up to the doctor. "You knew this?" The doctor again nodded.

Over the speaker, they heard Eislie yell, "I'm on my way up! Get medical down to the shaft area. And let the Gel know I have their leader as well!"

Tulo stammered for a moment. "Oh, okay, Eis, we'll be there."

The doctor turned and headed down, only to be blocked by Bosh standing in front of him. "I don't like people not following my orders."

The doctor pushed him aside. "I don't care, Bosh."

* * *

At the shaft, Eislie used one of the extractors to decontaminate them all. Tulo did a quick evaluation of Jace, who was now semiconscious. A group of Gel respectfully took the remains of their leader away. It took a few moments for Eislie to get the glyph suit off before she headed up to see if Jace was awake, only to be stopped by one of the Gel as she neared the med bay.

"Please, you must hear me," the Gel told her as she grabbed Eislie's arm.

"Get out of my way!" she yelled, trying to push her aside.

The Gel held firm.

"Let me go!" Eislie protested.

The Gel then spoke. "No, you must hear this. It is a matter of honor and will be heard."

Eislie stopped fighting for a moment.

"He gave his last power cell and helmet to help our leader survive. He did not push her away as she turned to dust. You brought her back willingly. You will know that you and he are not an enemy of the Gel. We are in your debt."

Eislie again was trying to break free. "Is that all?"

The Gel said, "No. But you wish to see if he is alive. We will speak later."

Eislie quickly pulled away as the woman released her arm but stopped. Eislie turned to say, "You're welcome."

When Eislie arrived, Jace was unconscious, but Tulo asked her to remain.

Several minutes passed before Jace opened his eyes to see Eislie sitting next to him.

"Hey, what time is it?" Jace asked drowsily.

Eislie leaned forward, touching his hand. "Just past lunch. You hungry?" Jace nodded. She brought him some food and took one of the rolls from the plate for herself, making Jace smile and shake his head. It was pretty quiet between them as they ate. Eislie seemed to stare away from him before giving him a concerned glare. "You're not going to ask how much, are you?"

Jace replied, "No, I don't care."

She was angry with him. "Seven hundred sixty-nine percent. Were you trying to kill yourself? That much radiation could have fried you."

Jace remained silent.

"Are you suicidal?"

"No, Eis, I'm not." He paused. "Me, you, down there, we would have had a chance. She didn't."

Jace pushed the tray away. "I had to give her a chance; she was just like us, stuck here. She was commissioned for only half a planet cycle. She was already going on two."

Eislie turned to him, tears falling down her face. "I really hate you right now."

Jace leaned back. "Get in line. I was here first."

The brief silence was broken when the doctor came in. "Am I interrupting something?"

Jace groaned. "Probably, but … Eis, let's finish this later."

She wiped tears from her face. "You know I won fifty shills from Bosh because of you."

Jace's anger left, and he smiled. "Good, you're buying then."

She laughed again, wiping a tear from her cheek. "See you later. He's all yours, Doc. Please do something painful to him; I'm really pissed at him right now."

Tulo laughed. "All right, if that's an order."

Jace laughed as the doctor escorted her out of the med bay.

Chapter 16

Pirates Again

Jace was ordered to be on medical rest, as was Eislie. Bosh had been behind closed doors for the past few days, only requiring light shift work for everyone. He allowed the Gel to prepare for the passing of their leader. The only good thing Bosh could salvage from recent events was that the situation now allowed the captain to intimidate the remaining Gel to work harder. Kasmae was helpful when the Gel became restless. Now with her gone, he could divide the remaining Gel. Bosh played things safe, since the recent production now gave him almost a full load of spide that could be shipped off world.

Jace was in his room and had slept for almost the entire day before something in his brain woke him. It was a nagging that he needed to finish what he started. When Jace opened his eyes he found the sight of the gray metal ceiling unnerving. The last few days had made him stir crazy, and he needed to see the sky again. He turned to see a small note on the floor by the door. He read it; Eislie told him she would be in her room if he wanted to talk.

On his way outside, Jace stopped by to see if Eislie wanted to join him. When she didn't answer, he became concerned. Eislie had told him she'd be in her room, leaving him a message while he slept.

Jace became worried that maybe she felt some residual effects from the radiation and went to see Dr. Tulo.

When Jace arrived, the doctor told Jace that Eislie was probably sleeping. When Jace pressed, Tulo explained that her people can only go for about fifty hours of waking time before their bodies start to shut down, and that with her recent recovery, she had well exceeded that limit over the past few days, even warning Jace that Terrans can only handle slightly longer before something similar would happen. The doctor was surprised he was awake and they were speaking after his recent ordeal. Jace's arrival prompted the doctor to take some additional readings.

Jace stared at the doctor as he worked and then asked for a favor. "I need to know what else is needed for medical supplies on a ship."

Tulo smiled. "Check the crate next to the ship next time you go to work on it."

Jace looked puzzled.

The doctor shook his head. "Arren told me. I figured I'd help. I told the guards I was putting radium extracts out for recycling. It's amazing how many people don't like being around radiation." Tulo paused before asking, "How long?"

Jace told him the engines seemed to be good, the ship had a complete working repair system, but the modifications were not something it could fix yet. The doctor warned him that Bosh was starting to watch them both closely and that Jace may want to hurry on their timeframe. Tulo also informed Jace that he had sent his report, prompting Bosh to request both he and Kala be replaced. Jace wasn't happy about the news, but he knew the doctor was right.

After waiting a few hours, Jace made it outside, even passing a few guards along the way. He was surprised when one of them nodded, then looked away as if not seeing him. *Guess I'm getting a reputation around here.*

Jace continued through the scrapyard. He waited till there was a shift change before heading back to work on the ship. The radium crate was right where Tulo mentioned, and Jace placed the supplies in the small hallway connecting the flight deck. His actions seemed to make the computer annoyed.

"Captain, this ship's medical system is fully capable of full surgical and biological regeneration."

Jace looked up. "That's great to hear. Can you repair mechanical and bio-linked systems?"

"Of course. The Takloh had more advanced medical than most spacefaring species. Those supplies are not needed."

Jace sighed. "Good. I want you to see if my translator implant can be modified not to accept that signal Bosh causes with those medals."

Ed paused for a moment. "The relative signal is linked to the power-regeneration system of your implant. It would be a simple modification."

Jace looked at the console. "You mean he's causing a back charge?"

The computer confirmed.

"It would be a simple modification; you could manufacturer the needed add-on with the supplies on board. Would you like to do it now?" the computer asked.

Jace thought for a moment. He didn't want to risk something going wrong and be discovered when they were so close to escaping. He declined the computer's offer.

"The modification can be done in a short time. This ship is quite capable with its facilities. In fact, the supplies you have stowed are not needed," Ed told him again.

"You know I'm from Earth. Then you should also know that I don't trust anything that needs power. On my world, a knife has many uses. You never know when you need something till you don't have it. Besides, what if the power is out, or you can't move someone?"

The computer paused. "Your argument is valid. Forgive my assumption."

"Don't worry, Ed, we're good. I just like to have something extra."

Jace sat in his chair, requested the star charts for Gilese, and worked on plotting a course. He wanted to keep his promise to Eislie. Jace had just asked the computer to estimate a travel time when he heard it say, "Intruder approaching." Jace went silent and slid down in the chair, grabbing the hammer he had left when he returned after saving Eislie.

Whoever entered the ship caused the lights to come back on, surprising Jace. He stood to see Eislie standing in the small hall onto the flight deck.

"Not planning on leaving without me, are you?" she joked.

Jace shook his head and walked over, pulling her into his arms, holding her tight. He relaxed, allowing her to push away. Jace smiled, hearing a moan of happiness as she pressed her forehead lovingly against his. He didn't know how much time passed before he asked how she was feeling.

"I'm still tired, but I wanted to see if we can get the ship running. I don't think Bosh is going to let us go."

Her words made the ship's computer reply, "According to Alliance records, you and Captain Jace have served your time and have been released, choosing to remain on neutral worlds."

"What?" Eislie yelled, then covered her mouth, realizing that she might give away where they were.

Jace explained that Bosh had covered all the angles and theorized that the captain thought his actions couldn't be traced. Jace also told Eislie that Ed discovered the same for all who were stuck on this planet. He also told her that Ed was very good at hacking systems, making the computer respond, "Commerce is as profitable as war. An old Takloh saying."

"Ed, you got some weird things going. I think we're really going to enjoy working with you," Jace said, making Eislie smile.

Jace looked at Eislie. "We should probably leave soon."

Eislie nodded in agreement. But as he turned to show her the charts, she looked down.

"Ugh, that's disgusting. Where did you get that?" she said, referring to the hammer he was holding.

Jace held it up. "Yeah, I haven't cleaned it from when I used it on the raza."

Eislie looked surprised. "That's the hammer you used to fight them off?"

"Yeah, I threw it into the scrapyard instead of using it on Butee. Apparently, I hit the ship."

Eislie looked down, remembering. "I watched you hit them with it. I kept thinking, kill them, get them off us." She paused. "Yeah, looking at it, it is pretty disgusting."

Jace laughed. "Yeah, should probably clean it off. The hammer still has wolf chunks all over it."

Eislie joked, "Yeah, it's a wolf-killing hammer."

Jace's eyes went wide with inspiration. "That's it."

"What's it?" she asked.

Jace looked at her. "We need to name the ship. Ed told me that when an engine or reactor are replaced in a Takloh ship, it has to be renamed."

Eislie looked at him and said, "Wolf killer?"

Jace paused for a moment, then shook his head, holding up the hammer. "Wolfhammer."

Eislie took a second and realized that the simple hammer had protected them both. It never broke, even smashing the metal-infused skulls of the raza, no matter how hard he hit them.

"Wolfhammer. Yeah, I like it," she told him

Jace smiled. "Ed, we have a new ship name."

"Captain and Captain, what is the ship's new designation?"

Jace's smile was ear to ear. "*Wolfhammer.*"

"Do both captains agree?"

Eislie laughed. "Yes, Ed, the new name is *Wolfhammer.*"

The computer paused for several seconds. "New ship designation is *Wolfhammer.* Do you also wish to add the Takloh hero, Restian, to the ship designation?"

"Who's Restian?" both of them asked in unison.

The computer then said, "Restian, leader of the Eston triad, the creator of the stars. Fabled to have used a hammer of the shadow wolves to strike the spark of creation by crushing blows."

"You're joking," Jace said.

"No, Captain, it is taught to all Takloh as children. It is the creation of all that is alight."

Jace and Eislie looked at each other. "I don't like Restian, too formal. Let's just go with *Wolfhammer.*"

Eislie nodded.

"The new designation is *Wolfhammer*, Ed," Jace told the computer.

The ship confirmed, and Eislie turned to Jace, excited. "We have our own ship!"

* * *

Several days went by, and things returned to normal. Eislie and Jace did what they could to stock the ship with food and other supplies for at least a few weeks. They tried not bringing too much attention to themselves as they continued to work as ordered. Butee had amazingly stayed out of their way, but even Jace noticed that when he looked at him and Eislie, the tiny alien was becoming angrier.

As Jace was stowing his glyph suit, he watched as Butee walked away, seething. "What the hell is wrong with that guy?" Jace asked.

Eislie simply replied, "I turned him down."

Jace turned. "For what?"

Eislie looked annoyed, but Jace quickly figured out what she meant, making him say, "Seriously? Man, that guy's got issues."

"Well, he's not a fan of you either." Jace nodded.

She explained that Butee's people are known for being single-minded. When they want something, they get it. Being told *no* is not something they take lightly. Several planets were destroyed because of disagreements.

"So, there's a whole planet of fucked-up assholes like him? You know, I understand there are medications for that," Jace said, making Eislie smirk.

"Remarks like that are why people don't like Terrans."

Jace pretended to pout. "What? They don't like our humor? That hurts my feelings."

Eislie laughed again before leaning against Jace. "I'll check with Arren to see if he has the stuff ready."

* * *

Butee was on duty in the west tower. He had watched Eislie bring out the latest crate of waste and place it out for the next recycling drop. He never liked the Alliance's way of keeping a world clean. His people had continued to do as they wanted for generations. When a planet became too polluted, they adapted or found another. But tonight, Butee was thinking of getting even. He had spent three days in confinement because of her and Jace, and he wanted payback. Seeing her alone, he decided to head down.

Eislie finished her work and looked up at the tower to see no one inside. Realizing Butee was on watch, she knew she had to get inside. He had already tried to kill her once; she knew he would try again.

As Eislie scanned the area, she could see Butee walking in the shadows toward her as she waited for the elevator doors to open. Like Jace, she had good night vision and readied herself as the small man approached.

Eislie pretended not to notice as the short alien paused to make sure no one else was around. Eislie became more alert when she saw a flicker of metal in his hand. Remembering her training, she removed the light jacket she was wearing and rolled it around her one hand, holding the free end in her other.

Butee wasn't very stealthy as he attacked. She wrapped her jacket around the knife, pulling it from his grip. She then kicked him against the metal wall, knocking him out.

"Jace is right. You are fucked up." She left him in the trash as the elevator doors opened.

As the doors closed, Eislie didn't notice several small lights appear over the horizon.

* * *

Jace had returned from the mine and was eating with the others. The Gel no longer considered him an enemy and were willing to sit nearby. He had taken his first bite when the whole facility shook. The central alarm was blaring, and he stood, along with many of the others, as the floor shook again.

One of the Gel turned to him. "What is it?"

They heard the general alert announcement over the speakers. "All defensive units to weapons. We are under attack."

Jace took several seconds before heading back to his room, but when he heard the shooting a floor above, he knew things were pretty dire. He grabbed the pack he put together and decided to find Eislie. He headed for the bar.

* * *

On the surface, several mechanized units stomped the ground. They fired at the main entrance, breaking through the sealed doors. Within moments, the machines were headed toward the storage facility down below.

Jace found Eislie at the bar. She was rushing to place some bottles in a pack. "Eis, if they're after the spide, they'll be coming right through here."

Eislie nodded. "I know. I just got finished dropping off my stuff and the supplies Arren had for us. I wanted to take some extra liquor."

Jace grinned. "You're a girl after my own heart, you know that? But we need to get scarce, now."

She agreed, but as they ran for the elevator, debris hit the ground before them, and seconds later, a mechanized unit followed, the impact of the machine throwing them both to the floor. Jace looked up to see the mechanized unit start toward the inside storage area. Another few seconds, and they were again jolted as another unit hit the shaft floor.

"They're going for the spide!" Eislie yelled.

Jace nodded. "Okay, perfect chance to escape. Let's go."

Eislie stopped him. "We haven't loaded it in the transport containers yet, remember? If those crates open while everyone is in here, then …"

She didn't need to finish her sentence before Jace started running toward the storage area, yelling back, "Tell Bosh, Arren, whoever, I'm grabbing one of the diggers!"

"Don't get killed!"

Jace mumbled, "Don't get killed. That's fucking obvious."

By the time he arrived, one mechanized unit was already heading back with a crate of crystals. The other seemed to be having trouble grabbing on to the container it focused on. While the pirate was distracted, Jace clipped on a harness and hopped onto a nearby digger. He used its arm and laser to attack the machine. He was surprised when the laser deflected. "Well, Arren did tell me these pirates were usually heavily armored."

Jace hit full throttle, and the digger sped toward the mechanized unit as it turned. The impact knocked it on its side, and Jace watched as the crate fell to the ground. The lid opened, spilling the load of crystals. With the arms of the digger, he quickly rushed to pick up the scattered crystals. He wasn't concerned with the disabled machine only meters away. Jace was more worried that radiation would kill everyone if it flooded the facility.

Jace had just closed the lid when his digger was struck from behind. He moved it away as the pirate advanced toward him. Jace got on the loudspeaker. "You moron, are you trying to kill everyone?"

The pirate laughed and fired a shot that hit dead center on the digger's windshield, smashing it away. Jace had the wind knocked out of him. He was trying to regain his bearings when the pirate reached into the open crate, grabbing one of the crystals. He brought it up, holding it in front of Jace, who merely stared at it.

Seeing the confusion on the pirate's face, Jace smiled and used the digger arm to smash the windshield of the mechanized unit. He watched as the radiation burned the pirate to dust and his unit dropped the crystal. Jace grabbed the shard, placing it back into the crate before taking it further down the mine.

Eislie had called Bosh and told him about the situation. The captain ordered her to head to the docking bay and load the remaining crystals already staged to be loaded. She was to meet Arren and make sure everything was on board. She didn't like something in Bosh's voice, and she instead went to find Jace.

Jace met her in the staging area. She told him about what Bosh said, making Jace say, "Yeah, he's probably going to leave us here and run."

Eislie nodded, and instead, they grabbed the pack with the liquor and headed to the *Wolfhammer*.

146

Chapter 17

Escape

Jace and Eislie used the elevator to head topside, careful to keep in the shadow of the mechanized unit escaping in the lift, hoping the pilot wouldn't notice. Once they made it out, they headed to their ship.

Jace opened the door, to be greeted by the computer. "Hostile forces detected. I recommend that we leave this location."

"No argument there, Ed," Eislie said as she sat in her chair. "Let's get the engines online." She then looked at Jace. "Any weapons?"

Jace nodded. "A drill and slag throwers."

"What and what?" Eislie asked.

"Ed, engine status?" Jace smiled before looking back at Eislie. "Slag cannons are kinetic rounds. And the drill has been modified. It's like the digger's drill."

Eislie looked at him. "You mean we have a dimensional-phased laser and shoot molten metal?"

Jace nodded. "Yep. The laser burns everything except spide. But it can be deflected, so we shoot molten slag."

Eislie looked at him. "Not normal weapons, you know."

Jace rolled his eyes. "Ed, engine status?"

"Engines online, tunnel drive online."

Jace smiled. "All right, weapons?"

"Slag cannons loaded and heated; the drill is charged."

Jace looked to Eislie. "We're not exactly your normal crew, you know. I'm a refugee left for dead, you're an enslaved worker, and Ed is from a dead planet." He paused. "No offense, Ed."

"Your assessment is correct, Captain."

Eislie looked back at Jace and could see his smile as he worked the controls. He turned toward her. "This is only the third real time I've piloted a ship."

She then said, "Maybe I should fly then."

As they were lifting off, the computer alerted them to incoming hostiles. "Recommend that magnetic shields be activated. Three vessels approaching, and the large vessel is primed with decaying orbit for its descent."

Jace hit the shields and said, "Sounds like the rest of the party guests just arrived."

Within seconds, they were airborne and could see a group gathered by the base's entrance. Unfortunately, their ship was hit by weapons fire, and they were thankful the shields were active. Jace did his best to keep the pirates in view, and when he had one in his sights, he fired the slag cannons. They both watched as the molten round hit the ship, knocking it sideways, the force of the round splitting the small ship open.

"Yeah, that's a really effective weapon. Next rounds we make smaller, Ed," Jace ordered.

Eislie looked at him. "That worked pretty well. Maybe we shouldn't."

Jace agreed, but they still had two pirates to deal with and the rest of the mechanized units. Jace flew after the others and dispatched them, each with a faster accuracy than the last. When finished, they headed to the dock, where everyone was trying to get on the remaining Alliance supply ships. Although the supply ships were armed, they weren't a match for the pirates.

By the time the two arrived, one of the supply ships had already left. Jace and Eislie took down the remaining attackers quickly using the slag cannons. Eislie noticed that the pirates had removed the transport crates and were loading them to one area. The ship's computer again warned them of the massive ship starting to deorbit.

"Probably heading down to land troops to take the base," Eislie said. "Ed, time to landing?"

"Approximately seven standard minutes."

They scanned the ground and could see Tulo and Kala helping Arren out of the facility. With the mechanized units gone, the guards were quickly herding the others onto the supply ships.

They landed the *Wolfhammer* and opened the rear loading door, greeting Arren and the rest.

"So, this is the ship? It's pretty old," Tulo noted.

Arren asked, "What'd ya name her?"

Jace laughed. "*Wolfhammer.*" He could see what Arren called brows raise and was surprised when the old man seemed more interested in the ship. "Yeah, it beat the slac out of the pirates so far. What are you using to get through the shields?"

He was going to tell Arren about the slag cannons when Eislie yelled to them, "Jace, it's a large dreadnaught coming down and a slac-load of more fighters. We have to get out of here!"

Arren told him to get a loader and grab that crate, pointing to a storage crate by the entrance. Jace dragged it over, and Eislie used the magnetic grappler to pull it on board the ship.

"Come on, everyone, let's get out of here," Jace said, pulling Arren forward. He was interrupted when he felt a sharp pain in his upper back. His eyes filled with anger as he turned to see Butee hanging on to a small knife that was now stuck in Jace's shoulder.

"You little shit," Jace said, grabbing the small man in a headlock.

Eislie rushed over and looked at Jace's wound. "Seriously, do you even feel pain?" she said as she pulled the knife out. Thankfully, it hadn't gone deep, only a centimeter or two, thanks to the digger harness Jace was still wearing. Jace tossed the small, green-gray man several feet. "You're lucky I'm in a rush to get out of here. Otherwise, I'd take my time killing you."

"Threatening a guard is punishable by one week in solitary!" Butee yelled back, only to be interrupted as a pulse of weapons fire hit him; they all watched as what remained of the guard fell to the ground limply.

"Ah, that kind of death is too good for a slac like him," Arren said as he shuffled toward the *Wolfhammer*.

Then there was another, much closer explosion and several others that blocked their escape to the ship. They were all knocked to the ground when one hit just about where Arren was standing. The old miner rolled across the dirt like a tumbleweed from the blast. Kala was the first to reach him. "He's alive but burned badly."

Jace went to grab his friend, but Tulo intervened. "No, we need to get him to one of the Alliance transports. I'd be able to treat him better there."

Jace knew he was right; they hadn't had a chance to test the systems on the *Wolfhammer* yet. Instead, Jace told them they'd cover them and let them escape. The doctor called some of the remaining guards to help move the old miner while Jace headed back, to Eislie's surprise.

"What happened?"

"Arren's hurt bad. They're taking him to the other ship."

"We could have helped," she argued.

"I know, but we haven't tested the med systems yet, remember?" he reminded her. "I didn't want to take the chance they wouldn't work."

She understood and watched as the others ran toward the remaining supply ship. She knew the computer had told them five standard minutes, but she closed the door when heavy weapons fire hit close by. They both rushed to the flight deck and secured themselves.

"Ed, where's the big ship?" Jace asked.

The computer replied, "One minute to landing. We have over thirty hostiles nearby."

"Well, geez, couldn't they make it more challenging?" Jace joked.

When they looked on the screen, they noticed the weapons fire now concentrated on the escaping supply ships.

"Eis, we have to give them a chance to escape. Our ship can take the hits," Jace said, making Eislie grit her teeth.

"All right, I'll fly, you shoot. You're still new at this."

Jace laughed. "Yes, Captain. Ed, flight control to the second chair. I'll take weapons."

The computer did as ordered, and they were off. Jace quickly took almost a dozen ships out using the slag cannons. Their actions allowed the Alliance ships to take off and head to orbit. He breathed a sigh of relief, but Eislie suddenly turned the ship. They nearly missed being hit by cannon fire from the dreadnaught. That wasn't the only thing they had to worry about as several shots hit them from all sides.

"Recommend evasive maneuvers or withdrawal, Captains."

Unfortunately, they were surrounded, blocked at every move they made. As the ship bounced off the pirates' shields, they realized the ship was trapped.

"Shit, we just got this ship running!" Jace said, then looked to Eislie, who was searching for a way out as well. She turned, seeing him staring back at her. They both looked at the screen as the massive ship headed right for them.

"Ed? Is the drill still charged?" Jace asked.

The computer gave a simple, one-word response. "Yes."

He looked again to Eislie. "They're herding us toward the ship. Probably figure we'd crash into them and break up."

She continued to fight as they bounced off the other ships that surrounded them.

"Eislie, don't fight them. Let's head for the big ship," Jace urged.

"Are you crazy? That thing will crumple us!" she protested.

"Ed, how much will full power on the drill slow us down?" he asked.

Several moments later, the computer said, "Power would decrease by approximately 27 percent but be fully regenerated after thirteen seconds."

Eislie looked forward, an unsure stare in her eyes. "We're going through, aren't we?"

Jace nodded. "Yep. When we get closer, I'll fire. I want full impact."

It didn't take long, and just as the other ships turned away, Jace said as he fired, "Ed, let's light up the sky, like in the legend."

Plasma surrounded the ship as it drilled through the giant pirate ship and emerged to see the darkness of space greet them. Eislie checked all sensors, and no ships were following them. They could see the planet through the hole they made in the massive vessel before it crashed on the rear viewscreen.

On the Alliance ship, Kala was staring out the window and saw the *Wolfhammer* emerge from the dreadnaught's back. Her mouth was open in surprise as she shielded her eyes from the brightness of the explosion, making Arren beam as he mumbled, "Tough little ship they got there."

Tulo overheard him. "They got lucky."

Arren sat up. "No, they didn't. I've been staring out that window watching them get hit with direct fire from that heavy ship, and they just blew right through it."

Arren pushed the doctor away as he lay back. "Doc, I wonder if they know about the legend of Eston Triad?"

"Who?" Kala asked.

The doctor turned with a smile. "The creator of the stars. I'm familiar with the legend. It was part of my studies at Covenant."

Arren smiled. "Restian, the one who set the skies alight using the shadow wolves' hammer." He paused. "I think those two lit up the sky today."

Chapter 18

Pirate Irate

The *Wolfhammer* exited hyperspace near an orange star.

"This can't be right. Ed, how accurate are these charts?" Eislie asked, confused by the sight.

"They are current as of the recent download from the facility."

"Show me," she ordered the computer, and the holographic screen appeared before them. Checking the display, she exclaimed, "We're off by more than forty arcs! Didn't you calibrate the system?"

Jace looked at her. "Not like I had a lot of time. I didn't get to it."

Eislie became frustrated. "We haven't tested medical, navigation's off. What else isn't fixed?"

The computer responded, "The cooling chamber in storage needs repair."

Jace laughed as Eislie stared forward in disbelief. Moments later, she joined him.

"Captain, did I say something funny?"

Jace caught his breath. "No, Ed, you're good. We're just a bit loopy right now."

"Loopy?" Eislie asked.

Jace explained that Terrans get this way when they're overtired and frustrated. Eislie did remind him that they spent a day running from pirates before using the tunnel drive to jump into hyperspace.

"You know, it's been over two days since either of us has slept," Jace noted.

He looked over to Eislie. "Ed, how long to recalibrate navigation?"

"About nine standard hours."

Eislie looked at the sensors, seeing nothing in the area. "Not the best place to hide right now. Ed, where is the nearest inhabited level-two or above planet?"

"Approximately two-hundred-seventy arcs, bearing 320, 24, 179. Type-three system."

"So, about two days with standard grav drive. We could be in worse shape," Eislie said.

Jace leaned back in his chair. "Guess we could head there if you want. Glad you knew when to tunnel out."

Eislie slumped in her chair. "I didn't. It just felt like something was off while we were traveling."

When she looked at him, he agreed. "Yeah, I was thinking about it too. I should have listened to my gut." He paused. "Ed, start recalibration."

"We will not be able to use the tunnel systems while calibrating. And the best speed for grav systems would be recommended to no more than one-quarter power."

Jace lowered his head. "Ed, we've already had the grav systems at a hundred percent with the reduction. What if we remove that?"

"Reduction? What reduction?" Eislie asked. When Jace told her the grav drive was from a racing hopper, she was surprised they weren't running full. "It'd take us less than a day to get there."

The ship's computer repeated, "But recommended safe speed is at one-quarter power when navigation is being calibrated, to prevent flight error."

Jace grabbed the controls and centered a star in the window. "Is that the destination star, Ed?"

"Yes, Captain."

Jace ordered the computer to remove the reduction, and he hit the throttle. "We keep the star in the viewscreen, and it gets us there."

The next few hours, Eislie and he took turns piloting. Neither of them had a chance to get any sleep, but surprisingly, they arrived at the star within five standard hours.

"This is a fast ship," Eislie praised.

"Yeah, I didn't even go full throttle."

They ordered Ed to scan for local planets and found the one the computer mentioned. They set course, only to be interrupted by the ship lurching sideways.

"Plasma weapons detected."

"Ed, on screen, who's attacking us?" Eislie ordered.

They groaned, seeing several pirate ships bearing down on them. "Let's get out of here," Eislie said as another shot hit.

The pirates moved in and were able to meet them at every turn. Both were exhausted from fighting and flying, and it was taking a toll. One hit shook them so violently, Jace was thrown from his chair, his side hitting hard against the front console, making him yell out in pain. As he sat back and buckled his harness, he held his side. "Shit, I think I broke some ribs."

The two found themselves trapped, and when the ultimatum came over communications, they knew they were in trouble. The fight had driven them closer to the star, and Jace had an idea. "Ed, you said this ship could mine stellar gas, right?" Jace said, making Eislie worried.

"Yes, Captain. We can direct plasma into the intakes for separation."

He turned to Eislie. "We make it look like we fell into the star's gravity well and burned up."

"You want to dive into a star?" Eislie protested. "No ship this small can enter a star."

"Captain, this ship can move beneath the star's surface approximately halfway for this type of class-M body. It has done so many times before."

Eislie smiled in disbelief. "You mean we *can* dive into a star?"

Jace nodded. "They're trying to kill us anyway."

Eislie looked at him. "The two of you are crazy." She paused. "Make that the three of us. What's your plan?"

Jace grabbed the controls. "Easy. We look like we are losing power and slide sideways toward the star. When we get close, use the mag and tunnel shields and find someplace warm and cozy to sit for a while."

They did just as planned, and the pirates watched as they fell below the star's surface. But instead of moving away, the pirates remained where they were.

"The enemy has sensors that can detect the density of the plasma. They are keeping track of us."

"We have to go deeper, don't we?" Eislie asked, making Jace nod.

As they fell further into the star, the cabin began to light brightly, making each search for something to cover their eyes.

"Ed, what's the plasma density like?" Jace asked.

"I can only partially detect their sensors, but they seem to be searching for us again."

"But our sensors are working?" Eislie asked.

"No, I am using plasma reflections to detect the ships."

Jace raised his eyebrows. "Neat trick. We're pretty deep, though, Ed. How long can we stay here?"

"Approximately three standard days, but the ship will heat past acceptable levels before that."

"Great. Any other good news, Ed?" Jace asked, obviously in pain.

"Yes. Controls can be transferred to the medical bay, and systems can be controlled from there. Environmental can be adjusted to remain steady for medical until the temperature returns to safe limits. It is a standard procedure during stellar mining. We can also enact the jump field to support the ship further."

"Do it, Ed. Transfer controls to the med bay," Jace ordered.

After the ship confirmed the commands, Jace needed help getting out of his chair. When Eislie turned on the med systems, everything seemed to be working. When she scanned Jace, she confirmed, "Yep, you broke two ribs." She used the knitter to repair the bones, but the regen wand was nowhere to be found when she looked for it. She touched his skin, just seeing the bruising starting to appear.

"Ed, where is the regen wand?" she asked.

"Captain, it is in storage."

Eislie rolled her eyes as Jace said, "I told you I didn't have time, geez."

But as she went to open the door, it wouldn't budge. "Ed, why won't the door open?"

"The temperature in the corridor is already exceeding survivable limits for your biology."

"You mean we're trapped here," Eislie said.

"No. You may ask me to leave the star, and when the temperature has normalized, you may return."

She returned to Jace, inspecting his side. Looking at the monitor, she said, "No internal bleeding. You'll just have to deal with it for the moment."

Jace looked up at her. "We have food, water, medical—um, mostly medical—a bathroom, and a bed. What more do we need?" He gave her a seductive look.

Eislie leaned down. "Sex in the middle of a star. Are you serious?"

Jace looked up at the window in the center of the med bay. "Yeah, probably not a good idea. But it'd be one hell of a way to go," he quipped, making Eislie laugh.

"Move over," she said as she crawled up next to him.

Jace placed his arm around her. "You know the doctor said the closer we are, the faster we heal."

She pressed her body against his. "Like this, I'll bet."

Jace smiled. "I have no idea, but I like it," he replied, making them both laugh.

He wiped some sweat from his forehead. "Is it getting hot in here, or is it just me?"

Eislie chuckled as Ed replied, "The temperature is thirty-six degrees Celsius."

Jace answered, "Hmm, guess it is getting hot in here." He then ordered the lights off to conserve power for the shielding.

Looking out the portal above, Jace could feel Eislie's breathing slowing as she lay next to him. When her head shifted against his shoulder, it startled him.

"Eis, you awake?" Jace asked. She stirred, lifting herself away from him.

"Sorry, drifted off for a minute." But when she looked at the clock, over an hour had passed.

She moved in closer and again nestled her head against his shoulder, now staring up through the window as Jace was. She watched as small flashes of light dimly flickered in the darkened room.

"It's beautiful, isn't it?" Eislie said drowsily.

Jace shifted. "Yeah, solar particles smashing against the shields."

Eislie sighed with a bit of annoyance before Jace continued. "Like raindrops of light, pinholes in the darkness."

Eislie moved in closer. "That's pretty romantic."

She ran her hand down his side before lifting his shirt. She could see the significant discoloration from where he hit the console. She gently pressed against it, making him flinch.

"Sorry, I didn't mean to hurt you. The med bay fixed the bones, but I needed the regen wand to fix the bruising. It has to go away on its own."

Jace snickered. "No, it wasn't that. Your hands are cold. I can't believe it's hot in here and your hands are cold."

Eislie gently hit him across his face with a pillow, making him laugh. "Ow, don't make me laugh; it still hurts when I laugh."

She rolled her body against his, holding him tight. Everything was silent, and he again felt her relax against him as her breathing slowed.

"Ed?" Jace said, his words slower.

"Yes, Captain?"

"Just in case I fall asleep, I'm ordering you to leave the star in one standard day and find someplace with an atmosphere to cool us down. Understood?"

"Order confirmed, Captain."

160

Right at that moment, Jace didn't want to change anything. They were free from being prisoners and had evaded the pirates. He had found some great adventure so far, and lying next to him was someone like him. But he was afraid this wasn't going to last; he had promised her that he would take her home. From there, he didn't know what was going to happen. But right now, he wanted each moment to stretch on for as long as possible. Jace did his best to stay conscious, but the lack of sleep finally caught up with him.

* * *

Jace woke with a start. The lights were on and the temperature much cooler.

Quietly he asked, "Ed, what's our status?"

The computer answered, "We are in the wake of a small comet, using its gas to cool the ship and hide us."

"Any sign of pirates?"

"No, they left over ten standard hours ago."

"Ten hours? How long was I asleep?" Jace asked.

"Eleven hours, eleven minutes, and six seconds."

"Yeah, too much info, Ed. What's the status of the rest of the ship?"

"All parts of the ship are accessible. The temperature has normalized."

He could feel Eislie still cradled against him and did his best not to wake her as he slowly slid out of bed. Jace lifted his shirt to see the bruising gone.

"I'll take that over the regen machine any day." He couldn't help but look back to see Eislie still sleeping.

Jace opened the door and headed to the control console. When he arrived, he was greeted with an ethereal sight as particles of dust and gas enveloped the ship. "So many wonders out here!" escaped his mouth.

A few hours passed before Eislie woke. She searched for Jace, almost falling off the bed as she did. When she asked Ed where he was and he responded, she quickly headed to the bridge.

Jace turned to see her rubbing her face as she walked in. "What's our status?"

"We're in the middle of a comet's tail. Ed tells me that navigation's fixed, so we can head wherever we want."

Eislie sat in her chair, then stared out into the sparkling veil that surrounded them. "It's beautiful, like sparks from a fire."

Jace smiled. He turned to see her starting to close her eyes again.

"Still groggy?" Jace asked.

She nodded, still feeling exhausted. "I don't know how Terrans function without sleep."

"I was out for over eleven hours. I don't know what you're on about," Jace grumbled.

"Really? Wow. That was long for you," she told him, seeing him nod. She glanced down with subtle concern. "Feeling better?"

Jace lifted his shirt, showing his now-unbruised side, making her smile as he said, "We didn't need the regen wand anyway."

Chapter 19

Keeping a Promise

Eislie and Jace landed on the nearest planet, as planned. They were in luck, finding it to be a neutral world known as Palanine Senka. After landing, they had to register and give an initial planet of origin. When Jace told them he was a refugee, the local authorities took pity on them. Although after hearing their ship was pieced together from older vessels, the local engineering league became intrigued. The world they found, Senka, was a level-three civilization. It was an industrial world with technology and systems that could only be found in Jace's dreams. The people of Senka had harnessed the power of their entire system. Even Eislie found it spectacular.

Since it was a neutral world, there were many races, but there were rules. Any disagreements were decided by logic and advanced computer algorithms. They were almost in trouble when Ed tried accessing the facilities systems after landing. Once the locals realized their ship had an older system, the incident resolved quickly, and as the locals put it, "It didn't know any better."

When asked how they would pay for the landing, rental, and supplies, neither answered right away. They remembered the load of crystals on board, and Eislie made a suggestion. When she mentioned they had extra spide, the locals became very interested in listening. Eislie asked for containment, and they could provide two large crystals for sale. That offer made the local magistrate question why a ship so small was carrying them. Eislie lied, telling them that the *Wolfhammer* was commissioned to bring them to a location, and they were to be paid on arrival. She mentioned that there were no ships at the rendezvous, only pirates. Seeing the scorching of weapons on the hull secured their story.

They informed the locals that the container was too large to be unloaded without some effort. The magistrate was happy to provide support, although they did become concerned the crystals were not genuine when Jace only took a few minutes to bring them out.

Jace knew what they thought and came up with a line. "We had some glyph suits ready to go. Been practicing putting them on. I don't like being close to those things." His statement made Eislie giggle.

When the magistrate inspected the materials, they were surprised at the quality and offered a very fair price of two million shill for the three provided. Jace and Eislie were more than happy to accept the offer.

As they were walking back to the ship, they began wondering if they should stay very long. When Jace mentioned, "They do know we have more spide on board," Eislie got his point. With that amount of crystals, they had a target on them. They quickly resupplied with food and water, some minor items, including crew jackets, before the star set on the horizon.

"Okay, we're a registered ship. We've got supplies. Where to now?" Jace asked as he buckled in.

Eislie looked forward silently.

"If you don't want to go back right away, we can stay," Jace tried comforting her.

She turned to look at him. "No, I want to go home."

Jace smiled, ordering Ed to plot a course for Gilese IV.

"Estimated time of arrival is five-point-four standard days from the current location."

Eislie groaned. "I didn't realize we were out so far. I thought this system was closer."

She asked Ed to check again. The computer confirmed their current location.

Eislie leaned her head back. "We were way off course."

Jace laughed as he guided the ship into the upper atmosphere. They waited until reaching the edge of the stellar sphere before using the tunnel drive.

During the first day, they were putting things where they thought they should be. But Eislie and Jace had several disagreements, almost always ending in them laughing at the discussion. By the time the third day arrived, they were both bored and were staring out into the energy ribbons' colors passing them.

"I'm getting a drink. Want anything?" Jace asked. Eislie shook her head.

While in the galley, he rummaged through the stores. When he found where Eislie had put the liquor, Jace thought it amusing. He grabbed a bottle and turned the label, trying to read it. The language was not one he recognized, so he decided to ask Eislie.

As he exited the galley, he walked right into her, bringing them both to the floor, with her landing on top. Though stunned, they both started to laugh, but neither tried to move from where they were. Jace held up the bottle. "I was going to ask you what this was."

Eislie laughed. "It's Taurian spirits. At least you didn't drop it. It's expensive."

They laughed for a few seconds more, and the small hallway fell silent as they looked at each other. Jace could feel the heat of her body against his through the new uniforms she had purchased. He watched as she kept a subtle smile, looking back at him. She moved to touch her forehead to his, then planted a gentle kiss on his lips before pressing her head against his chest.

Jace took a moment before saying anything. "You know, we're not on Charon anymore. And no one's chasing us."

Eislie took a breath and quietly said, "Ed?"

The computer didn't respond.

She threw her head back in annoyance before yelling, "Ed?"

"Yes, Captain?"

"Anything on sensors?" she asked.

"No, Captain. Nothing for thirty arcs."

"Really? Our sensors read up to thirty arcs?" was her reply as she sat up.

"Yes, Captain."

Jace shrugged his shoulders. Eislie looked at him. "Most systems go to ten, max."

"Ed, Jace and I are going to, uh … retire for the day. Keep us informed of any emergencies," she ordered.

Jace sat up, gently kissing Eislie, making her wrap her legs around him.

"Acknowledged, Captain."

Eislie stared into Jace's eyes, and he couldn't stop staring back into those light-blue eyes of hers. He shifted, lifting them both from the deck.

"I never realized you're not that heavy," Jace said.

Eislie laughed. "You're from a heavy-gravity world, dummy. I'm a normal weight."

She watched him smile before she kissed him passionately. Jace did his best to walk toward the cabin, almost stumbling before touching the frame to open it. Eislie snickered as she said, "Heavy-gravity world maybe, but not very graceful."

Jace placed his forehead against hers. "Oh, I'll show you graceful."

As the door closed behind them, the computer turned the corridor's lights down to conserve power. Over the speaker, the faint sound of the voice of the computer crackled. "Six days, thirty-one hours, and sixteen minutes. My estimate was off on these two."

The computer continued to navigate the ship. There was no one at the controls to see a small light flashing on the console. Above the tiny array, a small screen displayed "Message received and decoded. I will inform the crew."

* * *

Jace opened his eyes and reveled in feeling the warmth of Eislie against him. They had made love several times; neither of them wanted it to end. He turned to see her sleeping and relaxed. Brushing her light-blonde hair away from her face, he stared at her before mumbling, "You are beautiful. I can't believe I had to leave Earth to find someone like you." He ran his hand along her shoulder. "Definitely worth the trouble, though."

When he moved closer, she seemed to reciprocate, moving in to touch him. It wasn't long before he again fell into a deep sleep.

* * *

"Captains?"

Eislie stirred but remained asleep.

The computer again tried to wake them, turning the lights to high. It still took several tries, but as Jace turned over, he was finally awake.

"What is it, Ed?" Jace asked, hiding his eyes to adjust to the brightness of the room.

"We received a message for the *Wolfhammer* while you were … retired."

Jace turned, telling Eislie as she snickered, "Yeah, I noticed he hesitated saying that too. Want to bet he's been watching us the whole time?"

Eislie laughed. "That's not a creepy thought."

The computer paused. "As I mentioned, we have a message from Oppa. It reads: 'Duggor are on approach. Recommend that you not enter the system.'"

"The Duggor? But Oppa is a neutral planet. Why would the Duggor attack?" Eislie asked.

Jace shrugged. "Maybe there are Daak there." Then a chill ran down his spine. "Shit, there are Daak on Earth."

Eislie shook her head. "Any more to the message?"

"No, Captain, nothing more. Although it is in a Takloh format."

Eislie looked up. "Ed, how soon to our destination?"

"One day and four hours to arrive."

Jace looked at her as she said, "What? Oppa is on the other side of the galaxy."

She pulled herself close, and he again felt her press warmly against him. But she wasn't as relaxed as she had been earlier.

"You're worried about when we get there, aren't you?" Jace whispered.

Eislie nodded and pulled even closer. "What's to worry about? I'm a known criminal. I haven't seen my family in almost four cycles, my lover is Terran, and I'm in a ship put together from spare parts from around the galaxy."

Jace laughed. "Yeah, no, nothing strange there."

He felt her laughing as she hid her face before sliding over Jace, kissing him gently. "No, nothing strange at all."

* * *

It was almost a day before they were both back at the controls. The computer alerted them to the location, and they exited hyperspace just outside the stellar sphere. They used the grav drives to go the rest of the way.

As they neared the planet, they passed a beacon transmitting on an alert frequency. "What's it say, Ed?" Eislie asked.

"Daak territory, identify before entering."

"What? Daak, here?" Eislie yelled.

"Ed, can you confirm that there are Daak vessels nearby?" Jace ordered.

"Negative, only the beacon."

"No, no, no, please tell me the Daak did not take my world! Gilese IV is an Alliance neutral planet!" Eislie pleaded.

"I cannot confirm. The beacon does not have access to the planetary network."

Jace looked at her, and they decided to continue. They both knew the *Wolfhammer* was fast; in fact, it was probably faster than any Daak ship. As they approached, the computer alerted them to Daak activity nearby.

"Captains, there appears to be a Daak installation on one of the moons."

"Show me," Eislie ordered. Jace could see the fear and concern in her as she rotated the image.

"Have you tried contacting the planet, Ed?" Eislie asked.

"Negative. We have not hailed them yet, but it would be prudent to do so."

Jace looked at her. She was biting her lip, obviously worried at the recent findings. She looked over. "Let's call them now."

They opened communications, and the response was quick. When asked to identify themselves, Jace looked to Eislie. "I have no idea what I'm doing here."

She briefly smiled. "They ask for ship name, captain, planet of origin, and former destination."

Jace replied, "This is the *Wolfhammer*." He then paused. He was looking at her again.

"Just tell them you're the captain. It might be an issue if I say anything."

Jace smiled. "You troublemaker," he muttered, making her laugh.

"Gilese control, this is the *Wolfhammer*, Captain Jace Tucker. Coming from Senka."

A moment passed. "Planet of origin, Captain?"

Jace thought for a moment. "Formally of Earth, refugee status."

Another few seconds passed. "*Wolfhammer* is registered with the Alliance database. Senka is your new planet of origin?"

Jace responded, "For the moment."

"Cargo?"

Jace had to think, as they still had most of the spide from the mining colony on board.

"Salvage, here for sale."

On the comm, he then heard, "Nature of the materials."

Jace again paused. "Mining. Request containment when we land."

"Level of containment?" the controller asked.

Jace looked to Eislie again with her telling him, "Spide is level five. There are only five levels." So Jace requested level five containment.

There was a minute of silence before the operator returned. "Please proceed to dock seventy-one east port, and do not exit the ship until containment is in place."

Jace responded, "Confirmed."

They landed and waited for the shield system to arrive. Communication was handled through the comms, and eventually they were asked to offload the cargo. Jace and Eislie put on the glyph suits to make it look like they were running things safely. Besides, no one needed to know about their resistance to the radiation. The local team inspected the contents before again questioning its origin. The crate had a Charon identifier, and Jace told them, "We were in the area; we took out some pirates and helped the surviving Alliance ships escape. We picked this up from one of the pirates."

Jace technically wasn't lying.

The inspector argued with someone over the comm and then returned to them. "Your story checks out. A ship identified as *Wolfhammer* aided the escape of Alliance vessels evacuating the surface and reported to be in a battle with the pirates on escaping. The spide is to be considered salvage, and you are allowed to sell its contents."

Yes*sss!* Jace screamed in his head. Eislie remained in the background.

"The contents will be placed under secure lockdown until time of sale." The man handed a pad to Jace, who couldn't read anything on it. He gave it to Eislie, who nodded—telling him to place his thumb here to sign.

"Any ship repairs?" the man asked. Jace said there probably were, but they wanted to get a complete inventory first. The controller informed them that lodging was available. They did not need to stay shipbound if they chose. Jace was thinking of getting a room, just in case they couldn't meet Eislie's family. Then the man looked at Eislie walking next to him and interrupted, "Since the cargo is highly regulated, all crew must be logged. What is your name, please?"

Eislie froze for a moment before replying, "Eislie Licessien."

Jace watched as the pad the man held turned red.

"Eislie Licessien, you are a registered felon, with time served. What is your business here?" the man asked.

Eislie took a breath. "I am coming home. I wanted to see my home and family."

The man looked at her, and his demeanor softened. "Then, welcome back."

Eislie breathed a sigh of relief. "Thank you."

As they continued, Jace felt her hang on to him as if almost exhausted. He knew she was having second thoughts, but now he could tell she was relieved to be home.

Chapter 20

Meeting the Family

They stayed in the lodging for a few days to finalize the auction conditions, with the crystals' sale expecting to bring in over eighty million shill. Jace and Eislie knew they would be set for a very long time once completed. Eislie planned on paying off her family's home, but Jace had no clue what he would do.

Jace watched Eislie as they rode down in the elevator. He could see her clutching the small gift she had bought her mother. From the military registry, she found out that her father was assigned to a deep-space detail, watching for looters on a new artifact find. It would take him months to return home. The good news was that the ship's tour was almost up, and she was contemplating sticking around until he returned. She hadn't spoken to Jace much after she mentioned it the previous day.

"You okay?" Jace asked.

Eislie slowly nodded. He watched her wringing the small package between her hands.

"You're going to crush it, you know?"

"How are you so calm?" she snapped back.

Jace looked forward. "I'm not. I'm terrified about meeting your mother."

"It's been four years since I've seen her," Eislie said and reached out for his hand, fighting back tears. The rest of the ride was silent. When the doors opened, she hesitated. But as Jace stepped forward, it didn't take much for her to follow.

It took a few minutes to reach the front door, and Eislie hesitated before touching her hand on the frame. It unlocked, but she knocked anyway. Her mother looked annoyed as she approached, but tears started forming when she realized who was standing in the doorway.

"Eis, is it you?" Her mother's voice cracked.

Eislie looked at her and nodded. There were no words as they hugged each other. Jace felt his eyes tearing up as he watched.

Several minutes seemed to pass before he was invited in. Her mother didn't want to let go of her daughter until they made it into the living area. Jace looked around. "Nice place."

"Thank you …" Her mother paused, motioning for him to give her some information.

"Oh, uh, Jace," he told her.

"Flora. Please sit, sit."

They all sat before her mother asked if they wanted anything. Eislie looked at her and meekly said, "I'm dying for Talion tea, if there's any?"

Her mother smiled. "Sure. And you?"

Jace sat up. "Never had it before. Why not."

Eislie briefly watched her mother as she walked by, but before entering the kitchen, her mother paused to see Jace lean over and heard him say, "You all right?"

Flora continued to listen as they whispered between each other.

"I'm home. You actually brought me home!"

"I did promise," Jace whispered back.

She watched Eislie reach her hand out to his. "Thank you." She could see the tears on her daughter's face before she wiped them away. Flora's heart ached; she could see the connection between these two. She now knew they were much more than friends. Flora watched as Jace looked briefly toward the kitchen, seeing her standing in the archway.

Eislie's mother gave them a couple of minutes before returning with three cups of tea. She handed one to Eislie, then to Jace, and held hers securely as she sat. Jace took a sip. "This is good. We have to get some of this for the ship."

There were several moments of silence as Eislie stared down into her cup. Her mother then said, "You're Terran, aren't you?"

Jace nodded. "How'd you know?"

Her mother responded, "Good peripheral vision." She took a sip, remaining focused on Jace, who then looked back toward the kitchen. "You're Terran too, aren't you?" making Eislie scold him. "Not so loud!"

Her mother laughed. "Remember, Eis, you're part Terran."

Jace looked at Eislie. "I just realized that you never told me."

"Not the time, Jace," Eislie protested.

Jace smiled and took another sip of tea when her mother asked, "So, how long have you two been together?" making him choke.

Eislie laughed at him. There was silence for a few seconds before Eislie answered, "Officially, a few days. But …"

Jace took it from there. "It's a bit complicated," he added, making her mother nod.

"So, how was Etheois VI?" her mother asked, almost with a hint of anger, which Jace picked up on.

Eislie looked at her, confused. "Etheois VI?"

Her mother stood, walking over to the desk, and shuffled through some papers before producing a letter that she handed to

Eislie. "According to the military, you were released and requested to be stationed on Etheois. Why didn't you contact us?" She almost seemed hurt.

Jace could see the look of shock and confusion in Eislie's eyes and grabbed the letter. He didn't care what it said; he only wanted to know who signed it. Afterward, his eyes stared out into the air before him as he tossed it on the table.

"Bosh signed it. If that bastard didn't die in the escape, I'd kill him myself," was all he said.

Eislie looked almost in a panicked horror as her mother asked what was wrong. When pressed, Eislie threw up her hands as if to push her away. Eislie stood, rushing toward the kitchen, only to stop and release a scream of anger and anguish, her grip breaking the cup in her hands, and as blood fell to the floor, Jace jumped up, pulling her close. "It's okay, Eis. You're home. It's okay."

Her mother stood, putting her arms around them both. When she did, she asked, "What happened to her?"

Jace replied, "Like I said, it's complicated."

It took a while before things calmed. Jace bandaged Eislie's hand and told her mother what had happened—explaining that the letter was sent without Eislie knowing. And that the bastard who signed it was the one keeping her prisoner. Her mother became horrified, hearing that the Alliance military had enslaved her daughter.

"Why would the council do that?" her mother asked.

Jace replied, "Because of what she's capable of."

Her mother was angry. She informed them that her father was on deployment to another arm of the galaxy when Eislie had gotten into trouble. They had always wondered why she never contacted them, thinking that maybe she was ashamed of the protest.

"No, I'm resistant to …" Eislie paused, then leaned in. "I'm resistant to spide radiation. They were keeping me there against my will."

Jace spoke up. "And that was the same reason I was stuck there."

He also explained that all of those he found at the facility were there longer than they had to be. If not for political reasons, then for their resistance to the radiation.

Her mother tried to process the new knowledge and seemed to go numb from the news, only saying, "Not like that would happen on Earth."

Eislie looked at Jace after her mother spoke, to see him immediately roll his eyes. "Why do you do that when people think Terrans are warlike or crazy?"

Jace was about to speak when her mother interrupted. "Because he knows what it's like to be on Earth. It's not exactly the sanest planet."

A few moments went by before Jace and her mother both started laughing. Confused, Eislie asked, "Then why did you tell me it was so beautiful?"

Her mother looked at her. "Because it is. I've shown you pictures and vids. I never told you how bad it could be so as not to frighten you."

Eislie stared back in anger as her mother said, "Not that it would have stopped you from seeing for yourself. You're just as headstrong as I am."

Eislie chuckled. "I could never get a ride there. When I joined the research corps, they always went in the opposite direction."

"Then how did you wind up on the mining planet?" Jace asked.

Eislie looked at him and sat down. "It's not that long a story. I've already told you most of it."

Jace sat next to her but said nothing.

Eislie dragged her hands down her face and took a breath. "I protested having to join the military as a prerequisite to heading a research team."

Jace looked at her and then to her mother. "That's it? Pretty stupid reason to be sent to a mining colony. I thought you stole a ship?"

Eislie sighed. "Yes. I also stole a ship."

Her mother then spoke up. "Eislie, tell him everything."

Eislie looked at her and waved her hand as if to say *"I'm getting to it."*

"I also damaged several ships—and a control facility."

Jace nodded. "Ah, that makes sense. That's the crash you told me about. I presume your father was reassigned because of it?"

Eislie glared at him but was jolted to attention by her mother laughing. "Sorry, I couldn't help myself. Jace, I know for certain you're from Earth. Oh, I miss the logic of our home world sometimes."

Eislie looked confused, but her mother told her, "Do you know that it took them four months to decide on what to do with your father?"

She told them how Eislie's detainment was a demerit and that he would be shipped out to one of the deep-space research teams. He was told that to keep his commission, he would have to be in deep space for much longer. Eislie's mother understood and loved seeing her husband when he returned home. But she told them that Eislie being gone for over four years was something he couldn't understand.

"I tried explaining to him that they wanted to make an example of her and that she was probably being held on some trumped-up charges to keep her locked away. But from what you told me, even I was wrong. Something more sinister is going on."

Jace laughed, "See? She's not a complete delinquent," making Eislie punch his arm.

Her mother laughed. "Well, good to see that my daughter is aligned with someone with a sense of humor, though I question her taste."

Jace looked at her mother. "Not the first time I've heard that, you know."

Eislie's mother snickered. "I'm sure it isn't. Even I was questioned when I arrived."

They all started laughing, and as it subsided, Eislie's mother leaned forward. "I'm happy and grateful you helped my daughter return. But," she hesitated, "tell me why *you* were sent there."

Jace leaned back. "Well, fortunately, it's a short story."

* * *

A few days went by. Eislie had time to reach out to her father. The transmission would take several hours, but her mother was certain he'd be happy to see she was safe. Jace was staying at the house with Eislie, since her mother wanted to spend time with them both. Jace had been contacted several times by the auction board, asking where they wanted to start the bidding. He didn't know, and asked Eislie what she thought as she was talking with her mother.

"I don't know. What's the going rate? Did they tell you?" Eislie asked.

Her mother was curious. "Going rate of what?"

There was silence before Jace asked, "You want to tell her, or should I?"

Eislie huffed. "Spide crystals. We need to know the going rate."

Her mother had been on Gilese for years and was dumbfounded at hearing what she said. "Where did you get spide crystals?"

Eislie started to respond. "Well, we grabbed—" She stopped, looking at Jace, who replied, "We salvaged it from some wreckage."

Her mother then watched Jace smile, and she leaned back with a look of discernment. "Salvaged?"

Eislie looked at her mother, then to Jace, who replied, "Yeah, salvaged."

Her mother looked to Eislie and smiled. "You do know what he means when he says something like that, right?"

Eislie shook her head.

She leaned forward, looking judgingly toward Eislie. "You have to be from Earth to get the subtlety of the language. Especially in the way he's using it."

Eislie looked at Jace for clarification. "Well, I'm not lying. There was a crate, some wreckage. People were shooting at us. I'd say it's salvage."

Her mother laughed. "Oh, you are definitely from Earth."

They continued to talk. Jace again had to take a call from the auction board, and they agreed on a price point. Eislie told her mother about the prison and the bar she ran. She had conveniently omitted the part about Butee trying to torment and kill her. But when her mother asked Jace about the pirates and how they protected the other ships, he let it spill.

"Yeah, I modified the ship's extractors to sling hot metal. And it blew right through the pirates' shields. We were trying to load everyone on the ship, but Arren was injured, so we had to protect them until they could get him on the Alliance ship. That's when that little bastard that tried to kill her got toasted—"

"Wait, who tried to kill you?" her mother interrupted.

Eislie glared at Jace, who responded, "Yeah, no one makes shields strong enough to protect me from that stare. Apparently, I wasn't supposed to mention that." He walked away, hearing Eislie say, "Don't you have a call to make?"

Her mother looked at her. "Eis, who tried to kill you?"

Eislie simply responded, "I don't want to talk about it."

Her mother protested. "Eislie?"

"It doesn't matter. That little green bastard's gone. We both watched him fry."

Her mother hugged her.

"You know, he saved me more than once," Eislie said, holding back tears, pointing to Jace.

"You don't owe him anything; he knows that."

Eislie nodded. "I don't feel alone when I'm with him."

Her mother laughed. "I said the same thing about your father."

"I also heal quicker when he's around too." She unwrapped her hand, and her mother was amazed at the wound being almost completely healed.

"That's incredible. How?"

"It's called biofield compatibility resonance. I learned about it from Doctor Tulo. It's how his people came up with the regen systems."

Her mother was amazed. "You mean they found out because of the … starborn?"

Eislie nodded. "It's not that common, but it was enough for them to notice."

"Your father would love to hear that. Remember, he was almost considered a starborn, and he's about 35 percent Lyri."

Eislie thought for a moment. "Wait, then how am I 72 percent Lyri?"

Her mother smiled. "Because I'm a little over 40 percent, Eis."

She looked at her mother in disbelief.

"No one had even known until after you were born."

Jace walked in. He had just ended his conversation with the auction house and wanted to tell them the news.

Eislie looked at him as he sat next to her. He grabbed her hand, looking at it. "Hmm, almost healed. Imagine that."

She hit him lovingly.

"I guess she told you."

Her mother nodded.

Jace remained quiet, making Eislie ask, "What did they say?"

He took a breath. "Well, we have to be there for the auction tomorrow. But first, we have to set up a secured account to hold the funds. They gave me a few places that handle them. I have no idea how to do any of that."

Eislie then asked, "So, how much?"

Jace smiled. "Conservatively, about eighty," making Eislie squeal with delight.

Her mother stood to take away the cup from earlier and interrupted, "Eighty thousand is a lot of money. Spend it carefully, though."

Jace looked at her. "Who said eighty thousand?" he asked, making her mother stop in her tracks and turn toward him.

"Not eighty thousand?"

Jace shook his head. "Nope. Eighty million."

Flora's hand started shaking, and she dropped the cup she was holding. Jace reached out quickly to grab it, bringing a "Good catch," from Eislie before her mother sat down abruptly. "That's more than your father would make in his entire lifetime."

Jace asked, "How long is that?"

Eislie told him about seven hundred Terran years, and he said, "I'm just over thirty. I've only got forty to fifty max."

Her mother laughed. "You're not on Earth, Jace. You get about the same lifespan as them out here. I left Earth when I was about forty, and I'm almost a hundred."

Jace looked confused. "But you look young, almost my age. How old's Eis?"

She laughed at him. "She's about your age, a couple of years younger. Medicine is much more advanced out here. So, I think you'll like it."

Eislie then said, "Wait, you've been with Dad for over fifty planetary cycles, uh, years. Where were you the rest of the time?"

Her mother turned with a smile. "Exploring the galaxy with your father. Now, come on, I know a good counselor that can help you with setting up that account. I don't work as a bookkeeper for nothing."

Chapter 21

Auction Day

Flora helped them set up the accounts early, so they were ready for the auction later that day. They agreed to wear crew jackets, even though they didn't have a logo. Since they were considered a small, independent salvage company, no one would probably care who they were.

Her mother had taken copies of the paperwork to her husband's office for safekeeping, and Eislie was talking with her as Jace followed. When he entered the office, it was pretty standard: books, a desk, a computer screen, and several trophies. As Jace looked on the wall, his eyes focused on a small display case. The picture above was of an old Takloh ship. It looked just like the *Wolfhammer*. When he saw the small model below, he smiled.

"Hey, Eis. Look." Jace pointed to the model. "You know, I just dropped off the comm pads. I wonder if Ed's had a chance to sync them yet."

Flora laughed. "That's a Takloh mining skip. Her father did his thesis on their design. He's been dying to try and rebuild one. The radium reactors and engines are hard to retrofit."

Eislie laughed, telling her, "Then we have a surprise for him."

Her mother looked puzzled until Jace pointed to the model, saying, "That's our ship."

She looked at him in disbelief until Eislie nodded.

"Oh, your father is going to be so jealous! He's been wanting to get one for decades. They're extremely rare. And almost none of them fly."

"Yeah, well, I modified this one. New spide reactor, hopper grav drives. It'll outrun any ship in this area," Jace told her.

Eislie looked at the clock. "We have to get our crew outfits. You want to come along?" she asked her mother.

"Let me get an imager. Oh, you don't mind me taking pictures, do you?" her mother asked. Jace shook his head.

It wasn't long until they made it back to the ship, Jace grumbling at having to sign in at the front desk to let the dock crew know they weren't leaving. It also meant that they didn't have to file a flight report. When they got closer, Eislie's mother took one picture and spoke. "It's really a mining skip. It looks old. Is it safe?"

Jace laughed as he opened the door. Her mother continued to take pictures while Eislie ran inside to get the crew jackets. As they headed in, Jace told her, "Outside may not look pretty, but this ship will make it here and to the nearest star in only a few minutes."

Flora protested, "There is no way the grav drives are that fast."

She was startled when the computer interrupted her. "Distance from here to the nearest star is one point two arcs. Estimated time for arrival would be one point four semi-cycles."

"You have a Takloh AI ship?" her mother asked, making Eislie nod.

"Yeah, his name's Ed."

"How did you convince it to obey you?" her mother asked.

Eislie motioned to Jace. "He can sweet-talk anything."

Jace replied sarcastically, "Gee, thanks, Eis."

"Your father would have a field day here. Did you ever see the models he built for these ships? This is really rare to be operating."

Eislie looked around. "Hear that, Ed? You're rare."

The computer beeped. "I would agree. No Takloh ships or transmissions detected."

Eislie's mother looked at her as Eislie said, "He's a bit literal sometimes."

Her mother held up the recorder. "Can I ask its designation?"

The computer responded, "Captain authorization required."

Jace nodded. "Go ahead, Ed."

Flora walked to the control deck. Her husband had shown her where the computer interface was, and she stood in front of it. "What is your designation?"

She recorded the display. Its small lights flashed and faded as the computer spoke.

"Takloh artificial, Renner build, Taggusol consortium. Currently serving on Takloh stellar mining skip, designation *Wolfhammer*, Captain Jace Tucker, Terra, Captain Eislie Licessien, Gilese Four."

Eislie could see the smile on her mother's face. She continued to record as Jace showed her the engine room. She took a picture of the reactor and asked if it was actually working. Jace laughed. "It got us here, didn't it?"

"Oh, your father is going to hate me for sending these," her mother said, looking at Eislie.

Jace smiled. "Ed, any updates while we were out?"

The computer remained silent.

"Ed?" he asked again.

A few moments went by before Jace realized why the computer was waiting. "Uh, Eis, could you take her outside?"

Eislie looked puzzled, then remembered that Ed didn't speak to her until she was known as crew. Jace had told her that during their trip home. She hurriedly guided her mother out, with a bit of protest, but explained after Jace closed the door.

"Eis, what was that all about?" her mother asked.

"He won't talk with you in there. It turns out only crew can be notified of ship events," Eislie told her.

"Oh, I'll have to remember to tell your father that. He is definitely going to want to see your ship when he gets back."

Eislie tilted her head. "Maybe we'll go and see him?"

Her mother laughed. "No, I'll wait right here. But if you can get there fast, I can try and see if I can find his station."

Jace exited the ship, tossing Eislie her jacket as he inspected the right side of the door. "Well, what did Ed have to say?"

"We had a few visitors trying to break in. Ed activated the drives, tossing them about twenty meters that way." Jace pointed toward the flight area. "Whatever they tried using to get in only scratched the paint on the door. Two were injured when security showed up."

Eislie smiled. "Serves them right. Good boy, Ed."

Flora laughed. "It's really your ship, isn't it?"

Both of them nodded, and he handed Eislie a wrist comm. "Ed's got them working. The signal is able to be heard from anything planetside to the moons he can hear us or each other."

Eislie placed the comm on her wrist, and the molecular latches stuck quickly. "Ed, you online?

"Affirmative, Captain."

"Oh my, you have remote capabilities for your ship?" her mother asked.

Jace nodded. "Set it up the other day."

The comm beeped, and Jace looked at it. "Thanks for the reminder, Ed."

Eislie's mother looked at him. "What did he remind you?"

Jace laughed. "The auction begins in about an hour. We have to get going."

* * *

They reached the auction with only a few minutes to spare. Flora had parted with them to head home. She knew how secretive buyers could be and was concerned that if she was with them and her current benefactor was there, they may not trust her. Since her husband was off in deep space, she felt it prudent to part with Eislie and Jace at the door.

Jace stood next to Eislie as the attendants worked around them; both had been instructed not to speak with any bidders inspecting the merchandise on display but that they may have to answer questions during bidding. Jace was amazed watching several people press against the shield glass, trying to see if the spide crystals were fake, only to reel back in wonder, finding the material to be authentic. Jake tried not to laugh, hearing the discussions all around them. He heard one bidder threatening several others to leave, claiming that she would have them spaced if they drove up the price.

"Good to know that backstabbing is a universal trait," Jace whispered, making Eislie turn and look at him with annoyance.

"What? It's true; listen to them," Jace said.

"Not everyone is as intolerant as Terrans," Eislie said and immediately regretted it as two Earth military officers walked by with some Alliance officers in tow, making Jace smile.

The Alliance person told her, "We tend to be much more tolerant and civilized than those from Earth," making the Terran military roll their eyes.

Eislie laughed. "See, even they do it!" She looked smugly at Jace, who rolled his eyes mockingly, making her smile. She had to regain her composure before lightly hitting Jace.

"And you call *me* uncivilized."

When the auction started, it was just like any on Earth, Jace thought.

When the time arrived, the auctioneer introduced the crystals, and bidding commenced. It was more of a silent auction after that; they watched as several people operated displays. Jace didn't know what any of it said until Eislie handed him a translate visor. Jace could see the numbers as they climbed. The bidding slowed as two clients in the room continued to bid, and some on a few remote screens. They halted the auction when one bidder reserved to ask a question.

"We have a question from member 235," the auctioneer told them. "You don't have to answer, but it may affect the value." Jace and Eislie both agreed to their terms.

"The question is, what is your planet of origin?" Eislie looked at Jace to see his face with a sarcastic smile. "We're from different planets," making several in the room chuckle.

"The bidder wanted to clarify, to the male, what is your planet of origin, your circumstances, and how did you come about these materials?"

Jace thought before answering. Eislie whispered to him not to tell them they were prisoners. Jace agreed. "I am from Earth; I was left for dead by my people when the Daak attacked my world. As for how we came about these materials, we aided an Alliance ship in escape from a pirate attack. The items we recovered from the wreckage of the battle."

His words brought several bidders to their feet, and Jace watched as the Alliance and Earth military glared at him. Jace mockingly blew them a kiss.

After the room calmed, the Alliance bidder stood and offered a question. This time, Jace and Eislie had no choice but to answer truthfully.

"Is it true that you are both convicted felons?" Jace watched as one of the Earth military blew him a kiss as he had done before. Eislie looked unsure, and Jace told her he would answer.

"Yes, we both were." The room filled with a sudden grumbling. Jace waited a minute before continuing. "I was left for dead. I aided in saving Alliance personnel being held mistakenly by the Daak. And, for my actions, convicted of theft of a ship. However, instead of being sent back as a refugee, they sent me off to an unknown world."

The room again filled with murmurs, and Eislie looked around as she heard Jace say, "I didn't contest the decision and chose to go someplace unknown and alone rather than appease those looking to place a noose around my neck."

One bidder stood. "And why would you do that?"

Jace's face had a grin of victory. "I would rather face the unknown. Besides, if you didn't know the answer to that question yourself, perhaps you should retract your offer for bidding today." He then heard cheering from some in the room.

At first, he was startled, but when the auctioneer walked up and said, "Son, you know how to work a room," he watched Eislie's face fill with a smile as the auction price suddenly jumped much higher.

Soon after the bidding stopped and the auction cleared, they settled with the house. The fact that neither of them argued over the 30 percent fee made the staff very happy. They had complete royal treatment from there on out. When the accounts were settled, they walked away with a large sum of money.

Eislie was bouncing in the elevator as they headed home. "I can't believe we walked away with that amount!"

Jace's head was still swimming. "Well, technically, it's JESC Space Salvage's money. But wow, ninety-seven million shill; that's a lot of money where I'm from." He paused. "We just have to figure out how to use it now."

"We could buy my father a Takloh skip," Eislie said.

Her statement made Jace joke, "I know where we can get another for free."

She became silent, and Jace realized his joke wasn't as funny as it was intended. He apologized when she said, "We are not going back there."

As they walked off the elevator, Eislie leaned in and kissed him, but there was suddenly an uneasiness between them.

Jace looked toward the house. "You want to stay, don't you?"

She looked forward and put her head down, nodding. "At least for a while."

"I get it. You want to spend time with your mother. See friends and family. We can stay; I'm not going anywhere."

They made it to the front door of the house, where Eislie looked at him. "I don't want to keep you here either."

He responded, "We can go wherever and whenever we want. What's a little time on one world?"

They told her mother the amount received for the crystals—even speaking to her about what Jace had said when they asked questions. Her mother told them that Jace's response to the prisoner question was clever. Eislie said to her that they would look for their own place just outside the city. She wanted someplace high up, having been underground for the last few years. Jace agreed. Truthfully, he was exhausted from the auction and was looking forward to lounging around, doing nothing for the rest of the day. He laughed when Eislie held a pad in front of him, asking if he liked the first place she found.

Over the next few hours, they searched several locations. All seemed nice to Jace, but Eislie had things she didn't like about most of them. The others were more toward the bureaucratic side of town, and given that she was a known starborn, that could make things difficult. Jace, however, asked if they could find something close by the dock so they wouldn't have to go far if they wanted—or needed—to leave. Eislie had considered that and showed him a much smaller place that had an open view just outside the city. It was more expensive, since it was near a small body of water.

Jace put down the pad as he rubbed his eyes. He glanced at the door they had left open to get the seasonal breeze. "The air's much nicer here," he said out loud.

Eislie's mother said, "There's more oxygen than Earth, and gravity is lighter."

Jace smiled as he took in a deep breath. "I like that last one you showed me. It has a view of open ground."

Eislie soon joined him in the doorway, feeling the breeze as she held his hand. She pulled closer, whispering, "Thank you."

Jace smiled, but that quickly faded as he said, "We've been running and watching our backs for the last few years. I could use some normal life right now anyway."

* * *

It was almost a week later when Flora heard thumping outside; her daughter had gone shopping for furniture. Jace and Eislie had agreed to buy the home by the water. She was happy when they told her she could visit whenever she wanted. Flora missed the oceans of Earth, and this was something to look forward to. She looked at the report she'd sent on what Eislie and Jace had told her. They had spent yesterday giving their depositions to the Planetary Council on what her daughter and Jace had gone through. She was sure the information would be suppressed but was surprised when the statement made the planetary news feed.

Flora looked out the door to see Jace throwing a basketball hard against the backboard. As she exited the house, she laughed when he jumped, watching him hang on to the rim.

"You'll never make it as an all-star that way," she joked.

Jace laughed. "I would never have been able to do that back on Earth."

He threw her the ball, and she challenged him to a quick game. Jace promptly found himself outmatched and on the ground as she slammed the ball through the net.

"I'd claim foul, but I know you played already," Jace told her as he got up.

Flora smiled. "Yeah, when I was younger. Eislie told you, didn't she?"

Jace nodded.

She liked Jace. Even though he was from Earth, there was something she noticed. He had an easygoing way about him. She felt he cared about her daughter, but she still knew nothing about him.

"How bad were you on Earth?" she asked, making Jace look away.

"As bad as I needed to be when the Daak showed up."

She understood his hesitation and knew that losing Earth had affected him deeply. She had only been back twice since she'd left and had learned to control her empathy while on Gilese. She felt something in him, a dark sadness that was trying to get out. She knew he had been thrown away by their people. That alone would be enough to destroy anyone, but here, he was making jokes and playing basketball.

Flora's heart no longer ached; she now knew the truth about Eislie being imprisoned against her will. She had forgiven her daughter for a pain that she never inflicted over four years ago; now she felt the pangs of anger at knowing the truth.

Eislie's mother tried asking what had happened at the mine several times, and her daughter always looked away, just as Jace had done now. That made her wonder what really happened to them.

"So, you're letting her buy the furniture?" Flora asked, making Jace smile as he rolled his eyes.

She decided to press him for some answers and asked how her daughter was doing.

Jace gave a simple answer. "Fine." She felt a deep pain as he spoke, a rage hidden within.

"That's not what I'm asking. You care for her. How did they treat her?" she asked, suddenly feeling afraid of what he might answer.

Jace remained silent at first, but as she pressed, he hedged, "I'm trying to think of something nice to say," before he laughed nervously. There was a moment as he took a breath. "It was pretty rough for her, and when they tried to kill her …"

Flora felt her eyes fill heavy with tears as Jace looked out into the city. "No one stood up for her, for me. They were going to let her die. I, I couldn't let that happen."

She watched his shoulders become heavy and reached out to hold him, making Jace laugh. He returned the embrace and leaned on her for a moment.

When he pushed away, all he said was, "I didn't get a chance to kill that little bastard, but I got to watch him die."

She felt the rage he held and advised him, "Don't let that anger take you."

Jace took a deep breath before giving a subtle laugh. "It's nice here, with her, you, everyone. But some people still look at her and think she's trouble." Jace paused again. "Or worse, know she's a starborn."

Flora hugged him again as tears fell down her face. When she looked at him, he had a subtle smile of relief as he said, "When I was young, I looked up at the stars. I wanted to see them up close. But now, now we have a ship. We can go anywhere."

She wiped the tears from her face as she smiled back at the man before her. Eislie trusted him, and now she knew why. She instantly knew he was like her daughter, a starborn, and the call of the stars is what was keeping him alive.

"There is an archive that Oppa had provided the Alliance with on starborn," she told him. "If you and Eislie are going to stay, why don't you visit it?"

Jace nodded, then looked toward the sky. "I'm not sure, with everything that's happened."

She became serious. "Don't let them win. You can't. You're Terran, remember? We're as stubborn as they come."

Jace laughed. "Is that what you did?"

Her smile eroded as she said, "No. I had every intention to see for myself about our ancestry, but after she was born and Larat was found to have Lyri ancestry, he was punished by being passed over for promotion. I couldn't bring myself to endanger his career any more than it already had been."

Jace nodded. "I get it. I won't do anything to make it worse."

"No. You have to, for her, for yourself. They can't do anything more to us than they already have. You both may find something to make peace with what happened to you."

Chapter 22

Archives

Eislie laid the crew jackets on her worktable. She had been working on installing glyph generators in both since early morning. Jace had spent the last few days in the machine shop, working on another project for the ship.

"Eis, have you seen my jacket? I wanted to head over and work on the ship!" Jace yelled from the kitchen, his voice muffled as if he had something in his mouth.

"You're not eating more of that catlan fry, are you?" she yelled back.

Jace took a moment. She smiled, hearing his muffled response. "I have no idea what you're talking about."

Like him, she had been eating synthesized protein and poorly grown vegetables for the last few years. The taste of actual food was welcome. She smiled as he walked in, still gulping down the bite he had taken as he rounded the corner. Jace stared at the glyph circuits she had put together from parts all over Gilese.

"What are you doing?" Jace asked.

She huffed in frustration. "I'm adding glyph shielding to our jackets. No sense letting people know about us up front."

Jace nodded. It was a good idea.

"Besides, they may not want to deal with us if they find out. It also may come in handy for some other use later. And I've installed emergency breather veils."

"What are those?" Jace asked.

Eislie put her jacket on and zipped it up. She then pulled the small tabs on the collar, and a thin, transparent material rolled out. She placed it over her head and patted it down against the collar. Within seconds, the film inflated, and the jacket sealed around her jaw. He could hear her trying to speak. "It makes it hard to talk, but at least you won't suffocate right away." She then pulled the tabs back, and it returned to its original place.

Jace agreed. "Just in case something goes wrong. Good thinking. I knew there was a reason I loved you."

Eislie wrinkled her nose at him. They had been on Gilese for over three months, and like him, she found herself staring up at the sky more often than usual. She looked down to see a box of parts he'd been working on. "Hey, that looks like the old radium reactor."

"It was, well, at least some of it. It's a tritium decay reactor now," Jace replied.

Eislie looked at him. "Why? We have a spide reactor. What do we need another reactor for?"

It was Jace's turn to huff. "Well, I was thinking. Ed uses the main reactor for power. If it goes offline, he only has a few minutes of power storage. With this—" Jace took another bite of the drumstick he held and tapped the box of parts. "—Ed can run things. If I work it right, it will give us partial power if the spide goes offline. If someone tries to disable the ship, Ed could still do something about it."

She looked at him with her brows raised. "Planning on trouble?"

Jace shook his head. "No, but I don't like relying on just one power source. I mean, how many dead ships have we run across?"

Eislie looked around. "Not many, but … maybe you're right. I'm sure Ed would like it too." She paused. "And speaking of our delinquent computer, how is he?"

Jace laughed. "Oh, you know, he's bored. He spends his time hacking other ships that land too close. He's even been looking at the archives from Oppa."

Eislie suddenly became reserved.

"Eis, I think we should check them out."

She looked up at him, her eyes undecided.

"Look, Ed has a bunch of info, but he can't get to the hard-copy stuff. No one has put them in the system yet."

Eislie looked concerned. "They've had them for years. I wonder why?"

Jace tapped the box again. "Well, after I install this in the ship, maybe we should go and find out."

She stared at him for a moment before nodding. Eislie was curious about what they were hiding. She thought that maybe it was a trap to find unreported starborn but realized what they would do to her or Jace—put them in jail or send them off to a mining colony. She had been afraid of knowing about her discovered heritage. But now she was beginning to wonder why everyone hated starborn. Eislie looked to Jace before saying, "When you're finished with the ship, we should head over to the archive." She paused and grabbed what remained of the drumstick from him. "And maybe pick up some more catlan fry as well."

* * *

Jace opened the door to the ship. Ed greeted him as soon as he entered. A quick scan indicated that he was carrying new parts for the reactor.

"Captain, those are not required. The current configuration is much more efficient."

Jace placed the box down heavily on the floor. "Well, Ed, I was thinking. I wanted you to have a backup source if the spide went offline."

The computer was silent for a few seconds. "Will it allow me to power engine control *and* weapons?"

Jace laughed. "Not fully, but I think it'll get you from point A to point B. Maybe not as fast."

The computer analyzed the parts but wondered how Jace was going to attach the unit into the current power system without feedback. Jace had figured the solution out days ago but only told Ed, "Trust me, Ed, this will work fine. Besides, if someone does disable the main reactor, you'll be able to do something about it. But I do ask you to think before acting. I'd rather have you in stealth power, so as not to draw attention that you're active."

The ship's computer agreed, and Jace started the modifications.

It took a few hours, and Jace pressurized the tritium reactor before starting it up. "Ed, what's the current power output?"

The computer replied, "Forty-five percent and stable. I estimate drive systems would work at close to original function before your modifications." There was a pause. "Should they be tested?"

Jace smiled. "Ed, you don't even need to ask. I've already logged a flight plan. The dock knows we're testing a new power system, and they have recovery on standby." Jace paused. "Not that we'll need it." He then closed up the reactor housing and left the spide reactor offline. He called the controller, and they were off.

Jace looked out the window as the sky before him turned black, filling with stars. He put the new reactor through its paces, and it seemed to be working as expected. Rounding one of the moons orbiting Gilese, Jace wondered at its barren surface. It had a beauty all its own but was spoiled as he came upon the Daak settlement that darkened the desolate surface. He felt his hands grip the controls a little tighter as they flew over the base.

"Ed, I'm going to reactivate the spide. Let me know if there's any issues."

The computer confirmed the order, and Jace inserted the reactor crystal back into the core. Ed acknowledged the power increase and throttled back on the primary systems.

"Captain, I estimate that we can use the additional power to fortify shields. Would you like me to make the adjustments?"

Jace okayed the request and ordered Ed to remember to throttle the tritium reactor if they needed to stay scarce and record everything that happens on board if the ship is taken or shut down. The computer confirmed the commands.

"Oh, and Ed, if there's an emergency, no matter who is on board, do not hesitate to communicate. It could save us."

The computer confirmed the command, then asked, "Are you expecting trouble?"

Jace laughed. "Eis asked me the same question. The answer is, I hope not."

Jace leaned back and stared out into the stars. "So many to see." He then paused. "Let's head home." The computer complied, and they headed back to the surface.

In the dock, one of the repair crew asked how the modifications went. Jace told him they were working better than expected. The man offered to tune the systems, but Jace told him, "Nah, that's an older ship. It needs more finesse than repairs." When the man asked why he didn't buy a newer ship, Jace only walked away.

* * *

Back home, Eislie had finished installing the glyph circuits in the flight jackets. She asked how the reactor install went, and he told her about the flight. When he came to the Daak settlement, she became concerned with the anger in his tone.

"Jace, the Daak are a planetless society. They lost their world to the Duggor," she explained.

Jace inspected his jacket as Eislie walked up behind him. "Like another planet we both know about."

Eislie put her arms around him and snuggled into him. "Gilese is a neutral planet. All are welcome, even the Daak. Besides, the council has requested that they leave once a suitable world has been agreed upon for them. The Daak accepted the terms." She pulled in closer. "You've had me thinking about the archives since you left. Maybe we should go and check them out." Jace nodded and turned, kissing her.

Before long, they were at the archive building and were at the desk, searching for the location of the starborn records. For some reason, they couldn't seem to find them and had to ask. The woman at the desk gave them a fearful look. "I don't know what you are talking about." Eislie continued to question the clerk, who seemed to be resisting.

"Why won't you help us find the records?" Eislie asked.

The clerk looked up and whispered, "You don't want to go there. They are looking for people when they come. I was told not to say anything, but I don't know what they do with them. They never seem to come back."

Eislie looked at Jace before taking a breath. "I'm a known starborn, and I can appreciate you protecting people. Both of us do. Unfortunately, you don't want to know what they do with starborn."

The clerk looked up. "What do they do when they find them?"

Eislie looked down. "I'm not going to give you full details, but we just escaped from where they were holding us. Truthfully, I do thank you for protecting others."

The clerk started to show tears in her eyes as Eislie looked around. "We're trying to find information. We've already gone through what they had planned, and truthfully, if they try again, they'll have a fight on their hands. We just wanted to do some research, that's all."

Unfortunately, the documents they were asking about were considered rare, and anyone requesting them had to be logged. The clerk reluctantly asked them to identify themselves. But when the clerk heard their names, she looked up in amazement. "You mean the two people claiming that starborn are being used as slave labor?"

Jace smiled and nodded, making the clerk smile back. She then tapped on a small info pad and handed it to Eislie. "Gloves are required for handling the documents. I'll bring them to Exam Room C for you."

As Eislie took the pad, the woman grabbed her hand, not forcibly, but to thank her for standing up for starborn. "I've tried to dissuade people from viewing the records. I was afraid they were being used to catch starborn."

Eislie smiled at her and gently gripped the woman's hand in return. "Thank you. Please keep doing what you're doing until we find an answer."

The clerk nodded and pointed to where they needed to go, and she was quick to bring the records, so Jace and Eislie went to work.

Several hours passed. Eislie was still reading through the papers. She complained that this would have been easier with Ed. They had both tried to communicate with the ship, but something was affecting the comm signal. They were both a little on edge, knowing that someone was deliberately blocking transmissions.

Jace had been using a translator visor, since he didn't read Gilese or Oppa. Eislie knew much more. It was one of the languages she needed to learn to become a researcher. But even some things on the paperwork didn't make sense. She had put a page down, and when Jace picked it up, he immediately started focusing on something the visor picked up.

"Uh, Eis, did you see the coordinates on this page?"

She looked up. "What coordinates?"

Jace showed her the visor, and she continued to read. She noticed that it came right after the phrase "Suspected adjunct." Jace wrote the information on some paper instead of using the info pad and placed it in his pocket. Eislie wondered why he did things like that, but when they informed the clerk they were through, she finally found out. Eislie had been staring at the coordinates on the pad, only to see them disappear from the display. She showed Jace, who immediately looked around before saying, "Maybe it's for the best. Maybe they're right. We shouldn't have the information."

Eislie looked at him in disbelief, but as he strummed his fingers on his jacket just below the pocket, he again said, "Maybe it's for the best."

She smiled and nodded. "Yeah, maybe we should leave things alone."

They thanked the clerk and walked toward the entrance, Jace noticing there were at least four more guards than when they arrived. He nodded to them as they walked by. None of them made a move toward them.

As they headed home, they remained relatively quiet, just in case they were being followed. As they left the tram that ran past their new home, they exited normally. Eislie pretended to kiss Jace as she watched the tram move away. She observed three sets of eyes staring discerningly back at them.

Jace whispered, "I counted two."

She whispered back, "You missed one."

They finally got home, and both flopped themselves into the soft couch that she had purchased. There was only a moment of silence before Jace pulled out the paper. "Ed, you online?"

"Yes, Captain."

"I have a string of characters that I want you to process. It may be a travel command issue," Jace said, hoping the computer would get the inference.

"What is the string, Captain?"

Jace read the combination of letters and numbers all at once. "And, Ed, I do not need a remote acknowledgment. I'll stop by tomorrow, and we'll see if it works with the flight system."

The computer paused for a moment. "Command acknowledged. Have a good night, Captain."

Eislie then leaned against him. "You think he'll figure it out?"

Jace nodded. "Ed's a lot smarter than he lets on."

Eislie remembered stories of artificial personalities disobeying their controllers even after being programmed not to. "Do you think he'd go rogue on us?"

Jace shook his head. "No, he asked me to order him to delete himself and self-destruct the ship if we were killed."

Eislie looked in horror at Jace. "You didn't, did you?"

Jace nodded. "Yeah, I did."

She laid her head against him. "Well, it's good to know someone has our backs."

Jace replied, "Yeah. But where do we go from here?

Chapter 23

Road Trip

Both Jace and Eislie slept late. They had been up discussing the information they had found yesterday, and the thought that unsuspecting starborn were being targeted made them both uneasy. The only real question was how long they had been abducting starborn on Gilese. Eislie had also been up late speaking with her mother, learning that she had sent the pictures to Eislie's father, and he wanted to see the ship when he returned. The only catch was that he was supposed to be on tour for another few months at least.

Eislie clasped her hands around her nose, thumbs on her chin. Jace knew it was something she did when really concerned about something.

"What's wrong?"

Eislie took a breath. "My father is going to be on tour for another few months. He was supposed to be back in three weeks. They were assigned to protect a research mission from pirates."

Jace smiled. "He wanted to see the *Wolfhammer*?"

Eislie nodded as Jace handed her a cup of tea and took a sip of his own. "You know, we do have a ship; we can go look for him. Do you know where he's stationed?"

She shook her head. "It's classified. I just know his ship is the *Aranost*."

There was silence as they both tried to wake up. When Jace said he was going over to see if Ed had anything, Eislie told him, "I think I'll go say hi to Ed too."

* * *

Hours passed before they arrived at the *Wolfhammer*. Eislie opened the door. "Hi, Ed, how are you?"

"Greetings, Captain. My systems are functioning normally. It has been a while since you have been on board. Would you like a full report?"

Eislie shook her head. "No thanks, Ed. I just wanted to see how you were doing. Sorry for not visiting sooner."

"That is all right, Captain. This is your home world. I understand the situation and conditions that you were held in. My psychological profile systems are fully available if you need them."

Jace laughed. "You're a shrink now, Ed?"

"I do not understand the term *shrink*."

Jace explained that it was an Earth expression to describe a psychologist, in slightly derogatory terms, but he meant it endearingly. The computer understood and still offered his services to both of them if needed.

"Captain, I have information on that string command you gave me."

"Go ahead, Ed, whatcha got?"

"The location is a planet known only as Reothes, but there is no information in the Gilese Infobase at all about it. Only that it is a restricted location."

Jace looked at Eislie. "It sounds like that may be interesting. I presume you've already plotted a course."

The computer confirmed the location of the heavy cruiser *Aranost* as per the military subsystems.

"You didn't leave a trail, did you, Ed?" Jace suddenly became concerned.

"No, Captain, I used several jumps and other ships' computers to obtain the information."

"Wait, did you say the *Aranost*?" Eislie asked.

"Yes, Gilese *Aranost* Amanar cruiser. Would you like a crew manifest?"

Eislie shook her head. "No, Ed, but I do know at least one name on that ship. Commander Larat Licessien."

She looked at Jace with a smile and pleading eyes. "Please say yes."

Jace nodded. "Ed, what's the travel time to those coordinates?"

"Estimated time is fifteen days, twenty-nine hours, forty-one minutes; standard time."

The two lovers looked at each other. Jace would happily take her to see her father. The only concern was if they would be allowed.

They departed the ship, hoping to leave in the next few days, and headed over to see her mother.

"We were going to see if we could find your husband," Jace told her.

She laughed. "I've asked, and I have security clearance through my work."

Eislie looked at Jace for a second. "Well, we kind of found out."

Her mother looked at her suspiciously. "How did you find out?"

Eislie was about to tell her when Jace said, "Ed was bored, and he sort of came across some information."

Flora looked at Jace angrily. "That ship's computer of yours better not get her in any more trouble than she's already been in."

Jace smiled. "I did order him not to do things like that, but sometimes he just does. He's really helpful, you know."

Her mother was angry at him for a moment but then asked why they told her about it. Jace explained, "We thought you'd like to come along."

They watched her smile. "It has been a while since I've seen your father."

Eislie sat down next to her. "So, you want to go?"

Her mother shook her head, then said, "I do, but I can't."

When Eislie asked why, she told them, "If I show up, that means this was premeditated. You are showing up unannounced and without permission, especially in an older ship. That could be taken as coincidence."

Jace nodded. "You have a point. I was going to claim operator error for entering the wrong coordinates. I'm still a new pilot."

Both women looked at him, and Eislie said, "You already have an excuse lined up?"

Jace nodded. "Yeah. Sometimes, you just have to think ahead."

The women looked at each other, and her mother said, "I don't think your ship is the only delinquent."

Jace jumped in, "Yeah, I know, but I love Eis the same, no matter how bad she is," making them both laugh loudly.

* * *

Jace was loading the last of the supplies as Eislie walked up the ramp. "I've logged a flight plan. I told them it was a salvage recon. No one seemed to care."

"Ed, give me full status, power, drives, and weapons," Eislie ordered.

"Reactor is good, slag cannons operational but need to be refilled, and drill is functional."

She turned to Jace. "What about supplies?"

"At least two months' worth. We should be good."

He watched Eislie smile but noticed the redness in her eyes before asking, "You say goodbye?" She nodded. "We'll be back before she even knows we've been gone," Jace said, making Eislie roll her eyes.

"Did you just roll your eyes at me?" Jace asked, making Eislie defensive.

"No, I didn't."

Jace smiled as she closed the overhead bin of the storage and stormed away. He watched her look back at him as he followed her to the flight deck, hearing her repeat, "I did not roll my eyes," as she strapped herself in. Jace hit the controls once they contacted the controller, and they were off.

A few days went by, and the flight was uneventful. Eislie came back and sat down as she was finishing tying her hair back.

"I like your hair like that," Jace said.

She smiled. "I should keep it shorter, so it doesn't get caught in the helmet linkage."

Jace nodded, and they both turned to stare at the strands of energy surrounding them in hyperspace.

Several hours went by, and they felt a sudden surge, as if they hit something. The engines' gravity field wouldn't allow that, but when they entered regular space, they knew something was wrong.

"Ed, spide and tunnel drive status?" Jace yelled.

"Reactor operating at 103 percent. Tunnel drive functioning normally."

"Then why did we transition to normal space?" Jace asked.

There was a moment before the computer responded. "Quasi-space detected, recommend altering course."

"What the hell is quasi-space?" Jace asked.

Eislie tapped the display before her. "It's something we really should avoid. You need a Brenell engine to traverse quasi. You do it wrong, and you could wind up part of whatever universe it came from."

Jace looked at her. "So, what's quasi-space again?"

Frustrated, Eislie finally told him, "Technically, it's a dimensional collision. You sometimes find them close to the centers of galaxies."

Jace still looked confused.

"We can't go anywhere in it. We'd be stuck, and you need a different kind of drive. Grav drives wouldn't work. The whole thing is technically a great-big mix of gravity, matter, antimatter, and magnetism. It sometimes happens when a large drive system overloads. It's usually temporary."

Jace finally understood. "Got it. Don't blow the spide reactor."

She looked at him, shaking her head. "We were in hyperspace. We shouldn't have been affected. Ed, how large is the area?"

"Four-point-seven arcs, approximately. The nearest exit point is behind us."

"Can we maneuver with thrusters?" Jace asked.

"Yes. It will take fifty-one minutes to clear the area using thrusters."

Jace hit the reverse thrusters, and they started out of quasi-space. As the ship began to move, Eislie ordered Ed to map the anomaly.

"Geez, this thing is like a splatter in space; it had to be a ship explosion," Eislie surmised. "Ed, can you extrapolate the center?"

"Yes, Captain." The computer then showed the location and brought up a visual. They could see the remains of what looked like a ship. "From my database, it appears to be a Duggor Wrent class."

"Scan for Duggor ships now!" Eislie yelled, startling Jace.

"Already completed. No ships are in the area."

Eislie breathed a sigh of relief. She didn't want to risk being attacked by the Duggor. But then she muttered, "Wait, how come there's a Duggor ship here? We're nowhere near their space."

"Incorrect, Captain, Duggor space is approximately ninety-seven arcs, bearing 254, 192, 30."

"Shit, I didn't realize we were going through Duggor territory," Eislie said.

Jace looked at her. "Then we probably shouldn't stop."

The computer then gave an alert. "Antimatter detected."

"Where, Ed?" Eislie asked.

"Starboard, approximately seven hundred meters, and closing."

"Wait, it's heading for us?" Eislie asked.

"Correct, Captain. Our mass is enough to attract that amount of antimatter."

"Mass? How much is it?" Eislie became concerned.

The ship's computer then said, "Approximately sixty-one hundred metric tons."

"What! That'll destroy most of the hull!" Eislie yelled.

Jace then said, "Maybe we should turn on the shields," as he pressed the controls. Eislie yelled for him to stop, but it was too late.

The computer then announced, "Antimatter mass has increased speed. It will overtake the ship in eight-point-four minutes."

Eislie looked at Jace, biting her lip in a frown. "You never turn on magnetic shields unless you know the polarity of an antimatter field first."

Jace raised his eyebrows in innocence. "Oops."

They now had a problem. Eislie informed Jace that if the antimatter became stuck in the shields, they wouldn't be able to use the tunnel drive because they would be charged. And releasing the shields would probably send most of the antimatter straight into the hull. She tried increasing the thrusters, but that only bought them a few minutes.

"We're screwed. Probably wind up like that ship." Eislie sounded defeated.

Jace looked around. "There has to be a way out of this."

"We would need the same amount of matter to offset it. We don't have that much matter in the entire ship."

Jace looked around and focused on the extractor port. "Maybe we don't need that much."

Eislie looked to where he was staring. "What?"

"We only need to move faster to outrun it, right?"

Eislie nodded.

Jace grabbed one of the cartridges he had made to load the slag cannons. "What if we send a bunch of slag into it? Blow it away from us."

She looked at him. "We'd have a cloud of ionized metal slam into us as well."

Jace nodded. "Then we ride it like a wave. We'd get out faster."

Eislie shook her head.

"We're screwed anyway, right?" Jace said.

Eislie waved her hands. "Just do it."

Jace loaded the cannons and sat in his control chair. "Ed, where is the largest mass of antimatter?"

The computer showed the location on the display. Jace started firing and continued to do so until the cannons were empty.

"Let's turn the ship around. Ed, when the slag hits the cloud, fire up the tunnel field." Jace looked to Eislie. "It might protect us somewhat."

Seconds later, they watched as the slag hit the cloud, and the screen lit brightly. They were both pushed into their seats as the cloud of ionized metal gas hit the shields. The display of metal and antimatter sparkled all around them. The ride lasted only a few minutes, and they emerged from the quasi-space anomaly.

They did a quick inspection of the ship, and Ed confirmed that the ionized cloud had purged all antimatter. Jace sat down roughly in his chair as he said, "Let's not do that again."

Eislie agreed, and she fired up the tunnel drive to get them on their way. She thought out loud, "I wonder what they were doing that caused the explosion." She then asked the computer to run an analysis from the data they had. All the computer could find was that the anomaly also contained negative space. When Jace asked what that was, Eislie made fun of him. "I'm sure my mother has one of my old children's books explaining it somewhere."

After another few days, they entered standard space near Reothes and were quickly haled by the *Aranost*. Eislie pointed at Jace. "If they ask, you entered the wrong coordinates, remember?"

Jace laughed. "Sure, I'll take the blame."

She acknowledged the hail and changed to visual. "This is the *Wolfhammer*, sorry for the surprise. We ran into some quasi-space earlier and wanted to make sure we were still going in the right direction."

She could see the bridge and her father sitting in his chair. He started speaking. "You will leave immediately; this is a restricted area. Please identify yourselves for our records." He then looked up and suddenly stood, making Eislie laugh as he said, "Eis?"

"Commander, you know this person?" the captain said as he entered the bridge.

"Yes, Captain, she's my daughter," he said, his reply bringing a stern look from the man.

"Captain, Commander, forgive us for arriving as we did," Jace said. "I put in a new heading, trying to get to a Cygnus star cluster, but I think I entered it wrong after we hit the quasi-space."

"There are no cataloged quasi-space pockets in this area. They're lying," the captain scoffed.

"We can send you the data if you like. It appeared to be the remains of a large ship," Eislie explained.

"Send us the data. We'll decide for ourselves," the captain ordered.

Eislie did as requested and waved to her father. She could see him at another station, scanning the outside of the *Wolfhammer*. He was happy to see her, but this was a restricted area. The data she sent would be the only thing they could use to prove they weren't lying.

"Analysis?" The captain demanded an answer.

"Their data checks out. It looks like they were stuck in it. Their navigation may be off because of the interaction. They should recalibrate navigation if they haven't already."

Eislie thought fast. "It's an old ship. We had the same problem when we first flew it. Do you think you can offer assistance to calibrate the navigation?" She now had a way to get on the ship and see her father.

"Captain, they don't have any weapons, only a mining drill," her father told him.

The captain seemed not to believe him and checked the sensors himself. He seemed disappointed when he found the same readings. "Prepare to be boarded."

Jace nodded. "Okay."

They connected to *Aranost*, and Jace opened the airlock, only to have the barrel of a gun pointing him in the face, hearing, "Back away from the door."

Jace did as ordered and walked backward slowly. They both watched as several guards rushed in and quickly made their way throughout the ship. Eislie and Jace remained where they were. One of the guards held an identifier to both of them. "Licessien, Eislie, Gilese Four. Tucker, Jace, Terra."

Jace looked at Eislie; she could see he was going to say something but felt relieved when he only looked down at the floor. One of the guards connected to the computer and within moments said, "Ship navigation download confirms their story, sir. They did encounter quasi-space, and navigation seems to be off by almost thirty arcs." As he walked toward the captain, the crewman said to Eislie, "No wonder you're lost." He handed the captain the info pad, and he perused it.

Her father was the last person to enter the *Wolfhammer* as the captain asked, "Where were you headed?"

Jace said, "I read an article back on Earth, and we were heading to LS IV-14 116, planning on mining zirconium."

The captain glared at Jace before walking up to Eislie. "And you were teaching him to fly?"

Eislie suddenly felt unnerved by the captain's proximity and only nodded. When he turned away, she heard him mutter, "Damn starborn," filling her with anger, but she remained as she was. She focused on her father, who looked over the info pad.

The captain turned and took the pad from Larat. "Have a technician realign their navigation and get them on their way."

"Thank you, Captain," Larat said.

The captain walked toward the airlock. "You wanted to head back home to see your family. It looks like you got lucky, Commander. Sergeant, accompany the commander while he is on board."

As the guards left, only her father and the sergeant-at-arms remained. He walked up to her, and she smiled, looking away, only to say, "Surprise."

Jace watched as her father hugged her tight. "You really know how to get into trouble. You know that?" Jace could see the smile he had. "My little Eis, what are you doing out here?"

She remained quiet and hugged him again before saying, "I'm happy to see you. And show you the ship."

He laughed, looking around. "I never thought I'd be in one of these. You did a nice job of restoration."

He looked at Jace. "And you're not here just to see me, are you?"

Jace looked at him. "Well, sort of. It's on our way."

"And where would that be?" the sergeant asked.

They explained they were planning on doing some zirconium mining, but her father didn't fully believe them. In reality, he didn't care. He was just happy to see her safe.

"I'm sorry I wasn't there to help; we were both told that you served your time and left for a different planet. If I'd known, I would have come to get you. I'm so sorry for what they did to you." He pulled her close. "I love you, my sweet little Eislie."

When he broke the embrace, Jace could see a tear rolling down her cheek. Her father then turned toward Jace and walked over. "Flora told me how you saved her."

Jace felt his heart pained. "I couldn't let her die. I had to keep my promise."

He felt the man grab him in a firm embrace. Jace was surprised as the man pounded his back and heard, "Thank you," before Larat let go and composed himself. As her father once again stood next to the sergeant, Jace listened to the man say, "They're both starborn?"

Larat nodded. "It's all right, Garrett knows about you. Besides, not everyone is afraid, and there's no reason to be."

He smiled. "So, you're the man my little girl is aligned with?"

Jace suddenly felt a lump in his throat. "Oh, great, here comes the inquisition."

Her father walked over to Jace again, putting his hand on his shoulder. "It wouldn't be an inquisition; I use a firing squad."

Jace was about to speak when he looked to Eislie. "You know, I have never been threatened with a firing squad before."

Eislie jokingly scoffed. "Really? Never?"

Within seconds, everyone in the room found her response humorous.

Chapter 24

Pirates Attack

They spent the next few minutes showing her father and Garrett the ship, stopping in the reactor room to admire Jace's handiwork.

"You kept the radium reactor?" he asked Jace.

Jace smiled. "Nope, miniaturized a spide reactor. Has the same output of a cruiser ten times our size."

Her father gave a glare of disbelief before Eislie told him, "This ship can outrun any pirate skidders going full throttle while we're at half power. And I'll bet it'd outrun the *Aranost* easily on full."

Garrett laughed. "The *Aranost* is the fastest ship in the fleet. How long did it take you to get here, eight, ten weeks?"

Jace laughed. "Little over fourteen days. We got stuck in quasi-space for a few hours."

Garrett pulled up the info pad. "The logs state ten weeks." The sergeant was now looking at them both suspiciously.

Jace then said, "Ed, what was our travel time?"

The computer didn't answer.

"Ed?" Eislie asked.

Her father spoke. "You have an AI running your ship?"

Eislie nodded. "Yeah, Ed. He's the best program I've ever come across. He's helped us out a lot."

Her father looked around. "They were notorious for not speaking to anyone but the crew."

Jace looked surprised, then looked out the door and tapped the pad on his wrist. "Show me occupants onboard, Ed." The small screen displayed four individuals. "Ed, consider the two new persons as temporary crew."

Nothing happened.

Larat looked to his daughter. "You have two captains? They have to agree to override a hard-coded command."

"Oh, I confirm Jace's order, Ed."

The ship's computer came over the speaker. "Command accepted. Welcome to the crew, Larat Licessien and Garrett Yikk."

Garrett stepped back. "How did it know our names?"

Jace looked annoyed. "Ed? Have you been, ahem, *researching* again?"

"No, Captain, their names are clearly stated on their uniforms."

Jace smiled. "Good, just checking."

Her father looked at Eislie. "Researching?"

She leaned against his arm. "I'll explain later."

They walked back to the control deck, and Larat quickly headed for where he knew the main computer interface was. He looked at it and held his hands before it like a child looking at a new toy. "Oh my. It's in great shape. Almost as if it was never damaged. This is something special."

Eislie laughed. "Hear that, Ed? You're something special."

"It is nice to be appreciated."

Larat smiled, looking at the display, its lights flashing. "How did you convince it to obey you?"

Jace gave a subtle snicker. "Ed wanted to leave as much as we did. He's not a slave. He's one of us. Isn't that right, Ed?"

"As I mentioned, it is nice to be appreciated."

Jace showed the flight controls and asked for the display to show their current location. When the holo-display appeared before them, Garrett stated, "I have never seen an active holo-interface working before. They're a bitch to repair." His comments brought a stare from everyone. Garrett then said, "What? I like to work on old ships too."

They continued to await the technician to realign the navigation sensors. Her father used the holo-interface when he looked back at Eislie. "You didn't get lost, did you?"

She subtly shook her head and smiled. "I, we, came out to see you."

Larat smiled at her. "If they find out, you're going to be in a lot of trouble. And I won't be able to get you out of it. This is a highly restricted area. We're just outside Duggor territory."

Eislie looked him in the eye. "I know, but sometimes you just have to try something."

He caringly tapped his forehead to hers, and when he pulled away, whispered, "Must have taken you several weeks to get out here. It took us almost two months."

Eislie smiled. "Ed, what was our travel time from Gilese to here?"

"Our time, Captain, or what we are reporting?"

"Our time," she insisted.

"Fourteen days, three hours, and seventeen minutes."

"That's impossible; grav drives don't work that fast in hyperspace," Garrett protested.

"It is possible. The grav drives are enhanced, thanks to Captain Jace. We can compress the fields to a minimal effect in the slipstream."

Eislie looked annoyed toward Jace. "You modified the drives *again?*"

Jace felt her stare burning through him, and he desperately needed to move. Before rushing away, Jace said, "I'm getting a drink. Anyone want something?"

They continued to talk. Jace was showing them the battle with the pirate dreadnaught and how they escaped. Larat put his arm over his daughter's shoulder. "You're keeping him. Any engineer would kill to know how to do what he did for weapons." She rolled her eyes, making her father laugh.

As they finished watching the display, the technician showed up and started working on aligning the navigation sensors. Ed did his best to make the man work hard for his time, but eventually became bored and allowed him to finish his work. He had just closed the panel and was near the airlock door when the ship lurched. Ed started to close the door and the man ran into the *Aranost*.

"Ed, status?" Eislie yelled.

"Emergency, we are under attack. Sensors detect two dreadnaughts and thirty-plus skippers exiting hyperspace. Recommend a retreat to a safe area."

Over Larat's comm, they heard, "Larat, what's your status?"

"I'm still on the ship, and emergency doors are closed. I can be aboard as soon as we reattach," her father answered.

"Forget it, Commander, we've got this. You go hide somewhere safe. This is a fight; I know how you like to be diplomatic."

Jace looked at the comm on her father's arm. "A bit full of himself, isn't he?" he commented, making the commander laugh.

Jace suggested drifting away as if part of the ship, Garrett agreeing that was a good strategy. But when several massive plasma blasts hit the *Aranost*, Larat started to worry. Jace was about to sit down when their ship was hit with a direct shot. They watched the plasma arc inside the vent walls.

"Jace, let's move," Eislie said, then yelled, "Shields up!"

"Don't have to tell me twice," Jace said, strapping himself in. He turned back, telling her father and Garrett to strap in.

Ed turned on all systems and displayed the battle on the front screen and holo-display. They watched as the skips strafed along the *Aranost* as the dreadnaughts continued to fire. They could see the shields of the *Aranost* start to flex under the assault. "Why aren't they moving? They need a better firing position." Larat's question was only interrupted by the ship's computer announcing, "*Aranost*'s spide reactor is offline or damaged. The secondary is running the ship but is not synchronizing with the main engine. The pirates seem to be using an enhanced mag field to deflect the *Aranost*'s fire."

"What? I signed off on that two days ago!" Garrett said, sounding angry.

The computer then said, "Captain Voss ordered the reactor fitted again. You have a report against you on file with the fleet that was sent yesterday."

"Ed, what did I tell you about hacking?" Jace growled.

They watched as the dreadnaught struck again and again. Jace looked to Eislie. "We have to get rid of some of those ships."

Eislie nodded, then asked, "Ed, weapons status?"

Garrett noted, "But this ship doesn't have weapons."

"Slag cannons not loaded; drill charged," the computer replied.

Jace pounded the console. "We unloaded the slag cannons in that quasi-space."

He turned, looking back at the two men sitting behind them when Eislie said, "I've got this."

Jace smiled. "Gentlemen, I need your help to load the cannons." They quickly removed their restraints and followed him as he opened the storage panel and pulled out four cartridges that looked like water cans. They were deceptively heavy. He told Garratt and Larat to take two, then pointed to the ore-retrieval hatch. He brought the others to the port side and quickly heaved them up, locking the cartridges into the hopper.

"How's it going, guys?" Eislie yelled back. Jace turned to see the others struggling with the first cartridge. He quickly moved them aside and heaved them into place. "Loaded, Eis. Let's take 'em out."

Jace quickly strapped himself in and prepped the slag cannons. Eislie flew in close, and Jace starting firing. The slag rounds plowed through each pirate vessel, breaking them into pieces. That got the attention of the other pirates, and they began to focus on the *Wolfhammer*.

The ship shuddered. "Shields holding, no deviation," Eislie announced.

Jace added, "Let's hope it stays that way. We're taking a lot of hits."

* * *

On the *Aranost*, the captain ordered the repair crews to get the engines back online. The weapons officer did his best to protect the *Wolfhammer*.

"Captain, they're focusing on the other ship," the officer said.

The captain huffed and muttered, "Good, we'll be rid of that trash."

"Sir?" the officer interjected. "They're drawing our fire."

There was a frantic call on the comm as the crew planetside requested a fast retrieval. Two of the planet's team were injured when one of the damaged skips crashed near the camp.

"Alert the landing bay; send down a port ship," the captain ordered, only to be knocked from his chair as the last strike from the dreadnaught hit.

"Main landing bay's been damaged. We can't launch without lowering the port shields for secondary!" the officer yelled as the captain tried to stand.

The captain again ordered the repair crew to fix the engines as they watched the *Wolfhammer* being driven toward the dreadnaught. When the next shot hit, its force was enough to push the *Aranost* back. The inertia was enough to knock the captain from his chair, hitting his head and landing on the floor unconscious.

* * *

On the *Wolfhammer*, they noticed what was happening. "Jace, we're getting awfully close," Eislie warned.

"I know," was all he said before firing the drill, and they tunneled their way through the pirate's ship. The screen before them lit brightly and then suddenly turned to a dark, star-filled view. Eislie continued to fly as Jace thinned out the remaining skips. When the second dreadnaught fired, Eislie twisted the ship just in time to avoid being hit. However, a second shot clipped the back of the *Wolfhammer*, sending it into a fast spin. Eislie recovered control, joking, "I'm dizzy from that one."

They heard, "Any damage?" from her father behind them.

The computer replied, "Minimal, but secondary aft tunnel stabilizer will need repairing."

"Put it on the list, Ed." The ship confirmed his request.

They watched as their enemy fired again at the *Aranost*, making Eislie look at Jace. "We have to take out that other dreadnaught."

Jace nodded. "Slag cannons are almost out. We're going to have to reload. But I think most of the skips are gone. Let's go after the big one."

Eislie changed course and flew toward the side of the massive ship. Jace fired the drill. They were surprised to see a bright flash as the vessel used its tunnel drive to open an entry point. The remaining skips were already heading through the jump as the dreadnaught hit its engines. But Jace didn't miss, and they watched as the back of the pirate ship was gouged by the drill.

"Well, that's it for today's entertainment, lady and gentlemen. Please join us for our next show. Hopefully, never," Jace joked, making Eislie laugh.

Larat slammed his hand onto Jace's shoulder. "I love Terran humor." He looked at Eislie. "Your mother's the same way. They'll tell a joke when facing a crisis. I swear, I think your people would face a black hole head-on and laugh as they're being sucked in."

Eislie laughed. "They are strange."

Her father looked at her. "Remember, you're part Terran, young lady." Moments later, they all laughed.

Garrett spoke up. "Let's get back to the ship. It seems like we all have repairs to get done before the pirates come back."

"It's all right. We'll get you back on board. That stabilizer should be an easy fix," Jace said.

Looking at the *Aranost* and the damage to the hull, Garrett noted, "Maybe you can help us fix our ship then."

Eislie smiled and grabbed the comm. "*Wolfhammer* to *Aranost*, do you need assistance with repairs?"

The response was, "That's a tough little ship you got there. We could use a hand."

Larat took the comm from Eislie. "Braddart, where's Captain Voss?"

"Injured, sir, but stable. He's in the med bay. What your status?"

"Just bumped around. We'll be on board in a few. Garrett will head repairs, and you'll have some extra hands as well."

"Commander, there are injured down on the planet. They have requested a pickup."

"What happened to the port ships?" the commander asked.

"According to the team, both our landing bays are badly damaged. Does that ship have surface capability?"

Eislie nodded, her father responding, "Tell Subcommander Rallir we'll be down in a few minutes. Let them know it's not going to be a port ship."

"Acknowledged, Commander."

Her father handed the comm to Eislie and he looked around. This ship looked old, and it was smaller than most transport ships. All he said was, "He's right; this is one tough little ship."

The *Wolfhammer* entered the atmosphere. The orange glow of the shielding warmed the control room.

"What's this planet called again?" Jace asked.

"Reothes," the ship's computer replied.

Larat asked, "How does this ship know the name of a classified planet?"

Eislie looked back, shrugging her shoulders. She was smiling, but as they neared the planet, she felt uneasy. When her father said, "I hate coming down here. This planet is unsettling. There's no life here," she looked to Jace, who seemed to be having second thoughts. She watched as he kept his hand close on the cannon trigger.

They landed quickly, and Jace followed the others out of the back ramp. The research team met them, and Garrett said, "Feels good to be on a planet again." Eislie walked down the ramp, seeing Jace looking around as if something was there. She sensed there was something very wrong with this world. Eislie even noticed her father become uncomfortable as he slowed his pace. She took a few steps but froze, looking directly at the mountains off in the distance.

Jace also seemed to hesitate, her father taking notice of the two of them looking out into the distance.

"Is everything all right?" Larat asked.

Jace shook his head before tapping his comm. "Ed, ship status?"

"There is a fluctuation in the spide reactor, and grav drive is experiencing a low resonance."

Eislie continued to stare out toward the mountain range. "We should leave."

Garrett walked by her. "We just need to collect the research team."

Jace helped the others move the supplies on board but kept stopping to look over the plateau toward the mountains. Eislie continued to focus on the shadowed range before asking into her comm, "Ed, anything on scanners?"

The computer replied, "Rock, water, minerals, and five biologicals matching Gilesian signatures." The computer paused. "Inconclusive energy reading. I'm having trouble localizing."

Jace looked askance.

"Something wrong?" her father asked, seeing them both still focused on the mountains.

"Ed, any other life signs, anything?" Jace asked.

"Only life signs those previously mentioned."

"Commander Licessien, get your people on the ship as quickly as possible," Jace ordered.

Larat nodded and ordered the others to hurry. "There is something wrong, isn't there?"

Jace nodded. "Eis, you feel it?"

She nodded, only to turn and head back into the ship. "We should leave as soon as we can."

The commander watched his daughter help push the equipment up the ramp before he turned back toward Jace. "What is it?"

Jace continued to stare at the mountains. "This planet is dead for a reason, Commander." As he pointed to the hill he added, "And it feels like whatever did it is watching us right now."

The captain looked where he pointed, and an uneasy chill ran through him. "Right, everyone move. We're leaving now."

Chapter 25

Reactor Trouble

The *Wolfhammer* docked, using the starboard hatchway. The equipment would have to be offloaded later, according to Garrett. His main concern was the repairs to the *Aranost* and helping the injured.

"Welcome back, Commander, Sergeant."

"Damage report?" Larat ordered.

The news wasn't good. The repair crew still hadn't synchronized the engines with the secondary reactor. The ship was currently running on backup power, since the reactors weren't switched over correctly. The repairs that Voss had reordered had made the ship vulnerable during the attack. Both primary and secondary reactors were now offline at his command when the pirates attacked. Rallir had sent a secondary damage report base, and the response back was expected anytime.

"Sir, the main reactor is damaged; the actuator is not aligning. It was damaged when we tried to reseat it during the attack. And now, the secondary is not running anywhere near capacity."

"Engines?"

"Tunnel drive has minimal power. And grav drives are about 40 percent," Rallir told him.

Larat looked to Eislie. "Maybe you could get out and push."

Jace laughed at the joke, while others seemed to stare at the commander, wondering what he meant. Eislie pushed him with her shoulder. "You aligned with a Terran."

Her father shook his head. "So did you."

"Jace, by the look at your ship's power system, I'd say you know a thing or two about spide reactors. Why don't you take a look?" Larat ordered the crew to escort them down to the reactor room.

Jace nodded. "All right, I'll take a look. Eis, we'll get to the stabilizer later. Let's get them running."

She nodded and followed along.

"Sir, they're not Alliance personnel," Rallir told him.

The commander looked up. "She was, and from what I saw in that ship of theirs, he is a damn good engineer."

"They've been in trouble before. You trust them?" Rallir asked.

The commander nodded. "Yes! One's my daughter, and they saved our asses from the pirates, didn't they?"

* * *

In the med bay, the captain opened his eyes and groggily sat up. "Status report."

One of the medical team tried to push him back down. "Repairs are underway, Captain. The commander has things covered."

The captain leaned back. "Good. Has the research team been retrieved?"

"Yes, Captain. The *Wolfhammer* brought them back safely."

The captain glared at the medical staff. "They're still on this ship?"

"Yes, they are assisting with repairs."

The captain then looked annoyed at the woman's gray hand as she used the regen wand on the laceration she was treating. The captain stared on in anger as they continued to heal his injuries.

* * *

Jace entered the reactor room and looked up to see the extensive cooling system surrounding the reactor and power system.

"Damn, must get hot in here," Jace noted.

The engineer laughed before telling him, "It gets warm, but I try not to be in here when it is running full. The room's shielded, but you probably wouldn't survive."

Eislie snickered, rolling her eyes.

The extractors were running as they neared the reactor. The spide radiation was being held at bay but was still high enough not to allow them to work on the reactor without stowing the crystals. In a single glance, Jace could see the problem. The actuator track had fractured and was hanging loosely from the containment cylinder.

"We have to stow the crystal so we can fix it," Jace said. "What's your name again?"

The engineer answered, "Talin," before he added, "Let me get my suit."

They waited for the engineer, and he came out dressed in a full glyph suit. Jace smiled when the engineer told them, "I'd let you use the others, but they are for crew only."

"It doesn't matter," Jace said as he tapped the glyph controls on his jacket and walked through the extractor field, making the engineer yell for him to stop.

The engineer stood dumbfounded, seeing Jace looking back at him, asking if he had any gloves. When he turned to Eislie, she tapped the controls on her jacket. "Built-in glyph generators; we don't need full suits." As she walked through the field she said, "Let's fix your ship."

Jace grabbed the crystal and placed it into the safety container. The engineer inspected the damage and realized he'd have to weld the actuator to the cylinder for a temporary fix until they got back to base. Jace held the bracket as the engineer welded the part. He turned his head to avoid the brightness of the welding laser. Eislie was walking back through the extractor field to retrieve tools and saw her father standing in the door, so she walked over to give him an update.

"No spide radiation; that's good," her father said.

Eislie smiled. "No, it's about 140 percent. The glyph generators I made are good to about three hundred." She showed him the controls on her jacket.

"You don't need a suit? Just the jacket? That's incredible."

She shook her head. "I don't need the jacket at all. But it's a good show anyway."

Her father still couldn't believe that she was held captive because she could resist spide radiation. And here she was with her new love, fixing his ship. He brushed her hair back, telling her, "I'm sorry I wasn't there."

Eislie smiled. "It's not your fault; they lied to you."

"Eis, your mother told me what happened and how they tried to kill you." He watched her eyes remember the pain. "I'm happy he was able to save you."

Eislie looked down. "Yeah, me too."

Jace broke the touching moment as he walked up. "Well, the seals aren't fitting, but we should be able to get the secondary working."

Larat looked serious. "What's the issue?"

Talin walked up behind Jace. "You have to make me one of those glyph jackets. The field holds the suit back while extracting."

He paused. "As for the reactor, the iridium seals are gone on the main, but the secondary is fine. It's the exchanger bypass that's stuck."

Jace continued. "The good news is that if we replace the seal and close off the main reactor, the secondary exchange should open. You'd be down a reactor, but it'll get you a slow ride in hyperspace."

The commander asked, "Any chance we can get the bypass unstuck?"

Talin shook his head. "It'd be a teardown at this point; a week, maybe, if we were in dock."

He looked at Jace. "Unfortunately, it'd be the same for me, maybe a couple of days."

Larat shook his head. "With the damage, we'd be too tempting of a target. And we've been ordered to return to base for repairs."

Jace huffed. "Okay, option one it is. C'mon, Talin, let's go replace that seal."

The commander shook his head as Jace led the engineer away. "He's all work, huh?"

Eislie smiled. "No, he's not. He's just worried the pirates will come back."

Her father hugged her. "You know, your mother never told me how the auction went."

Eislie smiled. "Well, we made ninety-seven."

Her father smiled back. "Ninety-seven thousand? That's great. That'll be a good down payment for a home."

Eislie laughed and leaned in. "Mom didn't want to tell you in the comm, but it's not ninety-seven thousand. It was ninety-seven million shill."

Her father stood stock still, trying to form words. "Ninety-seven million?" He looked her in the eyes. "Did your mother tell you I would like to retire?"

She laughed loudly, making Jace look over. When he saw Larat hug her again, he knew it was something funny. He watched as Eislie started walking back and her father headed for the door. "Well, Talin, we should probably get working."

* * *

Outside the reactor room, the captain had left the med bay against the doctor's recommendation, and he ran into Larat as he was closing the door.

"What's the status on the reactor?" he asked the commander.

"The main seal on reactor one is ruptured. They're working on it now. The bypass is stuck, so we'll be down to one. Shouldn't be a problem unless the seal goes," Larat replied.

The captain nodded. "Good, give me an update on the engines."

The commander agreed and left for the lower engine deck. The captain then looked inside the door to see the three people working. A look of contempt filled his eyes. He then tapped the outside control panel, its computer voice saying, "Test mode active, shutoff bypass engaged. Silent alert engaged; door secured."

He then fixed his uniform. "Time to test the reactor feed to the engines."

When he reached the bridge, he ordered the navigator to plot a course for the Doren system. Half speed would hopefully get them there in a few weeks. But instead, he told her that he wanted to test the grav drives. The navigator did as ordered but hesitated. "Sir, we don't have repair reports from the reactor or engine room yet."

The captain lied. "I just spoke with them. Everything is working. Obey the order." The navigator did so and started the engines. But the captain pushed her out of her chair and then took the controls and pushed them to full.

* * *

Jace and Talin were placing the new seal down in the reactor room. They still needed to secure the fittings. The connection plates also had to be attached. They were startled as the secondary reactor went online. The alarms flashed, but there was no sound.

"What the hell?" Jace said as the reaction started. The heat from the leaking bypass was scorching. Jace slammed the reactor door closed. Unfortunately, the seal wasn't holding, and the spide radiation started to flood the area. All of them rushed past the extractor field and stood watching. Talin rushed over to the comm to call the bridge, but the captain shut him off as he started speaking, only telling the others, "Keep testing the reactor. We have to make sure it holds."

* * *

Back in the reactor room, Larat had run up the stairs to cut the power, only to find the door secured and the bypass enacted. He pounded on the door and was about to override it when the extraction field fell. The door went into safety lockdown, and that couldn't be removed until the area was clear of radiation. He watched as the engineer pulled at the door. The commander then pointed to his right, yelling, "Safety room! Safety room now!" The engineer nodded and led Eislie and Jace to the shielded room.

"We should be safe here for a while. The room goes up to 300 percent. The safeties should shut down the reactor before then."

Talin slammed the emergency shutoff, but nothing happened. He hit it several times before checking the panel on the wall. As he inspected it closely, he said, "Oh, no."

"What?" Eislie asked.

"Someone shut off the safeties. With the leak and offset, the core is starting to resonate. We have to get the chamber sealed."

"It's too hot to finish the install. What if we weld the cylinder?" Jace asked.

The engineer nodded. "That should do it, but we'll have to replace the whole casement when we return."

Jace scoffed. "So, die, fry, or weld. Your choice."

Talin nodded. "We weld." But as he grabbed the nearby laser, he stumbled and fell to his knees. Eislie turned him around only to see the effects of spide radiation taking hold of him.

"Shit!" Jace took off his jacket and placed it over Talin. The radiation effects subsided. He then grabbed the welder and said, "Show me how this works."

Eislie protested. "You're not serious?"

"Eis, we don't have time." Jace looked annoyed. "You know, I'd like just a normal day, for once. It seems like we're always doing something like this."

Eislie turned up the generator on Jace's jacket. "Talin, show him how this works."

Jace grabbed an armored apron from the wall, throwing it over his head as he put his hand on the door and looked back. "You going to be okay if I open this door for a second?"

Eislie nodded. "We'll be fine."

Jace heard Talin howl in pain as he opened the door and radiation filled the room. But it was only for a moment as they watched him run over to the reactor on the display.

"How is he alive?" Talin asked. "And how are you not being affected by the radiation?"

She bit her lip, looking worried before saying, "It's a long story, and I don't want to tell it right now."

* * *

Garrett watched as Jace headed toward the reactor. "What's he doing?" Garrett asked.

Larat replied, "He's sealing the reactor. We need to get them turned off now."

The commander turned and ran as fast as he could toward the bridge as Jace started to weld the casement closed. The heat from the running reactor he was experiencing was hellish, and Jace was beginning to feel it through the armored apron. As Jace continued to work, he could hear the coolant starting to boil as it tried to keep up. Seconds later, the coolant began to leak onto the bypass housing, filling the area with a cloud of thick, black smoke. The smoke choked Jace as he worked.

When he finished, Jace was covered in black soot, and he felt his eyes start to blur. He was startled as he felt something suddenly cover his face and the choking smoke no longer filling his lungs. He looked up to see Eislie wearing a breather mask. "You're not indestructible, you know?" Jace nodded, and they headed toward the door.

"What happened to your jacket?" Jace asked.

"I gave it to Talin. He needed it. He's still in the closet," Eislie replied.

Jace suddenly burst out laughing.

"What?" Eislie asked.

Jace laughed. "That last statement could mean something completely different on Earth."

Eislie didn't understand, but she laughed, seeing Jace laugh before pounding on the door. "Let us out of here!"

"We're trying, but the safety's been enacted," Garrett said.

Jace yelled, "At least shut down the reactor! The shutoff isn't working down here!"

Garrett told them that the commander was heading up there now. The bridge wasn't answering.

* * *

When Larat arrived, he was panting from running up several flights. The captain ordered Larat to stay away from the console, but he jumped over the front and pounded on the reactor's safety shutoff. He looked down to see the navigator nursing her arm as if it was injured.

"Subcommander, arrest the captain. I'm relieving him of command," Larat ordered with anger evident in his tone.

"Sir?" the subcommander asked.

"There were people in the engine room and reactor when it went on!" he yelled back.

"N-no, he told us it was clear," the navigator stammered, looking at Voss. "You told me it was clear."

"Voss, you're under arrest, and I am relieving you of command." Larat took a breath. "Rallir, bring him down. We'll put him in the brig later. I want to show him the lives he tried taking."

The subcommander restrained the captain and followed Larat to the reactor room. He could see the anger in Jace and his daughter's stares as they pounded on the door. It had taken a few minutes for the extractor field to remove the radiation before they were able to open the door. Jace continued to watch the level before heading back to grab the engineer. The medical team started working on him as soon as he exited. Jace was still coughing from inhaling the fumes of the burning coolant, and Eislie was standing there, glaring at Voss from the door.

When she heard Voss say, "How are you still alive?" she threw the breather mask at him and punched him hard across the jaw. She lunged at the captain again, only to have Jace grab her. Her love struggled to hold her back.

"Eis, stop," Jace growled as he continued to pull her back.

"You tried to kill us, you bastard!"

"Your kind shouldn't exist. You're nothing. You should die like remnants of the past," Voss growled.

Jace grabbed the captain's uniform and slammed him hard into the wall, the impact making the captain wheeze to regain his breath. Jace pulled his hands back slowly and stared at the captain before he started laughing. Eislie was looking at Jace like he'd gone insane.

Jace shook his head. "Thought I left shit like this back home."

Eislie nursed her hand, making Jace ask if she was all right as he wiped some of the soot from her face. She shook her head. "I think I broke my hand."

Jace looked at the captain. The man stood there, his eyes filled with a hollow sort of hate.

"Get off my ship, you slac," Voss again growled.

Jace stared back with a smile. "Why?"

"Starborn should not exist," Voss responded.

Jace walked up to him. "Well, I disagree; besides, it has some perks."

Voss looked furious as Jace walked backward. Larat then said, "Subcommander, you have your orders."

Rallir smiled. "With pleasure, sir." She then shoved Voss hard enough to make the man stumble forward, and she nodded to Eislie and Jace, saying a quiet, "Thanks for saving us, again."

Larat held Eislie and then ordered her to head to medical. "Captain's orders." He turned to Jace. "You've been watching her back like this the whole time?"

Jace nodded.

"Good, keep it up. Go on, head to medical, have them check you out. That's an order."

As Jace walked away with Eislie by his side, he yelled back to her father, "What, no firing squad?"

Eislie laughed loudly when her father replied, "Not today."

* * *

A few days passed. The *Aranost* was underway, but at reduced power. Jace had not had a chance to fix the burned-out stabilizer from the battle. They were getting close to a tunnel jump when they were ordered to disconnect from the ship. The *Wolfhammer*, unfortunately, would not fit inside the docking bay. Her father had given them some supplies and weapons from the research team. He'd explain the loss to Command when he returned. By then, the two of them would be long gone, and he knew that the damaged ship would be an easy dismissal of any missing materials.

"You're welcome to follow. You'll probably have to slow down for us, though," Rallir said to Jace as the captain said goodbye to Eislie.

When they walked over, Larat asked, "Where you two heading now?" Garrett walked up next to him.

"Well, we do want to see if we can get some zirconium mining done," Jace told them.

Larat laughed. "Should get a reasonable price if it's good quality. She told me how much you two made on the last one."

Jace snickered. "You told him the real amount?" She nodded.

Garrett asked, "How much did you net?"

Larat answered, "About ninety-seven."

"Ninety-seven thousand isn't bad for a first time."

The captain put his hand on the sergeant's shoulder. "That's ninety-seven million, not thousand. I made the same mistake."

The sergeant's eyes widened, and Rallir said, "I quit, Captain, I'm joining their crew," making everyone laugh. But eventually, there was silence, and Eislie said one more goodbye before they headed back to their ship. Jace and Eislie sat looking at the screen as they detached from the *Aranost*.

"That's a lot of damage they took." Jace paused. "Dammit, I forgot to fix the stabilizer."

"We don't need it right now anyway. It's the secondary." She paused. "Where to now?"

"Well, we should probably actually do some mining, and maybe head home. Might look suspicious if we don't," Jace said.

Eislie nodded. "It should be good quality zircon. We'd probably make a fortune for lining chambers."

Jace looked forward. "A few days mining, fill part of the hold, and then we can try out the, uh, other reason for being out here."

Eislie nodded. "Yes, let's hope we don't get ourselves killed."

Jace laughed. "Ed, set a course for LS IV-14 116."

Chapter 26

Duggor and Them

Jace and Eislie spent a good four days mining zirconium from a small dwarf planet near LS IV-14 116. The quality of the ore was almost as good as if it had already been refined. They filled several carriers with the mineral and were closing up when Jace stopped to look out across the stars. He could see the small, dying star off in the distance. The whole universe behind it lit up in a glowing red tone spotted with brighter stars—the dull blue from the nearby star looking eerily uninviting.

"Hey, Eis? You seeing this?"

Eislie walked down the ramp, holding on to the strut in the weak gravity. She paused to view the sight. The world they were on seemed so barren compared to her home. A moment of nostalgia came over her as she thought about the star that warmed her planet.

"It's quiet out here. It is beautiful, though," she said over the comm.

"We should get a picture of this," Jace said. "Ed, you recording?" Jace heard her grumbling through the comm.

"Yes, Captain. I was instructed earlier."

Eislie pulled on Jace's arm. "You have pictures. We should get moving."

"What's wrong?" Jace asked. "No sense of romance?"

She touched her helmet to his. "I do. But we've been working for almost two days straight. I don't know how you do this without sleep."

Jace watched her fighting to stay awake. "You're exhausted, aren't you?"

She nodded. "And I want a shower."

Jace smiled. "We could share."

Eislie smiled back. "I just want to feel the water and get some sleep."

Jace watched her swaying; her eyes took time to open as she blinked. Jace was beginning to wonder if he would have to carry her in when she leaned against him. "Eis, go. I'll finish up here and get things secure,"

Eislie nodded and turned slowly, using her hand against the wall for support. He laughed when she missed the door control on the first try.

It took him almost a half hour to get things locked in. Ed estimated the ore to be about fourteen metric tons of practically pure zirconium. It seemed to take longer to remove his environment suit. He stopped to rest for a moment, but several minutes had passed when he looked at the clock.

When he finished, he headed to their cabin. He could see Eislie already in bed. It looked as if she barely made it in before pulling up some of the covers. He walked around and pulled them the rest of the way over her. She was already in a deep sleep. Jace brushed the hair from her face and smiled. She was one of the most beautiful things he'd seen since leaving Earth.

He said nothing as he walked toward the shower, removing his shirt, only to trip on the boots that Eislie left by the door. She hadn't even put them aside; they were right in the walkway. He pushed them away with the rest of the clothes she left on the floor. He tossed his on top, feeling too tired to do any work.

Jace walked into the shower and tapped the controls. He heard the pump priming, and when the water hit his skin, he yelled and flailed toward the controls before slamming down on the lever to lower the temperature. He started laughing. "She had it hot again." Jace turned it down and felt the lukewarm water against his face. He increased the pressure, and the water pounded against his neck and back. He remained there for a few minutes until the water stopped. They had a usage limit set to avoid overwhelming the reclamation systems. He exited, and the air dryer took over.

Afterward, Jace sat on the edge of the bed, turning to look over at Eislie sleeping.

"Ed, any activity or hostiles?"

"No, Captain, just us."

"Great, Ed, wake me in eleven hours if I'm not up by then," Jace ordered the computer.

"Yes, Captain. Rest well."

Jace slid in next to Eislie. She never moved. Jace felt his eyes become heavy, and as he blinked several times, he eventually succumbed to exhaustion.

* * *

The computer watched as a small asteroid flew past, its sensors stopping on the little carbon star that held the dwarf planet in orbit.

I have never had a chance to observe a carbon star before. It has an interesting blue spectrum. I must remember to thank the captains for bringing me out here. I never had a chance to view such interesting things until these two came along.

The computer continued observing and analyzing the star; it took readings and set them aside for later to download when they returned home.

Now I know why those who built me revered starborn.

* * *

Jace was startled awake, feeling an arm around his neck. Once he felt the familiar sensation of Eislie nuzzling up to him, he relaxed. Waiting a few minutes, Jace turned over to see Eislie's eyes closed. A few seconds later, he touched his forehead to hers, and she opened her eyes. He took a few moments as he stared into those light-blue eyes of hers. She smiled and kissed him before moving her head under his chin. Jace said, "Morning," but then wound up with a mouth full of hair as she nuzzled in closer. Jace blew the hair out of his mouth, he could feel Eislie laughing, and she pulled closer to him.

Several seconds went by before Eislie asked, "Is it morning?"

Jace laughed. "I have no idea. I haven't even checked."

As Jace reached his arm over her, she grabbed hold of it to keep him there. "Mmmm, warm."

She held on to him as he turned to look at the ship's clock. It showed 1023 hours. They spent the next few minutes in each other's arms before finally getting out of bed. Jace dressed and headed for the control room. Ed updated Jace on the systems as he reloaded the slag cannons. Jace asked Ed to display the information on the route to Lyri. As Jace looked over the map, Eislie sat across his lap.

"That is not a recommended seating position, Captain Eislie. How will Captain Tucker fly the ship?"

She laughed. "Who said anything about flying a ship?" She then leaned forward. "So, what course are we taking?" Ed highlighted the recommended flight line; within moments, they were off.

As they neared the exit point, Eislie readied the slag cannons. They ordered the computer to keep an eye out for ships or anything hostile. When they returned to standard space, they were within visual range of the planet.

"Wow, look at that. It's beautiful," Eislie said. "Is that all water?"

Jace responded. "Not as much as Earth, but that is a sight. I can't believe we're here. Ed, take as many readings as you can."

"Yes, Captain."

Jace increased speed. "They had to see us come out of hyperspace; let's go half throttle for now. If we need to run, I'll floor it." Eislie agreed.

They spent a few minutes taking images of the planet but were interrupted as a Duggor fighter came up behind them.

"Proximity alert," the computer announced.

"Yep, we've outstayed our welcome already," Jace joked and punched the throttle.

The fighter gave chase and was keeping up with the *Wolfhammer*. Jace did his best to avoid the weapons fire coming from behind.

"You know, we really should have rear cannons," Eislie said.

"Yeah, I know." And he said the exact words together with her: "Put it on the list," making them both laugh.

The Duggor kept pace with their ship. When three others showed up, things started to get interesting.

"Three additional hostiles are approaching. Recommend evasive maneuvers."

"What the hell do you think I'm doing, Ed?" Jace said, trying to outfly the Duggor.

"Want me to fly?" Eislie asked. She was joking; she knew that it took a few seconds to hand over control, and by then, they'd be dead. Jace instead increased speed. He tapped the controls and increased the engine output to 120 percent.

"Captain, the engines will overheat in approximately seven minutes at this power."

"Noted, Ed. We're trying to escape, remember?" Jace growled.

Eislie looked at the holo-display. "Jace, they're boxing us in."

"Yeah, I noticed," Jace said through clenched teeth.

He looked out the viewscreen and saw the binary stars growing larger. And as they came around, they could see the stellar filament the stars shared.

"Would you look at that? That's amazing," Jace said. Eislie agreed, and the computer suggested they stop to examine it.

"Maybe another time, Ed, when someone's not trying to kill us," Jace said.

The computer responded, "That may be a while. Are you sure we can't do it now?" the computer's statement making them both break out in laughter.

There were several shots that Jace dodged, but one from the right hit directly to the top-right stabilizer. "Hope we don't need that anytime soon. The secondary is holding," Jace said.

Jace looked around and then at the stellar filament. "I wonder how plasma-proof those ships are?"

Eislie yelled, "You've got to be joking! You're not going to do what I think you are!"

Jace nodded. He then told her, "Hold on!" as he pushed the engines to 150 and flew toward the filament.

"It is recommended to enter stellar plasma at much slower speeds, Captain."

"Noted, Ed. Don't have much choice here. These guys are getting pretty fucking close," Jace argued.

He angled toward the lower end of the filament, and as he flew, a strange sensation came over him—a calm like he hadn't felt before. Jace asked the computer to find the gravitational balance point of the stream. He turned to see Eislie distracted before she turned to look at him. She seemed to be experiencing a similar sensation. As the computer calculated the balance point, Eislie pointed to the display on her side and said, "It's about here." The computer then displayed the exact position that she did.

Both of them looked at each other, and Jace said, "You know the strange part? Flying like this toward a dangerous plasma stream feels almost …"

Eislie finished his sentence. "Normal."

Jace nodded, and they flew toward the point on the screen.

"Firing up tunnel field. Should give us some protection from the flare," Jace said.

But as they reached the stream, something else happened. A hyperspace point opened, and for a few moments, the space around them turned into multicolored energy, nothing like hyperspace. However, as debris from the Duggor ships struck, it sent them into a spin. They witnessed several small explosions on the control deck. Jace fought for control before Eislie yelled, "Spide reactors resonating. We have to punch out of hyperspace now!"

She hit the emergency exit, and they were thrust into a spinning field of stars. It took several seconds for Jace to regain control of the ship.

"Ed, any hostiles?"

The computer didn't answer.

"Ed? You online?"

The computer finally answered. "My apologies, I had to go into safe mode due to a power overload. Checking independent sensors."

Eislie looked over the display. "No Duggor that I see."

"Where the hell are we?" Jace asked.

"I'm on it." Eislie looked at the current pulsar positions. "We're in the Proxima Five system?"

"That can't be right. It'd take us weeks to get here," Jace scoffed.

The computer responded, "Captain Eislie's assessment is correct. This is the Proxima Five system. The nearest level-two planet is Oppa. We are currently on the secondary reactor. Spide is offline."

"Any damage?" Eislie asked.

"Secondary left stabilizer and primary right are damaged and need repair. Power couplings on the grav drives are damaged but functional. I recommend half speed for travel given current ship condition."

Jace took a breath. "Well, not too bad. It sounds like we'll need to upgrade the couplings and do some repairs. And since it seems no one is chasing us at the moment, maybe we should get the spide reactor online and set a course for Oppa."

* * *

The *Wolfhammer* was a flurry of activity as Jace and Eislie fixed what they could, even using the tritium reactor to jump-start the spide quantum field. Eislie had previously questioned needing it. But she was now happy Jace insisted on the addition for the ship's computer, realizing it was something handy to have available.

Jace sat hard in his control chair as Eislie leaned on the back of it. "Okay, spide's up; let's see if the grav drive is going to cooperate."

Jace powered up the drives, and they were off. The ship's computer continued to monitor the drive systems and again recommended a lower power rate for the engines' current condition.

"It's going to take us a day or so to get to Oppa," Jace mentioned.

Eislie seemed to be thinking about something when he looked over, making him ask, "What's up?"

She took a breath. "When we were heading into the filament, I thought I felt something."

Jace nodded. "Me too. It was sort of like we had done it before?"

"That's it. Like I could feel the right point to enter the node or something," Eislie mumbled.

Jace heard her, and they both seemed to still be thinking about what it was. If they both experienced it, then they knew it wasn't something they imagined.

"I wonder if that's how the Lyri got to Earth. Maybe we should see if Tulo knows anything?" Eislie said.

Jace nodded. "Yeah, when we get there." He slumped down in his chair. "We should probably call ahead."

Eislie tapped the comm to contact Oppa space control about their current situation. They were asked the ship's condition and if they needed a pickup. Eislie only replied, "We should be good, just running slow. We should be hitting Oppa in about a day. Is Arren Yuonto still there?"

"Yeah, he's still here. You must be crazy if you think you can get him working on your ship. He's booked for a month right now."

"No problem. He's probably doing some mining as well. He's an old friend. We will make a call if we have any trouble," Eislie said as she ended communication.

"Good to hear Arren's keeping busy. I think that guy is going to work till he dies on the job," Jace said.

Eislie sighed sadly. "Resconasans usually do. They don't like to be idle."

Jace shook his head. To him, there was no sense in not enjoying life. He didn't like to be idle either, but continuously working, he couldn't understand. "We should drop in and see him when we get there."

Eislie nodded, holding back a laugh as she said, "Yeah, show him the damage we did running from the Duggor."

For the next few hours, they talked, joked, and enjoyed the quiet of not being chased or hunted. Even the ship's computer was silent most of the time. But when the subject came up about how they traveled several thousand arcs in a few seconds, the cabin seemed filled with an eerie sort of silence. The only input was from Ed, who told them, "Space seems to be much more compressed than hyperspace. It was difficult to get readings."

* * *

They finally reached Oppa. After docking, Eislie took a copy of Ed's readings of the jump and the damage report. Jace checked in with a repair team and a possible timeframe. He also checked with the registry to find out if Tulo was on the planet. Seeing he was, he looked for Eislie to let her know. When he asked about selling the zirconium, the clerk looked at him with annoyance. "All sellers must be registered one standard week before offering materials for sale."

Jace understood. They had to do the same back on Gilese, so why not here? He gave the information to the clerk and met Eislie at the repair shop.

Jace walked in to hear her say, "Let him know an old friend is here, if he isn't busy digging somewhere." The attendant didn't get the joke. As they waited, Jace looked around the office. "Why is everything gray here?"

Eislie laughed, telling him it was because they have a different visual spectrum.

Both of them smiled, hearing a familiar voice cursing the attendant from the back as Arren walked into the room.

"Blessed Talin, you two are a sight for these eyes." Arren jumped over the counter, and Eislie hugged him. Jace pounded the old miner's shoulder. They were happy to see him as well.

Eislie told him about the hyperspace encounter and the distance. He seemed perplexed, even saying, "Physics doesn't work that way." But when it came to their ship, he had other words for them. "You've been putting that ship of yours through some rough flying. Good to hear it's holding up. And I see you decided not to listen to the message I sent." He paused for a moment. "Try to avoid the Duggor next time; they have faster drives than you."

They showed him the recent encounters and the recording of the inside of the star. "You slept inside a star?" Eislie nodded. "Blessed Talin, the two of you are crazy!"

They spoke for some time. Arren rescheduled some jobs so he could check out the *Wolfhammer*. When the crew chief showed up, Arren was defiant, eventually telling him, "This is the ship I told you about that punched through a dreadnaught. Wouldn't you want to see what was inside?"

The crew chief was in disbelief, but when he saw the recordings, he became a believer. When they showed him the inside of a star, he suddenly decided to make a very high offer to buy the ship.

Jace and Eislie politely refused, and they showed him the battle with the pirates and the *Aranost*, Arren mentioning to the chief, "This is probably classified, so don't go mentioning it around Alliance personnel."

They talked some more, and Arren told them he'd get right on their repairs. He had an idea on the engine couplings and mentioned fitting the hopper engines with coolers. He then tapped Jace on his head. "That way, this idiot won't fry them overcharging the feed."

When they parted, Arren had a smile on his face. It made the chief ask who they were. Arren only said, "Some friends that have been through a lot."

* * *

In the Oppan command center, a meeting was going on that not many knew of. On the display was a fleet of large ships running at slow jump speed due to their size.

"Operant Saag, we have a large fleet on its way here. They seem to be a Duggor cleaver class." A man's monotone voice spoke from the darkness around the table.

"For those of us who don't know what ship designations are, what is a cleaver class?" asked one senator.

A blunt, annoyed response came from one of the Terran representatives. "It's called a planet cracker, Senator."

"Oppa is a neutral world. Why would the Duggor attack? We have not attacked them," the senator asked.

"We harbor Daak on this world, Senator!" another voice bellowed from the darkness.

"All races are welcome here, General, you know that," the senator replied.

"Yes, Senator, but at the moment, those welcomed individuals are a target for the Duggor."

"I see. We should issue a planetwide alert for security forces, and maybe some ships to evacuate the populace if needed. Can the Alliance help us with the Duggor?"

The Alliance representative stood. "We can bring in several ships to blockade the Duggor, but we cannot engage. We do not want to become involved with them as an enemy."

"So, you won't help if they attack us. Possibly killing billions?" another representative asked.

"If the Duggor attack, we can engage; however, not before," the Alliance representative replied.

The general ordered the security forces to be activated and any ships willing to ferry evacuees to be sanctioned.

"Chancellor Dedal, I think you should coordinate with the Alliance forces when the Duggor arrive," the operant said.

Dedal agreed and accompanied the Alliance command as they left.

Jace strummed his fingers on the wall, waiting for the elevator to reach its floor. "I can't believe they have a university 230 stories up." He paused. "And a pressurized building. This is cool."

Eislie enjoyed seeing him like this. She had been to Oppa before, but this was all new to Jace. When they reached the top, the doors opened to a light-gray-and-white hallway. There was a reception area on the right. They walked down the hall, passing doors and windows until they reached a small auditorium with about fifty seats. Students were writing furiously as the instructor spoke.

"Remember, starborn are bipedal, similar to individuals from the Terran and Gilese systems. Lighter hair and eyes, but that is not an accurate description. They can have darker-toned skin as well. These individuals are primarily from the Lyri B system. They lived much closer to their star. Although part of the same species, they developed defenses for the brighter light of their star. Unfortunately, destruction of that system due to the star having gone supernova in an earlier time of Oppa caused many to emigrate back to Lyri A system or explore different systems altogether as a result."

Jace leaned against the frame as they waited at the door. "That could explain a lot about the different people on Earth."

"What could? The destruction of the Lyri B system?" Jace looked at her. Eislie looked away as if not listening to him.

"What is it?" Jace asked.

She held up a small package. "I didn't know what to bring."

Jace looked confused. "What are you talking about?"

"He kept us alive. Remember?" Eislie was becoming angry with him.

Jace pulled her close. "He kept us alive. We kept each other alive. He also didn't do anything to stop Bosh keeping us there for a while as well." Jace paused, looking defensive. "I can't fault him for that."

Eislie leaned her forehead against his. "We never thanked him for helping us."

Jace smiled. "We did. We tried to keep them alive when things went bad. We took the heat so they, including Tulo, could escape."

Eislie looked into his eyes. She knew Jace was right. But then she felt they were being watched and turned to see several students staring at them, and Tulo had stopped talking. Jace turned to see them staring as well. He whispered, "I think they heard us."

Tulo looked annoyed toward them. "Since the two of you seem to be wanting to give a free show, why don't you come up on stage?" Anger filled his voice. Jace motioned for them to go, and she followed.

As they walked toward the front of the room, Tulo angrily said, "What gives you the right to interrupt my … class?" His words quieted and he ran down the small stairs to greet them.

He stood before them. "Oh my, it's you two! You're both looking very well."

Eislie laughed and reached out to hug the doctor. She told him, "We never really thanked you."

Tulo paused for a moment, and Jace said, "I'm man enough, come on," and reached out to Tulo, who pounded on Jace's back as a greeting.

"It is good to see you both. It looks like my class has some special guests tonight," Tulo said, looking over at the younger Oppan. "Students, let me introduce you to the two starborn who helped me escape the pirates on Charon."

There was a rustle of activity as students rose from their seats, but not to greet them. They pulled out sensing devices and started taking readings. Jace and Eislie laughed hysterically at the humor of the situation, but Tulo quieted them, telling them, "They are just excited to actually meet starborn. There's been a lot of interest in the program since I sent my report." He paused. "And of course, the revelation of what was happening on Charon." The doctor referred to the news from Gilese about starborn being kept as slaves.

Jace looked around the room. "Doesn't seem like many students. I thought there'd be more."

Tulo smiled. "This is the overflow class. We had too many for the weekly classes."

Jace nodded. "Oh, okay." Then one of the students walked up and looked at Jace. When the student looked behind Jace's head, he shifted his eyes toward Tulo. The doctor laughed. "He's trying to figure out why your hair is shorter than hers."

Jace said, "Men can have long hair. I'm just used to keeping mine short."

Eislie laughed. "Well, he likes mine long, and I like it too."

Tulo nodded. "I could tell the two of you would be aligned after a few weeks." He paused. "What brings you to Oppa?"

"Well, we came across something that we hadn't encountered and wanted to see if you had any information," Eislie told him.

"Please ask. I would love to hear about what you found."

Jace looked at the students. "We should probably do this in a more secure place. But we'd love to stay for the lecture if you'll let us. I know less about starborn than she does."

Eislie glared at him, and he added, "Admit it. You want to know too."

Tulo smiled and offered them a seat. "I'll continue my lecture, but would you mind staying to answer some questions? I'm sure my students have a lot of them already."

Jace looked toward Eislie. "Why not? But you know, we're going to have to be careful how we answer some of them."

Eislie laughed. "You're right; we'll probably have to edit some responses."

Tulo laughed at her joke. He knew what they were talking about, and he was sure his students were going to ask some inappropriate questions. He was looking forward to their responses.

Chapter 27

Meeting the Starborn

The doctor reveled at the recording of the inside of a star. He had only seen similar from probes Covenant had sent to take readings. But here, he saw it from not just the sensors, but through the med bay portal Eislie had recorded. "You actually slept inside a star?"

"It wasn't intentional, and we were both exhausted," Jace said. He then showed the data from their hyperspace jump before playing the recording. The doctor's eyes widened as he stared at the images of the multicolored display of energy that the ship's computer recorded. His heart paused, hearing Jace and Eislie fighting the ship for control until the screen became a mass of spinning stars, then steady darkness.

"Oh my, my, my." Tulo covered his mouth, then stroked his chin before saying quietly, "You were able to access the filament stream."

"Filament stream, what's that?" Jace asked.

"The Duggor have been trying to access it for years; so has the Alliance. The only people who are known to be able to access it are pirates and starborn. At least, that's the current theory. Any starborn suspected of having done so has disappeared."

"Great, we're not doing it again then," Eislie said.

Jace protested. "Eis, it's a fast way to get around."

"Jace, we have to figure it out. We can use it later," she retorted.

Jace agreed. They were spinning out of control when they jumped. Who knows where they could have wound up, without a way to get back. Neither of them thought that would have been a very good day.

When Tulo asked how they accessed the event horizon, both told the doctor: "It just felt right." Jace included, "I was aiming for the spot long before the ship's computer figured it out. She even pointed to it before then."

Tulo looked to be deep in thought. "That's something we never considered. A biological connection to the event horizon, to the filament stream itself." He paused, leaning back. "I am not going to publish that anytime soon."

Jace agreed. "Hey, we're hunted enough already."

They shared the additional logs well into the night with Tulo. He had turned away several students to continue to speak with them.

"You know, I should bring you to see the others. The Starborn Council will probably want to hear about this find as well." Tulo tapped a small data chip. He then wrote on a small piece of paper. "I have my students in the field tomorrow. Here's the location."

Eislie asked, "What's this for?"

Tulo chuckled. "It's the location where most of the starborn are. I want to introduce you to others like yourselves. Besides, how many starborn have you met?"

Jace thought for a moment. "One, and two halves."

Eislie glared at him before smiling and saying, "Maybe three or four?"

The doctor laughed at both of them. He had been working with starborn since his acceptance into Covenant. These two were unique, as far as he was able to tell. He felt obligated to unite them with the others. At his very core, he thought they needed to be there and was encouraged when Jace and Eislie agreed.

* * *

The following day, there was a lot of activity at the spaceport. Ships were readying, and Jace and Eislie had some difficulty getting out to the location that Tulo had given them. When they finally arrived, they found a site of simple housing. The heavily armed guards set an uneasy feeling in both of them. Jace asked, "I wonder if they're keeping people in or out?"

As they walked up to the entrance, one of the guards walked to block them from entering. When asked for identification, Jace and Eislie held up their crew identification. One guard looked at them with suspicion. They watched as an Oppan rushed out to where they were.

"They're waiting for you inside." She rushed to catch her breath. "They're clear to enter. Let them pass."

As they walked through the gates, both felt at ease, as though the air around them seemed filled with warmth. The sounds of everyone speaking and laughing were a welcome change to their recent experiences. But both noticed that as they approached, people became silent, some staring at them as they walked together. Eislie looked over to see a girl staring at her. When she nodded, the girl returned the nod in the same manner and cadence.

"This is feeling a bit strange. You know that?" she whispered. Jace nodded slowly.

He took a breath. "Rather than walking around, why don't we find Tulo."

They had reached an intersection and asked if anyone knew Dr.

Tulo. A man pointed in a direction but seemed annoyed at Jace's question. They headed toward a large, open area. People walking around looked like they could have been at an everyday marketplace, according to Eislie. But then they saw the medical sign and the small group of Oppan gathered around a tented area. When they saw people walking in and out, along with some of the students from last night taking readings, Jace joked, "Must be the place."

Eislie watched as one of the students treated a small boy, his pant leg stained with blood. Subconsciously, she grabbed her leg and felt unbalanced. Jace watched her start to sway before he held her hand. "You okay, Eis?"

Jace pulled back as a medic held a light to his face, focusing on his eyes. "You have green eyes, light but pigmented hair, some light-colored features." She looked at Eislie. "Light-blue eyes, very light hair, thinner features. Probably different clans. I suspect she is empathic." The medic paused. "I'm Doctor Timel. I head the southern point medical here. How can I help you?" She looked down at Eislie, holding Jace's hand very tightly. The doctor's eyes softened as she looked at Eislie. "Don't worry, it'll pass. I suspect you have been away from similar biofields for some time, judging by the force with which you are holding on to him."

Jace joked, "She hasn't broken my hand yet." Eislie squeezed his hand as hard as she could, trying to crush it, making Jace laugh.

Timel looked at him. "You must be Terran."

Jace was mildly insulted. "What does everyone have against Terrans? Geez, lighten up, people."

The woman turned around, subdued, anger in her eyes. "You do not take any situation seriously. People from your world are reckless. You joke in times of duress. And incredibly, you have managed to survive as long as you have on your world." She gave a dramatic pause. "You're not even ready to be off your planet."

Jace seemed insulted but then smiled, making Eislie tug on his hand. He took a moment before saying, "You sound jealous. You just have to get to know us; it's part of our charm."

The doctor sighed. "What seems to be the problem?"

Eislie spoke. "No problem, we're here to see Doctor Tulo."

Timel looked annoyed. "He's busy. Is he expecting you?"

Eislie feigned being polite. She was ready to grab the woman and shake an answer out of her. "Yes, he asked us to meet him here."

The doctor grabbed an info pad and tapped it a few times. "Your names, please?"

"We can see you're busy. Could you tell him Jace and Eislie are here?" Eislie started to sound annoyed. When the doctor processed her words, she looked up at both of them, almost as if she was in dereliction as she grabbed them both by their interlaced hands. "He's here. He's been waiting for you."

She led them along, dragging them to a small building. Inside, they could see a small group of people sitting in a semicircle. Tulo was answering questions when they arrived.

"Doctor Tulo, they're here," Timel hurriedly said, her statement making the others suddenly rise and approach. Eislie and Jace both stood ready to fight.

The people stopped. The one leading them held his hands up. "You are welcome here. We wish no harm to you. We are just excited by what Tulo has shown us. I'm Timon."

One of the women spoke. "We were informed of what happened to you both. We are so sorry for the torment you had to endure."

Eislie looked at Jace. She had a subdued smile as she looked back at the woman. Jace looked at one of the others who stood differently, almost defiantly, making Jace smile. "I get it now."

"Get what?" Eislie asked.

Jace pointed to the man. "You're from Earth," he said, and the man nodded.

Eislie looked to Jace as the man spoke. "Yeah. Name's Greyman. How'd you know?"

Jace smiled. "The way he stands; defiant. It's the attitude," he noted, making her laugh at him.

Tulo took out a sensor wand. "No biofield interaction. How did you know he was Terran?"

"Like I said, attitude," Jace replied. The man brought his arm up, and they pounded them together, creating a dull thud.

They overheard Doctor Timel speaking into her pad. "The subjects exhibited a physical, almost combative bonding behavior by using their forearms and pounding them together, seemingly with enough force to cause possible injury."

Jace turned around to see her typing something on the pad and she looked up, almost fearful. He heard one of the others say, "Ignore them. You get used to it."

As they introduced the rest, Jace and Eislie were asked to join them.

Hours went by. Jace and Eislie explained what they could about the filament stream, how they sensed the location much faster than the computer could even calculate it. They told them about their experiences at the mining colony.

"Thank heavens they didn't try and kill you," one of the women said.

Eislie suddenly became quiet as she looked at Tulo. "You didn't tell them, did you?"

The doctor looked ashamed. "I couldn't. You're one of my patients I almost lost." He then informed them of the gruesome details of Butee using the crane to crush her torso and drop her to the raza and how Jace defended her, taking on severe injuries as well. Jace watched as Eislie started to relive the encounter. He felt her squeezing his hand tightly again.

The same woman said, "But you survived. You fought off the raza."

Eislie shook her head. "No, he did." She leaned her head against Jace.

Jace watched her become unsteady. "Eis?"

"No, I watched them attack you. I couldn't move, only taste my own blood." Eislie started to cry, and Jace pulled her to him, holding her. She continued to tell them about the encounter. "I watched him pound the raza as they attacked. I watched as he used his hands to rip parts off of them. All I could do was watch."

"That's enough, Eis, stop." Jace became adamant. She looked at him and kissed him gently. "I never thanked you."

Jace leaned against her. "You never had to."

Tulo was fighting back the tears as many others in the room allowed them to fall. One approached and placed her hand on Eislie. She then knelt beside her. Within moments, all of the others had joined them in a huddle. Tulo wiped away tears that escaped when he noticed the energy readings on his pad. At first, they were erratic, uneven, but then everything suddenly formed into a single energy pattern, the frequencies and ripples smooth and flowing. He had seen this with families of starborn, but nothing on this scale. When he scanned them, all the energy was much higher, as though becoming one stronger entity.

"This is incredible," the doctor said, trying to explain what he had just witnessed.

The room fell silent before Jace said, "Well, that was a helpful therapy session, Doc." He turned to Eislie. "Maybe we let Ed do the next one. He's been dying to use his psychology program. Can you imagine him as a hologram sitting there with a small pad, jotting down notes?"

Eislie wiped away tears as she looked toward Jace before laughing loudly. "I can see Ed doing that. That would be funny." Within seconds, all of the others joined them laughing.

When everything died down, they got back to business. "We had an idea, but we'll need to make a drone we can pilot remotely. We still don't know where the stream will take us when we use it," Timon said. "We can use an entangled quantum transceiver to get the data and find out where it is. And remote-program it to synchronize on the same entanglement to return."

Jace looked up. "Like a beacon?"

They started to talk about a plan. Eislie mentioned that they could use a small scout class. It would have to be modified and released near a filament star. "Probably have to have real-time interaction." She was about to say something when there was an alert from both their comms.

"What is it, Ed?" Jace asked.

"There is a general alert going out. You may want to return. Oppa Space Command is asking for ships to help evacuate the planet."

"Doctor Tulo, we're being recalled to Covenant. There's an evacuation order out. The Duggor are heading here. They are insisting that we remove the Daak."

They heard shouting as people were running away, the sounds of pounding mechanicals suddenly filling the air. "We are requesting any who wish to evacuate to come with us. And any that have ships to help evacuate the planet. We will be meeting with the Alliance fleet."

Eislie stood. "We have a ship."

"Does it have weapons?"

Jace replied, "Not really. Mostly defensive. But we can help."

Timon placed his hands on their shoulders. "You can't fight. You both have work to do."

Jace looked at the man over his shoulder. "You're right, and right now, it involves saving as many people as we can."

"Eis, the ship can carry about forty or fifty people at a time. We can get them to safety," Jace said, and Eislie nodded. She tapped her comm. "Ed, warm up the engines. We're heading back."

* * *

The flock of people heading toward the dock slowed their arrival. Eislie and Jace held up their crew IDs, only to be corralled with other ship crews in the corner of the large, open dock.

"We need volunteers to stand as a defense for Oppa. If your ship has weapons, please head to your right. For others, if you have the room, you are requested to aid in the evacuation!" the chief yelled over the loudspeaker. Arren was down in the crowd, handing out emergency comms, when he spotted Eislie and Jace. "Bala, Jenti, those two, bring them over here," he ordered the two Resconasans he had been training as his replacements.

Jace stood face-to-face with the two Resconasans, and as he tried to walk around, they blocked his path. As he was about to push them out of his way, Jace heard, "Eis, Jace, here."

Eislie looked up, hearing Arren yelling, "Follow them!" and pointing to the two now blocking their path. When they finally reached Arren, he told them, "The ship's fixed. You can leave."

"We can take about forty people on board," Jace told him.

"You two owe nothing to anyone here. They won't stop you."

Eislie looked Arren in the eye. "We're helping, Arren. No way we're staying out of this."

The old miner smiled. "Had to try, Eis. Here's some emergency comms. Get loaded up; the controller will assign you to a carrier." Arren watched as they started toward the *Wolfhammer*. Eislie turned as Jace continued for the ship. "Come with us. You missed the last time."

Arren shook his head. "These two will get on later. I'm needed here."

Eislie felt a weight in her chest. "You sure?"

The old man smiled. "Yeah. We all have to save as many as we can. Someone has to stay here and get them on the ships." He winked at her. "Someone has to fly them."

She turned, only hesitating for a moment before again heading to the ship. When she arrived, Jace was already getting people on board. She stopped, looking back into the crowd.

"He's not coming, is he?" Jace said rather stoically. She glanced at Jace, placing her hand on his chest as she walked into the ship.

When they reached capacity, the deck crew told them to lift off. Eislie had contacted the controller. They were assigned to the *Allicar*. Since the *Wolfhammer* was small enough to fit inside it's docking bay, they were one of the ships carrying people who had difficulty moving or needed minor medical care. When they arrived, they contacted the vessels using the emergency comm. "*Allicar*, this is *Wolfhammer*. We have evacuees requiring medical level one. Where do you want us to dock?"

The comm crackled. "*Wolfhammer*, right loading dock. You're to unload and head back down as soon as possible. We have Duggor fighters coming in about two hours."

"Understood, *Allicar*, heading there now. Open the bay for us," Eislie replied.

Jace joked, "That sounded official," making her glare at him. "I know, completely inappropriate."

They offloaded everyone and were directed to another location on the planet. This time, the *Wolfhammer* was ordered to pick up dignitaries and some high-ranking officials. The two complied, but they quickly asked to be reassigned to the general populace as they left the planet again with these privileged individuals. The ship's controller listened to the demands of the people they had brought in and was considering the crew of *Wolfhammer*'s request. He was about to honor it, but Captain Radit overrode the decision. Jace and Eislie again headed down to pick up their next load of people.

Chapter 28

Duggor Strike

The *Wolfhammer* landed, Eislie even shoving one politician who insisted that they should have some alcohol on the ship available to passengers. Captain Radit had been standing in the access hallway that ran the length of the dock. When they came in, he called over the controller to see to whom the ship belonged.

"JESC Salvage. They're fast, seven trips so far. I'm sending them down again," the commander told him.

The captain looked at Eislie and swore he knew her. "Yalt, what are their names?"

"Uh, Jace Tucker and Eislie Licessien. Sir." The commander watched as a look of anger filled the captain's face. "When they arrive back, have security ready."

"Sir? Why security?" Yalt asked.

The captain muttered, "They're escaped criminals, Yalt. They're being locked up. We'll use their ship to continue the evacuation."

* * *

On the planet, Jace closed the cargo door. "Eis, we're full, let's go." They lifted off, only to encounter weapons fire. It struck the hull hard, and all aboard watched as the discharge arced inside the ship's structure.

"Geez, what the hell was that?" Jace asked.

Eislie looked at the screen. "Duggor fighters."

"Ed, weapons status?" Jace asked, the computer replying, "Seven shots loaded in slag, and drill is charging."

Eislie looked to Jace when he said, "Maybe we should just leave the damn things loaded."

"We can't land inside with weapons armed. The slag takes time to cool down," Eislie warned him. Jace knew it was a risk, but right now, they were under attack.

* * *

"Captain, Duggor fighters are attacking the evacuee ships," Resix said.

"Resix, get our fighters out there; protect those ships, now," Radit ordered.

As the battle continued, more transport ships were damaged or lost, and the Alliance was about to lose another when Jace fired a slag shot through the Duggors' cockpit. The vessel that was docking called to thank them for the assist. Captain Radit saw that they had a weapon that penetrated the Duggor defense shields and called down to the dock. The *Wolfhammer* now became more valuable to him, and he made sure Yalt had security ready. When Radit looked out the front viewer, the large cleaver ship came into view.

As Jace and Eislie landed, they hurried the passengers off and were readying to head back out. Jace was taken aback as his arms were suddenly pulled back and he felt himself being lifted off the floor after a restraining bar was slammed against his back. He turned to see Eislie restrained similarly as the guards pushed her forward. The captain soon joined them. "Jace Tucker, Eislie Licessien, you are escaped prisoners wanted for theft."

Jace looked up at the captain. "Who the fuck are you?"

"Captain Radit, and we're taking your ship. Maybe we'll throw it at the cleaver."

"Ed, emergency. Get out of here!" Eislie yelled.

They all heard the ship. "Acknowledged, I will continue with the rescue operations."

The ship started to lift from the deck as the door was closing. They watched as a guard jumped in, hitting the emergency shutoff for the spide reactor. The ship fell to the deck with a heavy metallic thud; the ship's computer appeared to shut down. The guard exited, lowering the powered door as he did. Jace knew they only shut off the spide reactor, but Ed was still online, only in stealth mode, as per orders.

Radit looked Jace in the eyes. "You two cost me a lot of shill."

Jace smiled. "Captain, you could use a breath mint. I mean, really use one."

Radit smiled before crashing his head against Jace's. There was a hollow echo from the impact. Jace shook his head. "Ow. That hurt." Jace watched as Radit stumbled back and heard Eislie laugh. "What, his head's harder than you thought?"

Radit walked over and was about to strike her when there was an explosion, making the ship lurch. Even with artificial gravity, it wasn't easy to stay standing.

Jace pushed back against the guards holding him. "How'd you know we escaped, Radit? Everyone else was told we already left after serving our time. You were working with Bosh, weren't you?"

Radit turned. "The ship is under attack. Yalt, get these two in the brig and prepare for battle."

The commander looked at the info pad and pulled up the information on both Jace and Eislie. There was no warrant for their arrest, and they served their time. Something didn't feel right to him, and he hesitated.

"Commander Yalt, is there a problem?" Radit growled.

"Sir, there is no warrant for them. We can't hold them," Yalt defended.

"They attacked me, Yalt. Didn't you see that he injured me?" The captain wiped the blood from a small cut on his forehead as he again ordered the guards to take them to the brig. They used the service hall to get them away from the evacuees. The captain was pausing for a moment, hearing Jace tell them to let them go. He pointed to the door behind him. "Just beyond that door is space. If you don't like the accommodations, we can always put you out there."

Jace looked defiantly toward the captain. "Good to know that assholes are a common thing in the universe."

The captain was about to strike Jace when the ship again lurched, this time more violently. The guards holding Jace stumbled, and he was able to get free from the restraint. Then, two more explosions, and the last one, none of them heard for very long. The entire area's atmosphere rushed by them as the outside door ruptured, exposing the hallway to open space.

Jace couldn't hear due to the pressure change and felt himself lift as the air rushed by. He felt a substantial impact as a body hit him in the chest, his instinct causing him to push it away. That action allowed him to grab the doorframe and stop himself from being blown out into space. He wasn't the only person who had caught the edge of the door; next to him was one of the guards. Jace watched him straining as he held on for dear life. Jace offered him his hand, which the man eagerly accepted. With all the strength he had, Jace pulled the man forward, watching him grab the inside of the sealed door.

"I'll push you in, then give me a hand!" Jace yelled; the man nodded.

Jace did as promised, and the man started to pull him through the door but was knocked away by another. Jace, in a panic, grabbed the edge of the door and tried pulling himself in. But when he looked up, Radit was leaning against the other side. Jace's vision filled with the silhouette of a boot as the captain kicked him in the face, the impact stunning Jace, making him let go.

Jace's ears filled with the fading sound of Eislie screaming, "No!" Within seconds, Jace felt the air escaping out of his lungs. His heart raced as he closed his eyes and fumbled to seal his flight jacket. He reached over with only moments to spare as he pulled the safety veil over his head. It sealed quickly, pressure and air returning to his lungs. He gasped, pulling in needed oxygen before looking around for something to grab on to, but found nothing.

Jace was floating in space. Without an environment suit, he felt the skin on his hands tighten. His clothing covered the rest of him with some form of protection, but the stars and ships around him spun as he fought to right himself. As he turned, what caused the explosion became evident. The remains of another ship had crashed into the edge of the dock. On Jace's next rotation, he saw where it came from; a jump carrier that had attacked the Duggor.

Jace yelled out as he witnessed one after another of the escape pods flying from it. As he continued to spin, Jace noticed the engines severely damaged, only to also see the spide core floating safely away into space. Eislie had told him some ships had separate reactors for internal power. That's what Jace designed for the *Wolfhammer*. Jace reached out as he fell closer to the ship; he was on a trajectory to hit it. *It must be my lucky day.*

Drifting closer, he reached out into the darkness. It suddenly became light, and he felt a searing pain as the unfiltered starlight scorched his bare skin. Jace pulled his hands in to cover them but had to bring up his arms to protect his eyes, the light causing a silhouette, and he could see the smoke weeping from his flesh. His moment of pain was stunted as he felt the impact against the ship. By reflex, he gripped one of the small handholds on its surface. If there had been air around him, they could have heard his howl of pain from orbit.

Jace made his way to the airlock and entered the ship. He never paused, pounding on the seal to close the door before hitting the emergency fill. Jace again felt the pressure of the atmosphere against his body and struggled to release the veil. As the denser atmosphere hit him, he gasped to fill his lungs. Jace grunted in pain, reaching for the med kit on the wall, and used anesthetic spray to numb the pain of his badly burned hands. But he was in an airlock, and he needed to get to an escape pod.

When he went to open the inside door, it wouldn't budge. A quick check of the status alerted him to the entire hallway being depressurized. He looked at the environment suit half hanging on the wall and shook his head, muttering, "Why can't anything be easy, huh?"

Jace did his best to put the suit on. He could still use his hands, but he needed medical attention. When he finally got the door open, Jace checked for escape pods but found none on the level he was on. He looked at the display and saw the cleaver ship looming large on the screen. He watched as it fired a powerful beam of energy across the planet.

Moments later, he heard over the emergency comm: "People of Oppa, you harbor an enemy of the Duggor. If you do not surrender them in one standard cycle, your planet will be purged of them and all who aid them."

"That doesn't sound good," Jace muttered to the empty ship. He looked closely at the screen. "Are those jump towers? They look similar. They must be using them to guide the beam." Jace looked down the hall and recognized something very familiar. "Shouldn't have locked me in that reactor room, Voss. Now I know what that sign means." He ran down the hall. "And if those are similar to jump towers, I've got a crazy idea."

Jace hit the door release and was greeted with the sight he had hoped for. "Anyone here?" he yelled. Of course, being in an environment suit hampered any communication. He walked along the room, seeing nothing but the console and monitoring equipment. Eislie had been teaching him Gilesian, and he knew what most of the words before him said.

"Okay, the reactor is working, engines are active but offline, no spide core. Already saw that. But jump engines are on standby." He turned to grab one of the consoles. "All right, let's see if we can get this thing flying."

Jace worked as fast as he could with his injuries. He found the controls and was able to access the thrusters. When he looked at the jump drive's status, he heard a warning over the ship's system. "Heavy magnetic field in vicinity. Cannot form jump field."

As he felt the ship move, Jace cheered. "Don't care, I only need the mag field inside the jump chamber anyway. I want to put this in the path of the Duggor ship."

Jace worked and was able to get the ship moving. He had planned to use the ship's jump chamber to deflect the energy beam when it fired. At least that's what he hoped to do. Jace still wasn't sure if the Duggor weapon worked like that. But seeing the jump-style mag towers, he thought it just might work. If not, he thought, *A few billion people are going to be gone real soon.* When he was able to get the larger thrusters online, he knew he had a chance.

As he moved the ship, he could see the *Allicar* on the monitor and wondered why they hadn't jumped away. When he looked down at the console, he answered his own question. "The Duggor weapon is not allowing the grav or jump drives to work. Must be interfering with their resonance."

Jace continued to pilot the ship slowly toward the cleaver ship. As he passed it, he could see the size of the weapon itself. Multiple reactors were powering it, and they seemed to be separate from the main section. Upon closer viewing, he noticed six large pipes running down the ship's length, each ending at one of the mag towers. "They have to be using them to direct the beam," Jace muttered.

Looking at the monitor again, Jace continued to steer the ship. He had thought about crashing it into the attacking cleaver, but the Duggor craft dwarfed the one he was on. That, and he was hoping to escape this without killing himself. Radit had thrown him out of the ship, and Eislie was still on board. Jace expected to make it back. He had some payback he wanted to collect.

He looked at the monitor. "Well, Eis, hope you're having a better time over there."

* * *

On the *Allicar*, Eislie fought with her restraints the whole way to the brig. They needed several guards and replacements to bring her there. Chancellor Dedal had been looking for Radit when he came across Eislie fighting the guards. Dedal knew her father and what had happened to him because of what she had done. Since she was little, he had known her, and was surprised she never took on being in Alliance service. But Dedal stopped when he looked at her face, and in his gut, he felt a twinge. The anger and sadness he saw was enough to make him take a moment to gather his own thoughts.

"You killed him, you slacs. Let me go!" she yelled, lifting herself from the floor. The chancellor was amazed at the strength she suddenly had. He watched as multiple guards fought to move her forward. He could only watch as they threw her into the cell. Empathically, he felt the impact as she hit the ground. But his heart skipped as she rose and ran toward the door, only to hit it hard as it stopped her. Dedal watched as the guards, some nursing injuries, walked away from the cell, leaving only one behind to guard her.

"What did you do to be treated like this, Eis?" Dedal muttered before walking toward her cell.

Chapter 29

Duggor Go Down

Eislie had finally released herself from the restraint. She rubbed her head from where she hit the door and peered angrily through the small port of the cell but could not reach out due to the mesh covering it.

"Let me out of here! I can still save him!" she screamed.

The guard ignored her as she pleaded for her release to save Jace. Eislie felt the tears drying on her face as she tried to force her fingers through the mesh to rip it away, only to bloody her hands in her attempt. Chancellor Dedal walked up to the guard and asked the reason she was being held. The guard only said, "Captain Radit's orders."

Dedal saw the blood on the floor and looked up to see Eislie clawing at the small grating that covered the access port.

"Eislie, stop!" he yelled.

He grabbed the guard. "You, get a med kit right now."

He then slid the grate up to allow the small access to open, and Eislie reached out, grabbing his arm. "Let me out of here. I might be able to save him."

Dedal tried to remove her hand, but even injured, she clutched his uniform, tearing it.

"Eislie, stop, you have to stop. Why are you in here?" He then grabbed her hand as the guard brought back the med kit and started to heal her injuries. Eislie fought to pull away but realized that the person holding her was a friend.

"Amous, it's you?" Eislie asked, disbelief in her voice.

The chancellor looked toward her, and he saw the fear and loss she was feeling. He finished healing her hand and watched as she pulled it back, slowly looking at it. She looked up at him. "Dedal, you have to get me out of here. He's still alive. I know he's still alive."

The chancellor felt her pleas in his bones. "Who's still alive?"

"Amous, please, let me go. Jace is still alive. I can get him. Just let me get him. I promise I'll come back," Eislie again pleaded.

Dedal looked at the guard, who handed him her info pad. The chancellor tapped it and again asked why she was being held. The guard gave the same answer, "Captain Radit's orders." When he attempted to find a reason for her incarceration, he only saw her previous record.

"Eislie, you didn't escape from your time on Charon, did you? And how long have you been flying with the Terran?"

Eislie growled quietly. "My sentence was up over three planetary cycles ago. I was left there."

The chancellor pulled up the info with a few taps. He viewed the records and checked the date, realizing she was correct. "You were due to be released three cycles ago; why was I told otherwise?"

Eislie looked through the portal. "Because they lied to you, Chancellor. They lied to you, my family, everyone."

Anger welled up in his throat as Dedal now understood what she was saying. When he asked why she didn't make an official investigation, Eislie slammed her fist against the door. "I did, many times, and you know what they told me?"

The chancellor remained silent.

"It was denied. Without reason."

Dedal looked at the guard to validate what he heard her say. "The base captain is not the kind of person to allow that, Eislie."

Eislie gave a smile filled with anger, and it showed in her eyes. "Chancellor, how much wealth does a single load of spide make the Consortium or the Alliance?"

Dedal stared at the wall as he comprehended what she asked. As a politician, he couldn't believe what she was saying. But as a friend, he knew something was wrong. "That's ludicrous. Your crimes were vandalism of state property. Your sentence to the mining field was for a term of one planetary cycle."

Eislie whimpered, "I was there almost four."

The chancellor now understood her anger and was appalled by the situation. "This was not meant to have happened. There are rules to prevent this. I'll petition to have the new charges removed and your sentence commuted."

Eislie looked at him, her eyes pleading to release her from the cell.

The chancellor looked down at his pad. "It was fortunate that Terran helped you escape. They can be dangerous."

Eislie now showed her anger, yelling at him. "What are you talking about? He saved several Alliance members; he chose the mine because our people wanted to give him to the Daak. His sentence was the same as mine, one cycle. The only thing he is guilty of is that he is like me."

The chancellor leaned in. "But he's Terran."

"Yes, but he's also a starborn. We're both resistant to spide radiation, and they threw him out the airlock, even after he saved someone."

She then pulled back and leaned on the door with both hands as if trying to push it open, tears again forming in her eyes. "Amous, you missed what I said. I told you exactly why we're treated this way." She looked over the bottom of the barred window with desperate eyes.

"Your resistance to spide radiation?" the chancellor mumbled.

Eislie nodded, giving a smile. "We only wanted to be free, Amous. We both served our time."

Dedal stared at the pain in her eyes. "You're aligned with him, aren't you?"

Eislie nodded.

Dedal knew something about starborn; his sister's daughter was considered one. Seeing the torment she was going through not being able to leave made him ask, "Were you compatible?"

When she nodded again, he felt a lump grow in his throat.

Eislie looked at him, her eyes filled with wonderment. "I have traveled with him to the outer arms. We've both seen the vast darkness of space. I've seen a solar wind make the dust from an asteroid glow like light-flies all around. I spent days lying next to him, listening to micro meteors tapping the hull of our ship. We watched as stellar particles flashed and crackled against our shields as we turned the power low to conserve energy and avoid capture."

She paused only to stand tall. "We were free. I'd trade it for nothing." Her voice was cracking.

There was a brief silence as the chancellor realized the implications of the actions of himself and Captain Radit.

"Open the cell door," Dedal growled. The guard looked at him, confused. "Do I need to repeat myself?"

The guard shook her head and opened the door. Eislie was standing there with tears in her eyes as she walked forward. "Maybe you're not so much of an idiot."

"Commander, we're taking this to Radit right now," Dedal said.

"It's Captain, Chancellor. I have my own ship," Eislie said as they walked toward the bridge.

As they entered the lift, the general alert alarm sounded. Dedal looked concerned as he said, "I hope that's not because the Duggor are targeting us."

When they reached the bridge, they heard, "Commander Yalt, I said move the ship to a safe distance."

Yalt responded, "We can't, sir, we're stuck in the weapon's magnetic field; we can't form a jump point. And grav systems aren't working."

The captain yelled, "Full thrusters then!"

"Yes, Captain, but we won't make it to a safe distance. We won't be able to jump until after they fire."

As Dedal entered the bridge, he asked, "Captain, what is the status?"

Captain Radit glanced at the chancellor and hadn't seen Eislie. "The Duggor are powering up that cleaver. They are going to destroy Oppa, and hopefully, the bulk of the Daak. Commander, let's get this ship to a safe distance."

"Are you crazy? There are billions of people down there, most not Daak!" Eislie yelled.

"How in Stellus did you get on the bridge? Guards! Take her back to her cell!" Radit barked.

"No, Captain, the commander, uh, the captain, is under my watch here, and I have some things I'd like to speak to you about."

The captain walked up, grabbing Dedal's arm. "You're not in

command right now, Chancellor. This ship and crew are under my orders. Your time for diplomacy is done. It's time the Daak burn."

The captain then ordered them to be detained, but the move was cut short when the collision alert sounded. The Terran officers looked toward the chancellor as Eislie glared over at them.

"Sir, we have a contact at twenty-three degrees," the navigator told them.

"Is it Duggor?" the captain asked.

"No, sir, it's one of ours; it's the *Baraont*," the navigator replied.

"That's impossible. That ship was damaged and evacuated. Recheck it," the captain ordered.

"Is it a danger, Captain?" one of the Terrans asked.

At that moment, the viewscreen came alive as Jace figured out how to work the comm for the ship he was piloting.

"Hey, everyone, don't move. I don't want to scrape your paint," Jace joked.

Eislie yelled, "Jace! I knew you were still alive!"

"Sir, he's heading right for us," the navigator warned.

"Don't worry. I'm gonna be close. I won't dent your ship or anything. Though that weapon's magnetic field is making it hard to steer," Jace complained.

"It seems that brashness and insanity are inherent in the Terran race," the captain remarked as the ship barely missed them.

"You realize that ship doesn't have jump capability, don't you?" the captain told Jace. Eislie remembered the star and how they used the ship's shields and jump field to reinforce the hull.

"Captain, I think he has a plan to save the planet. You have to listen," Eislie said.

Radit dismissed her. "Keep her quiet, Chancellor."

The whole bridge watched as Jace positioned the ship in front of the weapon's path. "That isn't going to stop that weapon. He's just going to get himself killed, and we'll have to avoid the debris," Radit scoffed.

Jace did his best to line the open jump chamber facing the beam.

"Sir, he's opened the main jump port," Yalt reported.

"Why? That ship doesn't have enough power to reach a reaction. And the mag field is too strong to do it anyway," the other Terran said.

"Captain, he's going to use the resonance chamber to deflect the beam," Eislie told them.

Radit scoffed. "Even if it works, at best, he's only delayed the destruction by a few cycles. It'll burn through the end. Keep moving to a safe distance."

The Duggor fired the weapon, and Jace did his best to line up the ship. The beam entered the chamber, but as power increased, the field started to collapse. It was only a matter of time until it burned through.

"Sir, he's turning the *Baraont*," one of the crew said.

Eislie jumped over the console and opened the comm. "Jace, you need seventeen degrees to clear."

"Got it. Thanks, Eis. How's it going over there?"

Eislie simply said, "The magnetic field is stopping us from jumping."

The captain motioned, and some guards pulled her away from the comm.

"What is he doing?" Radit asked, watching Jace's plan unfold.

She looked at him. "He's going to deflect the beam."

"That ship will be destroyed," Radit reminded her.

Eislie glared at him. "He knows that, but I've flown with him, and I know him. If he survives, you'll all owe him big."

"You've been hanging around Terrans for too long. You're starting to sound like them," Radit remarked.

Eislie walked back to stand by the chancellor, her demeanor reserved and controlled. "At least he's trying to save the people on the planet. Who cares if some of them are Daak?"

* * *

Back on the *Baraont*, Jace could feel the heat of the chamber through his environment suit. Jace worked fast, knowing that the Duggor would take time to power up for another shot. If the ship survived, Jace thought about ramming it into the Duggor, hopefully damaging the weapon. He turned as the beam started to breach the end of the chamber. The sudden creaking of the superstructure made Jace realize that he now had to find a way off, and fast.

* * *

The crew of the *Allicar* watched as a beam erupted out the aft of the *Baraont*. The field remained intact, deflecting the energy away from the planet. The bridge was filled with cheers as they started to celebrate.

"That sumbitch did it!" one of the Terran officers yelled.

The captain looked at the man. "Is your entire race insane?"

* * *

Back on the *Baraont*, Jace searched for an escape pod. "Where's a ship when you need one?" he joked as he slid down the ladder to the level below. He was lucky and found one of the pods still active. Jace heard the ship's groans as it started to fail. He jumped in and closed the hatch. As the pod launched, one of the reactors of the *Baraont* breached, the explosion forcing him off course, and Jace was stunned at his sudden stop.

"Probably should leave my number for the guy I just hit," Jace joked, but realizing he had just landed on the cleaver ship, he decided, "Maybe not."

The pod was damaged. Jace exited, hoping to push the small vessel from the Duggor ship. His efforts were hampered by the external gravity field holding it firmly in place. Jace found himself stuck and turned to see several Duggor in environment suits pop out of hatches and lock themselves onto the hull.

Jace stood with his hands down as they walked toward him with restraining rods pointed in his direction. He knew he was either dead or captured. "You guys came out to see me? I am overwhelmed. I don't know what to say."

Jace again tried to jump off the ship, but he heard an alert from his suit as he did, the pleasant computer voice saying. "Attention, you have five minutes of usable oxygen remaining."

Jace looked around. "Ah, hell, guys. I guess I've got five minutes to play with you." Jace then looked around, and as the first blow came, he grabbed the restraining rod and used it to fight back.

"Sir, the Duggor are recharging. The estimated time is zero point twenty-seven cycles."

Eislie moved to the sensor array and started searching for Terran life signs.

"Will someone get her off the bridge!" the captain yelled.

"Belay that order," the chancellor said firmly. "Captain, as I said before, she is under my watch."

"Then control her, Chancellor, or I will," the captain growled, and walked back to his chair.

"Why did you tell me that she was supposed to be a prisoner still, Captain? Her sentence was finished over three planetary cycles ago," Dedal demanded.

"This is war, Chancellor; we need all the advantages we can use. Besides, people with her attributes are rare."

"And the man who just saved Oppa? He had the same attributes as her, and his sentence was over two cycles ago as well. Why were we ordering them to be held longer, Captain?"

Radit straightened his uniform. "As I said, this is war, Chancellor. You do not understand. We can win against the Duggor."

"At what cost, Captain? That man has singlehandedly deflected their weapon." Dedal then looked at Eislie. "Communications, open a channel to the Duggor," Dedal ordered.

"Belay that order. Remove the chancellor and that … thing from the bridge!" the captain yelled.

"Thing? You consider me a thing?" Eislie seethed.

"You and those like you are only good for the attributes you have, nothing more. Your damn ancient blood is worthless when it comes to the rest of us. You should not exist," Radit proudly said.

"Worthless—blo—" Eislie stuttered in anger as she picked up a chair, throwing it at the captain over the control console.

"Restrain her!" he yelled.

As Eislie fought the guards, they all heard static and then some chatter on the screen.

"Eis, you there … Eis? You … there?"

Hearing Jace's voice gave Eislie enough strength to dislocate the guard's shoulder as she rushed for the comm. "Jace, where are you?"

"Yeah, crashed on the Duggor ship, could … use … pickup."

"I have to get to our ship. I don't think these assholes are going to help," she said, tears of joy running down her face.

"Restrain her. Someone, restrain her!" No one obeyed the captain's order.

"Captain Eislie, I believe your ship is in the holding bay. Ensign, take her to their ship."

"No! I'm countermanding that order!" Radit yelled.

The ensign only paused a moment before taking Eislie off to get to her ship.

"Commander Yalt, we are relieving Captain Radit of his command. You are now in charge."

Yalt stood. "An honor, Chancellor." After a moment, Yalt said, "Security, detain Captain Radit and take him to the brig. Chancellor, we will open communications to the Duggor as you requested."

Dedal stepped forward. "Good. Perhaps we still have time to avoid more bloodshed today."

* * *

Eislie and the ensign reached the dock, and Eislie paused before she touched the door release. "Now I get it."

The ensign asked, "Get what?"

"Why he feels so good seeing it. I get it now," Eislie said.

The door opened, and she rushed in. Checking the status controls, Eislie yelled, "Ed, you awake? We have an emergency."

"Captain, you have returned," the computer replied.

"Run a workup for a fast launch, Ed. We gotta get Jace," Eislie ordered.

"I presume Captain Jace is in trouble again."

"Yes, when is he, or we, not in trouble?" Eislie joked.

"It is good to hear your jokes again, Captain. I have been dreading these cretins trying to dismantle me."

"Good point, Ed. Uh, Ensign, uh … what is your name?"

"Ensign Resix, Third Fleet, Commander," Resix replied.

Eislie shook her head. "Not Commander, Captain. Here, I am Captain."

"Then is Jace your crew?" Resix asked.

Eislie shook her head. "Nope, Captain as well."

"Captain, all systems are functioning. Reactor point needs to be seated to return to full power."

"On it," Eislie said as she opened the engine room door. She was about to open the reactor compartment but was startled when Resix, in a panic, slammed the door shut. "Don't open that. It'll kill you!" he yelled.

Eislie rolled her eyes and worked to seat the reactor crystal. Resix watched as the radiation spiked to over three hundred times the deadly range, and Eislie was using the controls normally. She hit the extractors and cleared the compartment of radiation, channeling it into the reactor before opening the engine room door.

"Ed, you should have full power. Unless these assholes removed components."

Resix moved from behind the corner. "How are you alive?"

"You didn't remove or disable anything, did you?" she asked again.

Resix shook his head. "We only disabled the main power and took a lot of scans. We still don't know how this ship is flying. Again, how are you still alive?"

Eislie sighed. "Look, I don't have time to explain. Are you coming with me or not?"

"I'm coming with you," he said, still amazed she was standing there.

"Good, I need someone to run the scanners while I fly."

Within moments of sitting in her seat, they were off toward the cleaver ship. As they flew over, Eislie told Resix, "Look for Terran life signs. Jace said he crashed on the ship."

"What do Terran life signs look like? I see Duggor and Gilese."

"That's him. Gilese and Terran are very similar."

She switched the comm channel they used. "You there, Jace?"

There was a pause. "Eis, good to hear your voice. I'm a bit busy fighting some Duggor. I could use some help."

"We see you. Hold on," she said happily.

"Oh, and I'm down to about two minutes of usable air," Jace informed her.

"Dammit, Jace, can't we do something the easy way for once?" Eislie shot back.

They could hear Jace laughing. "I wish. Get me the hell out of here."

"I see him. He has about five Duggor surrounding him," Resix said.

"Prepare the winch, Ed. Fire it at Jace," Eislie ordered.

"Are you mad at him again, Captain?" Ed remarked.

Eislie laughed. "No, Ed, he's in danger this time. We have to get him out."

"Of course, Captain, winch deployed."

A small, magnetic mass on a thin wire headed toward Jace at only a few meters per second.

"Heads up, Jace, winch incoming," Eislie said over the comm.

Jace turned to see the grapple heading for him and grabbed it with his injured hands, making him yell out in pain.

"Sorry, I didn't mean to send it so fast," Eislie said.

"Not your fault. My hands and arm are pretty bad from the starlight."

"How bad?" Eislie suddenly became concerned.

"Let's say I'm definitely using two hands to hold on," was Jace's reply.

"Oh slac. Ed, ready the med bay," Eislie ordered. "Resix, keep the ship here and pull away slowly when Ed tells you."

Eislie entered the cargo bay and quickly put on one of the breather suits she purchased while back home. She pulled Jace in as the winch came up.

She removed his glove and saw the charring on his hands. "You'll be all right. We'll get you into a regen right now."

"No time; we can stop this. Power up the drill."

"What? But your hands!" Eislie pleaded.

"I'll be fine, but this whole thing is going to blow up in our faces if we don't do something. If the Duggor fire, it'll start a whole new war. Neither the Daak nor the Duggor will stop until everyone is gone," Jace said.

Jace jumped up and started toward the control room. "Ed, map the magnetics around that weapon," he ordered.

"Good to hear you again, Captain."

"Thanks, Ed, do as I ask, please," Jace said, leaning on the console.

"What are we going to do?" Eislie asked.

"You said it yourself. The magnetic field was stopping the jump field; we're going to destroy the weapon."

"How? That armor is too strong," Resix said.

"And who's this in my seat?" Jace asked, cocking his head.

Eislie looked at the ensign and motioned for him to move.

"Magnetics mapped."

"Good, display overlay on screen," Jace ordered. "See, the

power lines run to each of these towers. If we hit these connectors, the field will twist the ship apart."

Resix looked at the display. "That's brilliant," he said and held his hand up for a high-five.

Jace looked at him with confusion.

"I watched some Terrans do a greeting back on the ship."

Jace held his burned hand up, the charred flesh flaking off, making Resix cringe. "I'd respond, but, you know."

"How are you functioning?" Resix asked.

Jace turned to Eislie. "Where did you pick up this guy?"

At that moment, Ed stated, "My sensors indicate that the weapon is almost ready to fire."

Eislie looked at Jace as they both strapped in. "I picked him up on the ship, and we don't have time to argue. At least he was able to help." Eislie then asked, "What's the status of the drill?"

"Charged and ready."

"Good, target these points." Jace touched the screen with his injured hands, wincing in pain as he did. But he still took the controls.

"You okay to fly?" Eislie asked with concern.

Jace only stared forward. "Let's finish this, and then worry."

They flew close, and the Duggors' weapons deflected as they neared the towers. Jace felt the ship drift each time they came close. The first two towers were easy. But then the Duggor sent in some fighters, and Jace had his hands full. They had disabled three of the six towers and watched as the ship started to twist. The resulting failures caused the weapon's reactors to overload. The increased reaction caused the weapon's aiming field to expand, affecting the grav drives on the *Wolfhammer*.

"Ed, are we getting power to the drives?" Jace asked.

"Yes, Captain, but the magnetic field is concentrated in this area. We are unable to use any drive systems at the moment."

They watched as the back half of the Duggor ship disconnected itself and started to pull away. They were also having trouble fleeing.

"So, we have no engines?" Jace asked.

"Affirmative. I wish to inform the crew that the reactors of the Duggor ship are estimated to ignite in approximately twenty-two seconds."

"Ed, put all power to the mag shields and jump field. I'm going to use thrusters to maneuver."

"What are you going to do?" Resix asked.

Eislie shook her head. "Oh no, you can't be serious. Like the quasi-space?"

Jace nodded.

Eislie tightened her harness, turning to smile. "I hate you."

Jace snickered as the blast wave hit. There were several small explosions on the control deck as connectors and parts of the regulator systems overloaded. The sudden fireworks made Jace ask, "Got that list handy?" Eislie shrieked with laughter as Jace did his best to surf along the front of the wave before it dissipated.

When they finally stopped, Jace gave the grav drives a try to make sure they were working. Eislie put her hands in the air. "That was a rush. But let's not do it again. Okay?"

Resix watched Jace and Eislie celebrate and said, "The captain was right—all Terrans, crazy."

Eislie overheard him, and she turned to say, "I'm only part Terran."

Chapter 30

Oppa Saved

It had been four days since the Duggor ship was destroyed. The rest of the fleet had moved on. Jace and Eislie were on board the *Wolfhammer* fixing the power systems damaged during the explosion. Arren had given them full access to the shop so they could make replacement parts. Eislie was in the med bay, where she was using the regenerator on Jace's hand. She had just healed it, and he almost had it crushed when she slipped, replacing a circulation pump. She noticed movement and turned to see Chancellor Dedal walking into the ship.

"Amous, what are you doing here?" she asked.

"I just came from the Planetary Council. They want to see both of you." He looked around the ship. "It was a brave thing you both did."

Jace and Eislie looked at him. "It's too bad not everyone agrees." Dedal knew he was referring to the starborn, and how they were being treated. He also told them that the Duggor were very upset that such a small vessel defeated them so easily.

"Easily? We're lucky we survived," Eislie scoffed.

The chancellor smiled. "What you did, what this ship did …" He paused. "There was an entire fleet of ships trying to disable the Duggor, and you did it within minutes of climbing aboard this vessel."

Jace reached out, gently grasping Eislie's hand.

Dedal saw that and said, "I know starborn are seen as something lesser." He looked down. "My niece is considered a starborn, and I feel her pain every time she visits."

Jace looked confused, so Eislie explained. "Gilesian empathy increases as we age."

He understood but then said, "So what? What's wrong with being a starborn?"

Dedal reached out and placed his hand on theirs. "When I told her that you were both starborn, her eyes lit up." He took a breath. "I told her what Eislie did to rescue you and how you saved her, and what you both did to save Oppa."

Eislie hugged the chancellor. "So, she doesn't mind being like us?"

The chancellor shook his head, then looked up. "I can't believe you slept inside an actual star."

Eislie rolled her eyes. "Yeah, it wasn't our first choice."

Dedal looked at them. "This is an incredible ship. Who knew it could do the things it has so far?"

"Thank you, Chancellor Dedal. That compliment is much appreciated."

Dedal stepped back upon hearing Ed's gratitude. He felt concerned and said, "I thought Resix was joking."

Eislie laughed as she pointed up. "What, Ed?"

Dedal nodded. "This ship is older than most on Oppa, and none of them can do anything like it, and the two of you have." He looked at them. "You, him, this ship. I know you don't believe in fate, Eislie, but you were all meant to meet. Something in the universe brought you all together."

Jace hopped off the table. "Yeah, well, tell the universe to lighten up. It's getting kind of painful." Eislie laughed at him as he put his arm around her.

Dedal smiled, seeing the two of them together. He remembered the birthdays when he had visited, back when her father was planetside. The chancellor's wife was good friends with Eislie's grandparents, at least the ones on Gilese. He was even present when she protested the service requirements for ship assignment and was there during her sentencing when she protested having to serve additional military time before she could get her own command. His heart ached, knowing how much she had to endure while a prisoner.

"They are investigating Radit, and I just heard back that they cannot confirm Devlin Bosh is dead." Dedal waited for that last bit of information to sink in before saying, "I'm sure someone is going to pay, but it probably won't be who's really guilty."

Jace took a step forward. "Well, Chancellor, we'll just have to see what comes up next." He looked back at Eislie. "We probably shouldn't keep the council waiting."

* * *

When they arrived, several people they knew as starborn met them at the door. They told the two how starborn were now allowed to join as crew on ships and travel. Greyman shook Jace and Eislie's hands, telling them that his first assignment was beginning tomorrow. Jace asked, "When did you become a leader?"

"Hey, someone has to head up the research you two proposed."

Eislie and Jace felt a warmth in their hearts at the news. Dedal told them that the decision was made the day the Duggor officially left. He also informed them all that the Duggor now see Oppa as a protected planet. The force on this world warranted destruction, but when they lost the cleaver ship, the Duggor decided to leave them alone, at least for now.

They could see the Oppan space representatives and a few Alliance sitting discussing something as they entered the council chamber. To Jace, it seemed like they were just arguing. One of the Oppan stood, motioning for them to approach. The rest of the starborn that had accompanied them remained a few meters behind.

"Thank you for bringing them, Chancellor. Have you informed them of the news?"

"Only some, Councilwoman. It was the decision of the Terran and Alliance representatives that they be brought here to inform them of the rest," Dedal replied.

The councilmember nodded and sat. "Very well. Please take a seat."

Jace and Eislie listened to the news. They again were informed that all starborn on Oppa would be allowed to fly as crew.

When Eislie asked, "Why not their own ships?"

Greyman answered, "We have to get some first. Who knows, maybe we'll piece some together. Seems to be working for you two."

Eislie and Jace laughed. The *Wolfhammer* was an odd ship, but it was a good ship. They continued to update them on the Duggor fleet's status and that the Duggor had decided to allow the Daak to stay for now.

Eislie watched as one of the councilmembers walked toward the small, curtained area that led to the council's exit. She returned, whispering to the head of the panel before she sat.

"On a more interesting note, we have some additional guests that would like to thank you for your efforts as well," the councilman stated as several Daak representatives walked into the room. They stayed a distance away from Jace and Eislie, as well as the Terrans. Only one of them moved forward.

"On behalf of our people, we thank you for stopping the Duggor. You have preserved the lives of millions of Daak and the billions of Oppan who aided us."

Jace felt the anger sticking in his throat, seeing the Daak standing there. "Great, then leave Earth."

Eislie grabbed his arm as she turned to him with concern. "I know you're angry. Let's hear what they have to say first."

The Daak stood and bowed as Eislie held on to Jace. "The anger is understandable. We have consulted and wish to inform all Terran interests that the Daak have made an error. We attacked your planet under a misguided decision. The Daak had only wished to help your people. You were destroying your own world needlessly. We did not understand the subtleties of the hierarchy of the Terran people. Please know that we have made available the resources of the Daak to rebuild what has been destroyed."

One of the Terran officers stood, seeing the message on his comm. "The Daak have stopped attacking Earth."

The Daak continued to look toward Jace. "And you were involved in the attack and injury of Daak."

Eislie felt the muscles in Jace's arm tense, and she held him tighter.

"We understand that you did not fire on the chase ship and that you were acting in a manner to preserve life. We are also aware that you are of Lyri descent."

"So what?" Jace muttered.

"When your actions were verified, all charges were removed. The Daak do not see Lyri as an enemy. In our history, the Lyri have been of assistance to us, as we are also without our home world."

Eislie then muttered, "Technically, they're like us. Starborn."

Jace gave a heavy sigh. "Still not an excuse for attacking Earth."

The Daak turned toward the council. "When we were informed

of the proceedings of Jace Tucker and understood that his actions were of self-preservation, we were surprised that he chose exile rather than to be aided by our people as per our request."

"What is that supposed to mean?" Jace snarled.

"You were not informed by the Terran Council that we would have aided you in relocating you to a neutral planet as a known descendant of the Lyri."

Jace suddenly looked puzzled and turned to the Terran representative as the Alliance members asked what the Daak was insinuating.

"On the discovery of Jace Tucker being a Lyri descendant, the Terran and Alliance Council were informed and requested to allow the defendant to choose if he would like to leave or return to his planet freely. It has also been concluded that the Alliance Tribunal was negligent. They did not inform Jace Tucker of his choice to be set free as per the request of the Daak."

Eislie didn't need to be a total empath to feel the anger Jace was holding back. The Daak turned toward them again. "We suspect that's the same reason that you, Eislie Licessien, were also held against your will." The Daak's statement drew several glares of accusation toward the Alliance representatives.

Eislie suddenly felt conflicted and released Jace's arm, only to feel him gently grasp her hand. She was confused, feeling him suddenly relaxed.

"Representatives of the Daak, you are welcome for the assistance. But regardless of the circumstances, I do not harbor any blame on the Daak people," Jace said.

His statement made the Terran representative stand. "They attacked Earth, killed millions of us. And you're all right with that?"

"No." Jace took a breath. "People of the Daak, you are again welcome. It doesn't matter what happened; you can't dwell on the past. If I had done as you mentioned, we would not be standing here. The Duggor would have destroyed the Daak settlement and most of Oppa. Also, Earth would not be free." He paused. "The Daak retaliated against Earth because they were attacked by those fearing a loss of power. And we were held and used by the Alliance, I suspect, by people with the same fears. In truth, right now, right here, this is the best outcome all of us could hope for."

Jace looked around the room. "To the people of Oppa and the Alliance, we thank you for allowing us to be here."

The room fell silent. Dedal placed his hand on Jace's shoulder. "Ever think of taking up politics?"

Jace laughed. "Not going to happen, Chancellor."

The Daak representatives all bowed to Jace. "The Daak thank you," they said, all in unison.

Greyman placed his hands on both their shoulders. "All of us do."

The Daak remained, and Jace and Eislie spent the rest of the hour listening to the council on their plans to help the starborn, promising to include them in the current population. Jace did ask something that he didn't expect an answer to. "When I crashed onto the Duggor ship, they didn't try to kill me. It seemed like they were just trying to capture me."

The Daak replied, "You are Lyri. They would not kill you."

"Why?" Eislie asked.

The Daak hesitated. "We are not able to tell you." When Jace pressed, the Daak remained silent, their actions causing a stir of confused looks.

When the council ended, all the starborn headed out with Jace and Eislie. When they reached the dock, Arren greeted them.

"What, a party, and you didn't invite me?" the old miner joked.

Eislie hugged him before heading to the ship. "You are invited, old man. I'll be back. I've got the drinks on the ship. Let's celebrate."

Everyone cheered, and they partied through the night. When morning came, Eislie and Jace were sitting on the dock's ledge, looking out over the horizon. The light of the star was just starting to fill the sky.

When the light hit the ship, Ed alerted his captains to the time. "My bio-sensors indicate that you have not slept. But it is zero five hundred. You asked me to wake you around this time."

Eislie waved back to the ship. "Thanks, Ed." She leaned against Jace, who sat, still looking up at the sky. She then said, "I like it better when it's dark out. You can see the stars."

Jace leaned his head against hers. "We've been here almost a week. You know that, right?"

Eislie smiled. "Where should we go?"

"I'm not sure I'm ready to go back to Earth. Although, I'm not as wanted a man there now."

Eislie mentioned a trinary star system about three days' flight, and she had always wanted to visit since she heard about it. She smiled. "The clerk's office opens in a half hour. I can go let them know we're leaving."

"Okay, I'll get a few things then meet you there."

An hour passed as Eislie waited for the clerk to open the flight office. Ed had notified her about a message her mother had left. She informed her that her father had made it back to Doren and asked if they were in the area. Eislie wanted to mention it to Jace. She had already filled out the paperwork and was standing there when Jace walked in.

"Still waiting?"

Eislie nodded before telling him about her father having made it back to Doren. She was delighted when Jace said they should bring him home.

The clerk was annoyed seeing them standing there as she walked in but was able to process their paperwork quickly. She handed them the permit, and they were on their way back to the flight deck. Eislie gave the dock director the ticket and told them they were leaving right away. He followed them, his complaining getting the attention of Arren, who was already working on another damaged vessel.

The director showed Arren the permit. The old man yelling to Jace and Eislie, "You leaving already? I have some engineers waiting to see that ship of yours!"

Jace yelled back, "Tell them they can see it when we get back!"

The old miner then asked, "Well, where are you going?"

A few seconds went by, and Jace and Eislie both pointed up, but in different directions. Arren was laughing so hard, the director thought he'd lost his mind.

As Jace sat, Eislie was already plotting their course, and he could see the trinary star they spoke about clearly visible on the holographic display.

"I thought you wanted to pick up your father," Jace said.

Eislie nodded as she entered the coordinates. "We are, just adding a slight detour."

Jace chuckled as he went to grab the controls, the recessed panel making him realize Eislie had transferred flight systems to her side. She laughed, watching him as he searched for the controls in a humorous, animated way before pointing to herself, saying, "My turn."

Jace finished his pantomime and looked forward. "Okay, so where are we headed?"

Eislie pointed forward, and Jace sat back, his hand mimicking the same direction. "You have the controls. We'll go that way."

The *Wolfhammer* lifted from the deck as Arren turned from the ship he was working on to watch it become a small dot over the horizon, the subtle smile of joy on the old man's face making the engineer next to him ask, "Where are they heading?"

Arren said reverently, pointing toward the small dot in the distance, "They're going to light up the skies."

ABOUT THE AUTHOR

Stephen has experience in technology, engineering, and sales spanning over 30 years. He has been writing science fiction and fantasy for far longer—his work primarily for role-playing and short stories personally, using his knowledge and imagination within his life. He is always known to have a story to tell and it's usually sprinkled with a hint of adventure. Through his character's eyes, you find that life can be an adventure, and it's always better with a bit of science and magic.

Wolfhammer is his jump into the science fiction genre and something very familiar. The universe can be a big place, and many universes even more so.

Jace and Eislie are at it again. But unfortunately, they haven't cracked the mysteries of filament travel. At least, not yet. But, when Jace feels the effects of an unknown illness, they set a course for Earth.

Jace is returning home, and Eislie can finally visit the planet her mother came from, although, as usual, things don't go as planned.

Join Jace and Eislie on another adventure.

Filament

It's a stellar ride across the galaxy between being chased by the Alliance, pirates, new and old enemies. They even find the discovery of a lifetime. Filament is the second in the series for Legends of the Starborn.

For more stories, please visit: www.wolfhammer.com

For even more stories and a bit of magic, visit: www.afairyslight.com

www.ingramcontent.com/pod-product-compliance
Lightning Source LLC
Chambersburg PA
CBHW070557260626
47161CB00002B/636